DRAGON'S CALL

DYSTOPIAN FANTASY

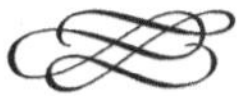

ANN GIMPEL

CONTENTS

DRAGON'S CALL

DRAGON HEIR, BOOK ONE

A Dystopian Fantasy

By
Ann Gimpel

Tumble off reality's edge into myth, magic, and dragons

Copyright Page

BOOK DESCRIPTION, DRAGON'S CALL

After her Celtic kin proved too big a bunch of bastards to bother with, Rowan sought solace among witches.

The first book in a magic-laced, fast-paced fantasy trilogy. With dragons.

After the Breaking, not much was left. I assumed it was a case of magic gone bad—until I discovered my goddess mother had broken the world. She didn't like it that I'd turned my back on the pantheon. My long tenure among witches rubbed salt into the wound.

After a confrontation where Mommy Dearest fessed up —and lacked the decency to bat an eyelash about the widespread destruction she'd caused—I was digesting what to do next when a dragon showed up.

Yes. A dragon.

The beast didn't talk with me or anything, but it flew overhead wreaking havoc on a goblin horde. Witches are old souls with kind hearts, but they're not particularly strong magically, so I was grateful for the help.

And suspicious as hell. Why a dragon? Why here and why now? More importantly, why was he—she?—helping me? Part of me didn't want to know, and another part was certain I'd find out anyway.

If I seem to be on a dragon kick here, it began long ago. My first runaway bestselling trilogy, Earth Reclaimed, had dragons in it. So did my almost-as-successful Dragon Lore series. Dragons have made cameo appearances in other books as well.

Well, maybe slightly more than cameos in the Ice Dragon series.

Beyond dragons, I've had a lifelong love affair with both the Celtic and Norse pantheons. While writing one long-ago book, I swore no Celtic gods. Nope. Nary a one. Well, along about Chapter Five, who should come strolling out of the wasteland but Fionn MacCumhaill, Celtic god of creation, protection, knowledge, and divination.

I gave up to my muse thereafter. She hasn't led me astray yet.

Welcome to another series that blends the Celtic and

Norse pantheons. In my imagination, the deities all know one another. It was a pretty intimate circle filled with petty—and not so petty—squabbling. Add enough acts of unbelievable valor to keep things on an even keel, and the foundations of a story magically appear.

CHAPTER ONE, ROWAN

I huddled deeper into a luxuriant clump of gorse bushes and drew my hood over my head to hide my bright hair. Thorns were a problem but a small enough price for protection. I'd tried, goddammit, but I hadn't been quick enough reaching the cave I called home. Bugles from the Wild Hunt blared. Clanking chains, creaking saddle leather, and the whoops and cries of Odin and his contingent of long-dead faeries and warriors filled the air.

An invisibility spell was a crapshoot. The Hunt smelled magic like hunting dogs scented prey. Hard to do nothing, but safety lay in holding my position, in barely breathing—until the Hunt had flown by.

Not that they couldn't return in a flash, but—

"*Rowan?*" Tansy's terrified voice exploded into my mind.

Goddess blast it, so much for not drawing power. Telepathy didn't take much, but still... "*Hush.*" I ground out the single word, hoping it would shut Tansy up.

So few witches were left. Tansy might be the last of them. Barely thirteen, her moonblood had just begun to flow.

Blood.

I sucked in a breath sharp as glass scrapings. The one thing the Hunt would zero in on faster than magic was blood. They soared right above me now, blotting out half a moon and all the stars. The pungent stink of horse sweat and drunken men wafted down, and I silently urged them to keep on flying. So far, so good. The horses' hooves churned air, finding purchase somehow. Hunger streamed from the ghost army.

Hunger for warmth. For the living to feed on, so they could ride forever. As if to validate my thoughts, they broke into a rambling Norse drinking song, one I'd heard in the odd tavern or two back before the world broke.

Best not to go there. If I do, I might cry. Once I begin, the tears will never stop. I'd cry so much, I'd become one with rivers raging through the Scottish Highlands. Not such a horrible outcome. Better than ending up fodder for the Hunt.

Or the gargoyles or griffons or goblins or trolls. Wicked things that had grown so brazen, they showed up in daylight. No time was safe to be about. Not anymore. I closed my teeth over my lower lip hard enough to hurt, stopping shy of piercing my skin. Blood was a very bad idea with the Hunt overhead.

A misplaced magical casting—and a very powerful one—had broken the balance point between bright and dark energy. At first, I'd been certain the witches could fix it, but

I'd been wrong. Not that I'm exactly a witch, but I blend in better with them than anywhere else. Anyway, we wasted a whole lot of time and magic before we gave up. By then, survival hung by the barest of margins.

The Hunt wheeled in the night sky, forming a circle. A fist squeezed around my heart until pain filled my chest. Caught. Odin knew we were below him. Fucker. Bastard. Saliva departed, leaving my mouth sandpaper dry.

Everything slowed as I watched Tansy emerge from a magical shrouding.

Hard to blame the girl. She must have been scared out of her wits, but she'd summoned magic. Between that and her blood, we'd had no chance of escaping notice. None at all.

I pounded a fist into the damp dirt. No wonder the Hunt had stopped.

Tansy rose unsteadily to her feet. She was dressed in the same motley collection of rags all of us wore. Blonde hair streamed down her slight form, and her breath formed clouds of steam in the chill air. Since she'd already been discovered, she began to chant in a clear voice that only trembled a little.

I knew the incantation, and the child's courage seared me. It was a witch's last-ditch attempt to save herself from death. My heart ached for Tansy, but I was proud of her too.

The aerial ballet circled, coming closer to the ground with each pass. I could see them clearly now, skeletal fingers, eyes like burning coals. I smelled their charnel pit breath, and what little was in my stomach curdled into a sour knot.

If I was going to act, my grace period had just expired. I

had to make a move and do it now. Another few seconds, and the lead rider would latch onto Tansy. What they'd do to her would be worse than death.

Far worse.

A girl on the brink of womanhood would be passed from rider to rider in a never-ending circle of lust. Theirs, not hers.

Cursing to give myself strength and project the illusion I was a total badass, I bolted to my feet and raced toward the clearing twenty meters away, stumbling over tangled roots.

"Take me, instead, you bastards," I screeched, shaking a fist at the riders.

Tansy turned a startled expression my way, her green eyes rounded into small moons. "Aw crap, Rowan. You don't need to—"

"Yeah. I do."

I reached Tansy and looped an arm around her shoulders, drawing her shuddering form close as I warded us. My spell wouldn't stand up to concerted battering from the Hunt, but it was the best I could do.

"I—I'm sorry," Tansy stuttered.

"Be sorry later." I narrowed my eyes, thinking. There had to be a way out of this.

Who am I kidding? I just offered myself. It gives them permission to take me.

Bile splashed the back of my throat. I swallowed it down. I refused to puke in front of Odin and his ilk. I'd stand proud, and I vowed I wouldn't show distress. Not in front of this batch of rotters.

"Let the girl leave." I squared my shoulders and looked

Odin right in the eye, no easy task since his fiery one-eyed gaze seared my corneas until I feared I'd be blind afterward.

"Aye, and is this a bargain freely requested and freely given?" he boomed in heavily accented English.

Tansy clutched at my arm. "You don't have to do this. I'll go. I'm the one who was stupid. I'm who—"

I rounded on her. "Shut up." Tansy's eyes filled with tears. I felt like a shit-ass. What I wanted was to drag her into my arms and comfort her, but comfort wasn't part of the new world order.

Hadn't been part of any world order I remembered. No one had ever offered me solace. Rolling my mental eyes, I shut off my pity party. Yeah. Life was a bitch. So what? Suck it up and keep on keeping on.

Tansy trembled where she leaned against me. I switched to shielded telepathy, hoping Odin and his merry crew wouldn't pick up on it. *"I may have a chance of returning, child. They'll eat you up alive."*

I stood so straight my spine cracked in protest. Before Odin had to ask me again, I said, "Yes. It's a bargain freely requested and freely given. So long as you allow the child free passage."

Whoops and cheers rose from the riders. A slimy creeping sensation wracked my body. What would they do to me? Would I have enough cunning to escape? Magic wouldn't be enough. I'd need luck, timing, courage. And a plan.

At the moment, I had nary a one of those four pesky items.

One of the horsemen angled his steed my way, dropping lower. I held up a hand, palm outward, and strengthened the ward around myself and Tansy. "Not so fast. The girl goes free. I would see her safely out of here."

"Ye're a lying, conniving slut," Odin sneered. His eight-legged steed, Sleipnir, pawed the air a few meters above my head.

"I resent that. I'm a witch, and I live and die by my word. I shall meet you back here in one hour, but you must leave between now and then. I do not want you privy to where we live."

I tossed my head, and my hood fell back. Oops. I wasn't all that recognizable—not after all the crap I'd lived through—but Odin was sharp as a fox. It would look bad if I made a grab for my cape, so I ignored it. Careful to enunciate each word clearly, I asked, "Do we have a bargain or no?"

Breath steamed from Odin, and he extended an arm, index finger pointing dead center at my chest. "I know that hair. Whose get are ye?"

"No one's." I slipped a knife from a sheath that hung from my waist and let the blade hover across my open palm. "Deal or no? I shall seal it with my blood." I avoided holding my breath, or looking too anxious. If the specter of my blood didn't move things along, nothing would.

Damn if Odin hadn't picked up on a resemblance. I remembered him visiting Mother occasionally. Him and those damned ravens of his. Not too many had hair like ours. Curly, shining red with golden streaks, it highlighted our golden eyes. I hooded mine and sprinkled a pinch of obfuscation into my warding. Normally, I employed a glamour, but magic wasn't limitless.

Mother had been gone from Earth since just after the Breaking. Time and chaos might have faded Odin's memories of her. Maybe

Tansy edged behind me and tried to jerk my hood back into place, except she wasn't tall enough. Good move on her part for a couple of reasons. If it had worked, she'd have tucked my hair back under cover. More importantly, though, any additional space between her and danger would help if Odin decided he wasn't up for bargaining with me. If that happened, I'd scream at Tansy to run, and then I'd hold my ground, offering what resistance I could as the Hunt swooped down on me.

I expelled a tight breath and waited. I'd done all I could, and the ball had left my court. My unusual hair fairly sang Ceridwen's name, but I downplayed that part of my bloodlines.

More than downplayed. I hid everything but my hair and had done so long enough it had become second nature. Turning my back on a hopelessly patriarchal pantheon, I'd done my damnedest to blend in with witchdom. My unusual locks hadn't posed a problem since no one remembered what any of the Celtic pantheon looked like. No one living anyway, which counted Odin out.

Not that he was dead, but he rode with the dead. It was kind of the same thing.

He angled his head to one side, eying me speculatively through his fog-colored eye. His dark hair was braided close to his head. Bone showed through the lower part of his face, skeletal bits with whiskers still growing out of them.

At least he'd stopped nattering on about who I was and where I'd come from.

I waited, my mouth dry and my chest so constricted I had to remind myself to breathe. Time dripped past. The other Huntsmen were growing restless, throwing taunts and graphic descriptions about what they'd do to me once I was in their clutches.

Some were still lobbying for Tansy. Virgin's blood, and all that crap.

I wanted to slice their dicks off, but this wasn't the place to let my temper loose. I was strong, but not against so many.

"Well?" I raised one brow, resisting the temptation to tap a foot. Now that I'd picked a path, I had a handle on my fear. All that remained would be to see how my gambit played out. Would Odin let Tansy and me leave? Or would we duke it out right here? Launch a fight certain to alert every magic wielder within a twenty-league radius. Not that the Hunt wasn't likely to prevail, but it wouldn't be the easy pickings I was offering, nor without losses to Odin's skanky tribe.

He chopped his extended arm downward and bellowed, "Go," adding "*Raus hier*," for good measure.

Outraged howls rose from the other Huntsmen. Odin swung the mace and flail looped around one wrist, narrowly missing his steed. The spiked ball connected with the skull of one of his men, cleaving it amid the sickening sounds of rotten bones crunching as they splintered to dust. The unfortunate target cantered off into the night, headless but still screeching. Odin took off after him with the rest of the Hunt scattered behind.

This wasn't a time to tarry. I hooked a hand beneath Tansy's arm and dragged her into a shambling trot. "Hustle up."

"You can let go. Goddess's tits, he beheaded his own man." A trill signaling the beginnings of hysteria burst from Tansy.

"Breathe," I suggested. "Nice deep breaths and don't think about this. Any of it."

"But we won. You don't have to go. He didn't take your blood oath." Relief laced through Tansy's words.

I tucked the knife still clutched in one hand back into its sheath. "Oath or no, I gave my word."

"Pfft. To a thief, a murderer, a soul-stealer. None of the—"

"Silence!"

I didn't slow until we stood within the entrance to the first cavern. Not many buildings had survived the Breaking. Caves were a better bet, but some of them were unstable. Ours was an extensive system dug deep into the southern flanks of Ben Nevis. From the looks of paintings on its stone walls, it had been here since the beginnings of time. Built and reinforced with magic, it should last through the ages, Breaking or no.

So far, I'd been right about that.

I stepped in front of Tansy, blocking her way, and draped a ward around us, so no one would overhear. "You owe me for tonight, yet the boon I request is small."

Tansy's green-eyed gaze skittered away. "You're going back—to that monster."

"What I'm doing—or not doing—is none of your affair. You will go to your pallet and prepare for bed. If anyone asks why you were so late returning, tell them you lost track of time. Apologize for your carelessness. Assure them it will never happen again."

Tansy bobbed her head once in acquiescence. "What if they ask about you?"

"You never saw me. Got it?" I dropped my hands onto Tansy's shoulders, wincing at how the young woman's bones almost poked through her skin.

"Got it." Tansy scraped her gaze off the floor, her eyes widening. "Your eyes. They're golden. Why did I never—?"

"Because I employ a glamour. Now go."

Tansy hesitated. Her eyes filled with tears, and she threw her arms around my back, hugging me hard. "You saved my life. How can I go on knowing you gave yours in return?"

I wanted to hold Tansy, offer what comfort I could. Instead, I pried the child loose. "You will keep going. Anything less than your best effort will squander my gift. Besides, no one knows the outcome of anything until the game is done. Don't count me out yet."

Adopting a jaunty expression I was far from feeling, I watched Tansy hurry the length of the cavern and vanish from sight. While I waited, I untangled the rest of the spell I hid behind to mute my high forehead, stark cheekbones, and taller-than-average height. Borrowing from the remains of magic powering the glamour, I teleported to the small side cavern I'd claimed as mine.

I didn't have either the time or inclination for questions from anyone, so I muted my presence—and sealed my door. We'd all been existing on the ragged edge of annihilation for years. Dodging evil day and night made it impossible to grow food. We'd raided stores vacated by scores of dead humans, but that resource wasn't limitless. Beyond that, we hunted. Rabbit. Deer. Racoons. Rats. Meat was meat, and we had to survive.

No one knew whose side anyone was on, so we distrusted other magic-wielders. Annoyed by how the witches had painted themselves into a fatal corner, I lifted the spell that concealed a plain wooden box. Not just any wood, though. Hawthorn. My mother had fashioned the box, and I hated to leave it behind. The wood warmed beneath my touch, almost as if the tree were still alive.

Who knew? Perhaps it flourished on some borderworld where Mother and the other Celts had sequestered themselves after the misshapen spell broke all that was pure and good on Earth. Scents I associated with Ceridwen— mint, vanilla, amber—soothed me as I removed an onyx amulet on a golden chain and placed it around my neck. I slid a ring with a matching stone over my index finger. Lastly, I draped a small, golden circlet around my forehead.

I took my time letting go of the box. It reminded me of warmth and home. What a fool I'd been to walk out on the pantheon. And then I reminded myself what a wasteland it had been. I'd left because I had no choice. Not really. If I'd remained Mother would have finished killing off my soul, sucking me dry as the mood struck her.

I settled my mouth into a resolute line and tucked the box away in a dark corner. Absent my magic, its glow would fade. Ready as I'd ever be, I kindled a spell and visualized the spot on the moors where I'd last seen Odin.

Maybe because I'd held it at bay for so long, Celtic power jumped to my command. The earthen walls of my grotto fell away, replaced by open moorland. So far, the sky was empty, but it hadn't yet been an hour.

What would I do if Odin didn't come back? Pick up the tatters of my glamour and go on as if nothing had happened, while we all slowly died of starvation? I shook my head, filled with sadness and determination.

Someone had to do something. I'd known it for over a year. The someone had to be me, and maybe tonight's confrontation was the beginning—

"Yeah, but of what?" I mumbled. Before I launched into a buck-up-buttercup lecture, the distant sound of horse hooves reached me. I stood tall, proud, every inch my mother's daughter. Hood back, my hair gleamed in light from Arianrhod's moon. Seeing me without my glamour would give Odin grist for his mill.

I might be a lot of things, but I would never become one of his lackeys.

The swoosh of wings beating fast made my head swing around. Wings had no place here. I gave myself a brisk mental slap. Valkyries rode with the Hunt. They decided who lived and who died in battle, but I'd always suspected they picked off the pretty ones to ravish at their leisure.

According to lore, they were maids, but the lore often overstated such things.

A pair of the winged warriors, fair hair streaming behind them, bore down on me, landing a few meters away. "We propose a test." The one with silver armor angled a speculative gaze my way.

"What kind of test?"

The other Valkyrie brayed laughter, displaying a mouthful of yellowed teeth. "What other kind is there?"

I took a measured breath. "Are you proposing I fight both of you?"

The Hunt roared into view and formed a rough circle in the air above us, the men jockeying for prime positions where they could have the best view.

"Never mind." I muttered. "I withdraw the question. Will I have a weapon? Both of you have spears. And armor." While I talked, I began weaving an illusion, one that would create two more of me.

Might be enough to even the playing field.

"Aye, the wench catches on fast," the first Valkyrie said.

The one with bad teeth made a face. "I thought this was stupid when Odin ordered us to do it. Should take less than five seconds start to finish." She dusted hands with cracked, dirty nails together and cackled like a mad thing.

"You're absolutely right," I crooned as I put the finishing touches on my working and readied myself to fight. "I thought Odin wanted me to ride with him."

"He has us," one of the duo hissed. "And our sisters."

"Aye, he has no need of you," the other winged warrior chimed in.

I was ready. I whistled once, the cascade of notes a linchpin. Air shimmered and swirled, forming an opaque curtain amid guttural curses from the Valkyries as they tried to figure out what I was up to.

Waiting was a bad idea. I jumped on my small advantage. Spinning to one side, I gripped the amulet to concentrate my power and set wheels in motion to animate my doppelgängers.

"What in the bloody fucking hell?" one of the Valkyries bellowed and charged, spear extended.

"Not that one," Odin shrieked from his aerial perch. "She's on the left, stupid."

I gritted out a string of Gaelic curses. Of course he'd be able to see through my ruse. Of the bunch, he was the only one whose magic was strong enough.

Keep going. Ignore him. Maybe he's not as smart as he thinks he is.

I nimbly traded forms with the twin he'd fingered. I could do this for a while—and fight too—but not for very long. The dual castings pigged up power like mad. I sidestepped the charging Valkyrie and aimed a blast of magic at the back of her neck.

It bounced off her helmet. With a roar, the woman twisted and charged, her face screwed into a mask of hate. I switched places with one of my twins right before the Valkyrie drove a spear through the illusion. It reformed a few meters away, grinning merrily.

"Fuck!" The other Valkyrie twirled in a circle, spear extended in front of her. "Which one is her?"

"They're all me."

I skinned my teeth back from my lips and took careful aim. The armor must be spelled, or my magic would have penetrated it. I jumped to one of the doppelgängers, sighted, and let a lethal blast fly from my outstretched fingertips.

Augmented by magic, my aim was true. I hit the small, exposed spot beneath the Valkyrie's chin, and she crumpled to the ground.

"Now that's more like it," I muttered and hopped to the doppelgänger nearest the other Valkyrie. Driven by fury, bloodlust in her eyes, the woman ran full tilt toward the place I'd just been, driving her spear through illusion—again.

The Valkyrie raised a fist skyward. "I'm done. That's no witch."

"Hold. I did not release you." Odin flew lower.

"I don't care. If I remain, that bitch will kill me."

"Truer words were never spoken. The next piece of magic is all yours." I tightened my grip on the amulet.

The Valkyrie threw down her spear. "I surrender. You killed my sister. I'm the last of my line, and—"

I lowered my hands and cut the flow of magic powering my likenesses until just one of me remained. "Go. I understand about being the last." No longer worried about the winged warrior, I raised my gaze to where Odin hovered in the air above. The Valkyrie may have been an enemy, but she'd given her word, and I'd heard truth in it. To murder her after she'd surrendered wasn't my style. Odin's, perhaps, but not mine.

Odin circled lower and lower until his steed's feet touched the earth, and then he jumped down and strode to where I stood.

"Ye're Ceridwen's get. Do not deny it," he growled.

I inclined my head. He'd speared me with a truth spell and caught me dead to rights. Nothing to be gained by lying. "True enough," I snarled. "Why is it important to you?"

"She has unpaid debts." He slitted his eyes.

"They'd be hers, not mine. I walked out on the Celts eons ago. Before the Breaking."

"Aye, but ye know where she is." His expression turned shrewd. "I propose a bargain."

I had no idea where Mother was, but I wasn't about to tell him that. "What kind of bargain? I'm not generally the bargaining type."

"Ye'll like this one well enough. I shall release you from your blood-sworn oath to join the Hunt."

I pursed my lips, not bothering to mention there'd been no blood-swearing anything. "What do I have to do?"

"Get what your mother has that's mine and return it to me."

"Care to offer up a clue as to what it is?" I angled a sidelong glance his way. "Mom can be cagey when she wants to hang onto something."

"She'll know. Ye have until this time tomorrow night." He turned toward his stamping black destrier.

"I don't think so." I planted myself between him and the horse, ignoring the animal's angry whinnies and hoping to hell it didn't take a chunk out of my shoulder. With its eight legs, it was capable of moving in unexpected directions. "I need at least a week."

Odin pushed around me and jumped astride his horse. "Two days. Final offer. Take it or leave it."

"Deal," I shouted after his retreating form and then kicked myself. Bound by my word, I had to comply. If I'd refused, though, he'd have insisted I join the Hunt. I'd have pointed out the niggling problem about him forgetting to bind me with blood. He'd have gotten angry, and we would have been off and running.

Yeah and maybe he'd have taken me hostage—until Mom ponies up whatever she stole from him.

The Hunt circled where I stood before flying north. The Valkyrie must have taken her fallen sister because the moor stretched around me was empty.

Two days.

I sank into a crouch and dropped my hands onto the damp, rocky earth seeking answers. The Celts were on a borderworld, but which one? There were hundreds, most sporting unbreathable atmospheres. If I guessed wrong, I might be in search mode for two years, not two days. Meanwhile, Odin would decide I was the cheating, conniving whore he'd labeled me, and the next time I set foot on Earth, he'd be waiting for me.

Hell, he'd probably set snares keyed to my energy that would tell him the second I arrived. A long, annoyed breath steamed through my teeth.

Never mind it was needle-in-haystack territory, I needed to get moving. Straightening, I gripped the amulet, letting magic boil around me. I'd start with the only borderworld I knew and take it from there. The minute the airless void between worlds surrounded me, I remembered how much I hated travel away from Earth.

Breathe through the amulet.

Easier said than done, but it was the only game in town. Not that lack of air would kill me. Last I checked, I was still immortal, but it didn't mean I couldn't suffer just like if I were human.

Feeling beleaguered and thoroughly disgusted with Mother for whatever she'd screwed Odin out of, I settled in to wait out my teleport spell.

CHAPTER TWO, ROWAN

Blech. Norse pantheon. Celtic pantheon. They weren't much different. I assumed if I ever stumbled across gods from the Roman or Greek ones, I'd have the same reflex antipathy.

I'd had a weak moment back in the witches' grotto, but it was easy to forget what arrogant assholes my family were when I hadn't laid eyes on them for a long while. Beyond that, Earth could have used a spot of divine aid after the Breaking.

Did anyone bother to show up?

Hell no. Not the Norsemen, unless you counted Odin, and he was only passing through trolling for spoils. Certainly not my kinsmen. The Celts had been absent since right after the world broke.

My lungs seized reflexively as I sucked nonexistent air.

I've always been a bit of a black sheep. Or maybe more than a bit of one. Mother didn't exactly parade me around.

Nope. The antithesis of a proud parent, she hid me away—until I was old enough to escape from her gilded halls. She never admitted what she was doing, the sequestering me part, and it took me a while to figure it out.

I assume I wasn't the result of immaculate conception. Even the gods require assistance producing young. But I knew nothing about who my father might have been. I asked. Many times. Ceridwen either changed the subject or left the room.

It used to worry me. The only reason she would have been so secretive was because she was ashamed. My father might have been a monster. Or a demon. Once I tried to call up an image of him in the cauldron. It blew up in my face—my casting, not the cauldron—in more ways than one. First and last time I tried my magic on that piece-of-crap urn.

When I finally snuck away and left Mother's home, I felt guilty. I might have been about ten at the time. I knew I'd done something wrong, but I wasn't willing to give up my only taste of freedom, either. I kept expecting Mom to show up and drag me back by the scruff of my neck.

Never happened.

Finally, I got hungry and made my way back to her domain. The Celts all lived in something like the Faeries' version of Underhill back then. A world within a world that humans had no idea existed. To mortal eyes, it was the ruins of Inverlochy Castle, but behind the illusion protecting it, the enormous, rambling stone structure was hale and hearty.

I anticipated a reprimand or at least a question about where I'd been. Nope. Mother just glanced up from her cauldron and then went back to it. When I thought about it later, I was certain she'd known precisely where I was. The magic urn would have told her.

After that, I left whenever I pleased. Eventually, I moved in with the witches. I felt more at home there than I ever did with my own kind. They accepted me without a whole bunch of questions, but more about them later.

Ducking my face into the folds of my cloak, I willed oxygen molecules to jump from the fabric to my lungs. It helped—a little. The choking sensation lessened, and I rolled out onto rocky ground. Standing creakily, I gulped air and crossed beneath the rune-carved arches of my first choice. I blinked, but nothing came into focus. The world had gone dark, but at least I could breathe. It didn't take long for me to determine no one was here. Not even shades.

I visited three more borderworlds in quick succession, finding exactly nothing. Hunger nagged, but thirst dogged me. I'd been a real dumbass not to bring a water bottle. This world was inhabited, so I set off in search of a stream. Besides water, I needed a better plan than random guessing.

I was crouched by a small brook, drinking from my cupped hands, when a flaxen-haired elven youth joined me. "Who are ye?" he asked in archaic Gaelic.

I swiped a hand across my mouth and stood up. "Ceridwen's daughter. Do you know which borderworld the Celts occupy?"

"Left at the first star and straight on till morning." He giggled, pleased by his own joke.

I grinned. "I know *The Little Prince* too, but I need to find my mother."

"They bide on the next world southeast of us," he told me.

"Thank you." I tossed my arms around the elf and hugged him hard. His startled expression was priceless and made me laugh. "Who lives on this world?" I asked. So long as I was prowling about, I may as well learn something about nearby realms.

I hadn't even considered leaving Earth since the Breaking. Maybe it had been a bad idea. After zero aid was forthcoming from any quarter, perhaps I might have unearthed ideas if I'd gotten off my duff and gone exploring. I exhaled noisily. I hadn't left because survival was so uncertain. Not for me, but for the witches. I was afraid if I left them for long enough to accomplish anything, they'd succumb to some unnamed danger.

They'd been kind to me, treated me like family. And so I'd remained, offering help as I could. If I'd wanted to leave, the time would have been shortly after the Breaking. Before rations thinned and foul magic grew far bolder.

"My lady?" The elf nudged me.

I nudged him back playfully. "Yes, I still want to know who is here."

His open expression developed suspicious edges. "Why?" The planes of his face and his tone reminded me he only looked like a child. He could be centuries old.

"I live on Earth—" I began.

He bent two fingers into a sigil against evil. "The bad place," he said firmly, as if he knew all about it. "The place evil runs free." The elf made shooing motions as if my presence would sully his world. "Go away. Leave."

He whistled shrill, high notes. A unicorn galloped toward him, and he swung onto its back. I stared after the horned horse. Even though I'd been spurned, the sight of the magical creature, shimmering in shades of white and gold, heartened me.

What the hell? Had Earth developed a reputation as a devil's world? The elf had acted as if I would wreck his world too, if I remained very long.

Shaking my head, I loped to an open area to launch my next spell.

This trip was shortest of all, the elven world fading as the next one formed around me. I'd no sooner cleared the borderworld's lintels than Celtic magic blasted me. The sensation brought me to my knees, and waves of emotion swept through me. These were my people. This was where I belonged.

Stop. It's compulsion. Pay it no heed.

No fucking way had I come this far to turn into a maudlin fool.

I straightened, determined to locate Mother with magic, state my business, and be gone from here. Ceridwen saved me the trouble. "There ye are, Daughter. I knew ye'd come. I saw it in my cauldron."

She hadn't changed one whit over all the years since I'd seen her. Garbed in soft, buff leather trousers and a linen tunic with runes seared into it with magic, she stood tall, regal. Her feet were laced into calf-high boots. Absent the fact we were dressed differently, it was like looking into a mirror. My same telltale hair—cherry red with golden streaks—cascaded around her. Golden eyes, twin to my own, stared back at me. Rings circled most of her fingers, and a golden torc sat at the base of her throat.

I resisted an inane desire to throw myself into her arms, but Ceridwen wasn't the huggy type. Never had been. She hadn't wanted me anywhere near her when I was a toddler. Nothing about that had changed.

"Good to see you, Mother." I tried for a positive note to conceal my inner turmoil.

"Aye, ye as well, lass."

"If you foresaw my coming, do you also know why I'm here."

Ceridwen nodded. "I did an ill-advised thing. Dabbled where I should not have. Unfortunately, Earth has paid for my folly, but 'tis finally time to set old wrongs—"

Understanding slammed into me. "What? You're who broke the world?" I stared at my goddess mother, unbelieving.

"I may have, but—"

"But what? How in the hell could you stand by and do nothing? All these years. You could have helped," I sputtered, too furious to watch my words. "Was Odin's bauble the linchpin that caused the Breaking?"

Ceridwen looked annoyed. "All that happened long ago. Why drag out old bones to gnaw?" After a hesitation, she added, "Daughter."

I started to announce I was no daughter of hers, but it would undermine my whole reason for being here. I came by my temper honestly. If I angered her, she'd toss me out on my ear. I settled for, "If you knew, why didn't you return Odin's bauble long before this? Christ on a crutch. Do you have any idea—?"

"Silence! I will not have ye speak thusly to me."

I ground my teeth. "Give me whatever it is, and I'll be on my way."

"Nay. 'Tis a task we must do together."

Suddenly suspicious, I asked, "Why?"

"I'm ready to depart." Ceridwen offered a smile with a lot of teeth and zero genuine feeling. "Coming?"

"Where are we headed?"

"Earth," she replied.

Too angry to trust what might emerge from my mouth, I nodded once and felt Ceridwen's familiar power settle around me, soft, nurturing, full of promises that would never materialize. At least it would cushion the journey through the space between worlds. Once I'd craved her attention, until I learned it came with a very high price tag. Her touch was a velvet-lined trap with steel jaws and the reason I'd left so long ago.

Mother ceded power to no one. Not then, and not now, either.

We emerged in the ruins of Inverlochy Castle, the site of the Celts' erstwhile domain, in the Scottish Highlands. Other than smelling musty, it hadn't changed in several centuries. Carpets and wall hangings depicting various Celtic victories lined the floor and walls.

Ceridwen breathed deep, spreading her arms. "Och, I've missed this place."

Yeah, but not enough to lift a finger to stop the evil spreading its contamination across Earth. I buried the thought deep and spaded magic over it. She was more than capable of reading my mind.

"When do I get the full story?" I crossed my arms beneath my breasts and glared at the woman who looked just like me.

"When did ye grow so ill-tempered?"

I shrugged. "Watching half the world die has that effect."

"Are ye finally done with your ridiculous witch fixation?"

Eyes widening in realization, I gasped out, "You're jealous."

Ceridwen strode close and jabbed my chest with her index finger. "Ye are mine. Mine. Do ye understand me? I allowed ye to leave thinking ye'd get over your fascination with witches once ye saw how weak they are, but it never happened."

Already near boiling, my temper erupted. I jabbed Ceridwen back. "I am no one's woman but my own. You're why I left."

"That's impossible. Ye were young, full of hubris—"

I chopped a hand through the air between us as the whole, unbelievable picture took shape. My autocratic bitch of a goddess mother had engineered breaking the world to force me back to her side. When it hadn't worked, she'd herded the Celts to safety and left everyone else to rot.

"I'm ashamed to be related to you."

"I offer you one chance to take those words back, *Daughter*." Mother's golden eyes caught fire. "Do. It. Now."

"Or?"

Ceridwen's features turned menacing, any beauty long gone. "Or the banishment shall become permanent."

A painful arrow lodged beneath my breastbone, but how could I lose something I'd never had? I kicked my shoulders back. "Fine. Have it your way, *Mother*. You always do. Give me Odin's trinket, and I'll never darken your door again." I paused for a beat. "Just so we're clear, you didn't banish me. I left of my own free will."

For scant moments, Ceridwen's mask slipped. If I hadn't been looking right at her, I'd have missed the shock—and the hurt. The goddess tilted her chin at a defiant angle I remembered only too well.

"While we're at it," I forged ahead. "If this is the last time I'll ever see you, who the fuck was my father? You owe me that much."

"I owe you nothing," Ceridwen snapped back.

Before I could say anything, the big doors at the end of the hall slammed against their stops. Odin strode in, chains clanking and leather chaps creaking as they brushed against each other. His two ravens, Huginn and Muninn—thought and memory—rode on his shoulders. For once they weren't cawing up a storm.

Obviously, he'd known where Mother was all along. I'd been played.

"Well met, Goddess." He mimed a parody of a bow in Ceridwen's direction

She barely glanced his way. "As usual, your timing couldn't be worse."

He shrugged and trotted to where we stood. "Fine. I see

ye've been reunited with your errant spawn. Pay up, and I'll be on my way."

"Pay up?" I shrieked. "What the unholy hell? This whole thing was nothing but a charade." I launched myself at my mother, tugging her hair and punching her wherever my fists landed. Somehow, she was in cahoots with Odin, and his story about a bauble she'd stolen had been pure fabrication.

He rubbed his hands together. "Och, and I do love a good cat fight. Get cracking, wenches." The ravens quorked merrily, apparently sharing their master's opinion.

My next punch landed square in the middle of Mother's nose, but the one after that blasted through empty air. Ceridwen was gone. I wrapped my arms around myself. Sobs wracked me. Fury? Loss? Relief? I felt like a chump. A fool, but I couldn't stop crying.

Odin grabbed my shoulders and shook me. "Where'd she go? Poxy slut never paid me."

I drew magic. Enough to make him let go fast. "That would be your problem. Watch who you bargain with."

One of the ravens divebombed me. Before I could flatten it with magic, it hustled back to Odin's shoulder.

"Mayhap, I should take you with me after all." He regarded me speculatively out of shrewd eyes.

I shrugged. "No blood bond. How do you think you're going to accomplish that?"

"Ye're a woman of your word. Unlike your Mother—"

"I'm nothing like her," I agreed. "Thank every god or goddess who ever walked, but it doesn't mean I wish to join the collection of dead things that trail after you."

"Watch it. Ye're talking about my men."

"So." I slitted my eyes. "That night on the moors, you were hunting for me?"

He brayed laughter. "Aye, and ye fell into my lap unexpectedly, right after I found the young, succulent one with blood running from her." He laughed harder. "Hell, she'd never have noticed a touch more blood after I took her maidenhead. I sacrificed a whole lot when ye showed up, and I figured out who ye were."

"Money trumps sex, eh?"

"Every damn time, lass." He leered at me. "Never got my money, but mayhap I can still have t' other. Ye're no maid, but ye'll do—as a consolation prize." He patted his groin.

Before he dragged out his cock, I said, "I propose a bargain."

"Ye're scarcely in a bargaining position, lassie." One hand had dipped beneath the skins draped around him, digging for his member.

"Maybe not. Do you know who my da was?"

He stared at me, lust yielding to surprise. Out of all the possibilities that could have come out of my mouth, he hadn't expected that question. At least he quit grappling with his dick.

"Well?" I pressed. "Do you?" For good measure, I cast a hasty truth spell and tossed it about his beefy shoulders. It disturbed the clumps of rotting hides he wore when he led the Hunt. For long moments the stench of death filled the Celts' hall.

"Say I did, ahem, have access to that prime bit of knowledge—" he began.

I anticipated his question. "I would join the Hunt for a

limited time. One month only. During that month, I would ride with you, but no man will touch me. No woman, either."

"Two months." He showed me a mouthful of teeth. The stink in the room thickened into a nauseating brew.

I shook my head. "One month. Take it or leave it."

"Ye drive a hard bargain, lassie."

I bared my teeth at him. "Will ye tell me or no?" I aped his brogue. "Or are ye still playing me when ye have naught to tell but conjecture or outright lies."

"Celtic bitch," he snarled.

"Norse bastard," I countered and blew out a tired breath. "This is stupid. I'm done. I'm leaving."

"Are ye quite certain? Anyone with sufficient power can determine bloodlines."

I cocked my head to one side, regarding him. "True enough, yet I can't unearth my own. I've tried."

"They're hidden." He sharpened his gaze. "I can see the shrouding. Breaking through it should be simple enough."

"No thank you." The thought of his slimy magic touching me turned my stomach. As things were, I'd be off my feed for a week. Maybe it wasn't a bad thing, since the larder was nearly empty.

He'd begun rattling off all the things he was god over. I stopped listening after the dead, inspiration, battle frenzy, and ecstasy. Of course, he'd have to toss that latter one in. He hadn't given up trying to fuck me.

Before he could come up with other inducements, I stood tall, focused my power, and instructed it take me back to the witches.

My family.

My home.

At least I didn't have to face the void between worlds a third time. Inverlochy Castle wasn't far from my cave. Though the castle lay in ruins, invisible to men who marched over its grounds every day, being there had given me an idea. My teleport magic was slower to respond than I would have liked, but Odin's burly form finally vanished.

A harsh smile forced its way out. Before, I hadn't known what kind of spell to look for to neutralize the Breaking. Now I did. Perhaps I could defuse Ceridwen's damage, no matter how many ways my mother had reinforced the casting.

It was at least possible since we held the same magic.

Somewhere along the line, I'd unearth the truth about my father. I hadn't thought about him in a very long time, but he'd rocketed to the forefront of my mind.

Why now?

Was everything connected in some way I had yet to figure out?

Before the walls of my room shaped themselves around me, I could have sworn I wasn't alone with my spell. The impression was fleeting, so brief I chalked it off to exhaustion.

No one followed me into my chamber. Once I'd sealed myself in with magic, I pitched facedown on my narrow bed and willed myself to sleep. If I hadn't, I'd have replayed my interaction with Ceridwen.

Over and over again.

I'd always known what a self-absorbed bitch she was, but even a salamander was a better mother than mine. She'd rained destruction down on mankind to drive me back to her side. For what? Not because she loved me. I wasn't anything more than a possession who'd strayed from her circle.

I ripped off the amulet, ring, and circlet. Tomorrow, I'd bury them deep and never, never use them again. My pillow was damp with tears before I finally, mercifully, fell into a restless sleep.

The rich earthy smell of Vanaheim's air billowed around me as I swung my broadsword in an arc above my head.

"What?" Jarle smirked. "Are you posing for a painting? Or are we sparring?"

Medium height and barrel-chested, he'd been my arms instructor all my life. At least the part of it where I could heft a sword. His thick black hair had been braided out of the way and fell down his back to his knees. Clad in dark brown hunting leathers, he'd strapped a light coat of mail over his garments. Vambraces covered his lower arms. A length of leather cording was tied around his forehead to keep sweat out of his hazel eyes. Like me, he was barefoot.

I planted my right foot so the heavy weapon wouldn't unbalance me and swung. Low, fast, and from the left.

Jarle parried my blow easily. Shifting his own blade to one hand he made come-along motions with the other. I knew that gesture. It meant I should try harder. I did. This time, I put my back into it and was rewarded by a muted grunt. I swear, Jarle is just like Yggdrasil, the One Tree. It doesn't move, either, and its roots bind the Nine Worlds together in ways too convoluted for my magic to follow or understand.

We sparred beneath a tiny section of its magnificence. Smaller trees, probably offshoots, grew in a grove around us. Green, rolling moors extended out from Yggdrasil. In the distance, massive snow-capped mountains shot up from the valley floor. Although they're not visible from here, deep canyons cut into the ground between where we are and the mountains. Fissures that make travel on foot impossible.

Ten blows later, my breath came hard. Sweat trickled down my forehead, and I was sorry I'd forgotten my own leather band.

"Two more," Jarle urged.

My arms felt like they didn't even belong to me anymore. I gritted my teeth and hefted the blade. Because it took less effort than a swing, I cleaved it straight down. Jarle hooted laughter and sidestepped me easily enough, but I'd anticipated his move.

For once I guessed correctly and swiped him from the side. My sword clanged against his armor. I hadn't hurt him, but maybe he'd have a bruise across his ribs. A small one.

A herd of wildebeests sashayed by. Followed by the tiny birds that feed off their hides. Above us, the occasional dragon winged past, bugling.

"Nice work." Jarle bobbed his head my way.

My eyes widened. Praise from Jarle was so rare as to be almost nonexistent.

I was still panting, but I managed, "Last time you said something nice was a dozen years ago."

"Eh, you're a slow learner."

I laughed, but his words stung. I was a wizard by trade, not a warrior. "Why can't I use magic?" I asked for the millionth time. "The blade would be lighter. I'd be faster, and—"

"Because magic can run out," he spoke over me. "If you've grown dependent on it, you'll be lost if you run it down to nothing." Stomping toward me, he yanked a flask from one of his many belt hooks, drank deep, and handed it over.

I downed a few swallows of mead, savoring the rich honey-based brew. This batch tasted of heather and clover. Every vat was different depending on what the bees had been eating.

I sank to a crouch. Jarle unbuckled his mail and knelt next to me; I gave his flask back. For a while, we traded drinking and getting our breath back. Vanaheim is very different from Asgard. That world is in the sky, and the gods there think they're better than we are.

Of course Vanaheim differs from Midgard too. Humans live there, and that portion of the Nine Worlds is in deep trouble.

A while back, magic got loose and did a whole lot of damage. Mortals called it the Breaking, and it killed off over half of them. Not much of a loss, if you ask me. They'd been breeding like rats for far too long. At first, we were convinced it was the dark gods' work. Or the Devil and his minions had gotten bored enough to leave Hell and kick up their heels. Notice I said Hell. It's very different from our Hel, which is ruled jointly by a goddess of the same name and our dead. Yes, they have a role too. I believe the modern term is self-governing.

Another rumor behind the Breaking was that Tantalus got loose. Remember him? He's who cooked up his children and fed them to the other gods in a stew.

I glanced at Yggdrasil. The One Tree contained the roots of everything, of all life. I'd examined it closely after the Breaking and been relieved only Midgard had been affected. So far.

"What are you thinking about?" Jarle asked.

I snorted. He was certain I'd bemoan what a poor swordsman I was, but for once it wasn't foremost in my mind. "The Breaking," I replied.

He rocked back on his heels. "Why? It didn't impact us."

"Of course it did," I retorted.

"How?" Jarle furled his dark brows. "Mortals come and go. Surely, you're not concerned about a few million dead."

I exhaled slowly. How to explain the concept of dynamic balance? "You know how watching your opponent is critical?" I asked. At Jarle's nod, I went on. "Midgard's woes shifted the balance among the Nine Worlds, much like the crux of a battle alters when one fighter moves out of the way."

"Are you saying that the sheer volume of dead left a vacuum?"

"Of sorts." If I said much more, I'd have to own up to the

many trips I'd made to Midgard after the Breaking. Far more than anyone suspected.

Maybe it was time.

Jarle was waiting, but patience was one of his long suits. He could wait for days and not bat an eye.

"We discount mortals," I began as I thought how to say what I needed to in as few words as possible.

"Aye. That we do. So what?" Jarle countered.

"Human energy is mostly a source for good. I agree it's negligible until there are a whole lot of them. Then it makes a difference. If only a few thousand of them had died..." I shrugged.

"But it was over a million, was it not?" Jarle asked.

I nodded. "Many times that number. The fabric of their society crumpled. Most of their buildings collapsed. Their big cities have become rubble heaps filled with rats and opportunistic thieves. The seas have risen, and they're choked with rubbish. Nearly everything that lived in them is dead too."

Jarle leaned close. "I have heard the Hunt flies almost every night, seeking spoils."

I had heard the same, but I was reluctant to criticize Odin. He was our god, and if he was leading the Wild Hunt through Midgard with far greater frequency than in the past, he must have his reasons.

"There is a point to this," Jarle pressed. "What is it?"

"I have perhaps spent more time in Midgard than you know about," I said slowly as I tried to select the best path. Until now, I'd been closemouthed about my suspicions. Who would I have told? Not Odin. He was busy picking meat from Midgard's bones.

Jarle's gaze developed the shrewd aspect I associated with a thorny sword move. "And?"

"Two things. I am convinced Celtic magic was behind the Breaking."

A sharp intake of breath told me the revelation startled Jarle. He was unflappable, so I gladly took the point I'd scored.

"Why are you so sure?" His hazel eyes bored into me. He might be short on magic, but he was long on common sense.

I don't know why I'd expected he'd take my word for it, and a small part of me was hurt he didn't trust my wizardry. I had absolute confidence in his warrior talents, but this wasn't a tit-for-tat contest.

I raised my gaze and looked right into his eyes. I didn't want any doubts about my veracity—or my interpretation of magical footprints. "Because I have traveled to Midgard a lot, perhaps a hundred times since the Breaking. Once the initial damage settled out, I hunted for clues. The wreckage was so pervasive, it took me time."

Jarle curled his hand in a get-on-with-it motion. "Fine. So you've been haunting Midgard."

I didn't care for the word haunting, but it wasn't worth quibbling over. "One day, I found something eerie and unusual," I went on. "A definite splatter of Celtic magic. The Celts were long gone at that point, so their power should not have been there. Unless someone established a time-linked spell that would continue to wreak havoc with no one to sit on top of it. I looked deeper and found one Celt—a woman—

residing with a bunch of witches. The magic was similar enough, it might have been hers."

"A woman, eh?" A knowing smile curled the edges of Jarle's harsh mouth.

"Yes, and she's...amazing, but the magic wasn't hers. A relative's perhaps, but not hers. I cast a few seeking spells and found the spot where Celtic power broke the world. They'd obviously done their research because the place was where plates supporting Midgard's surface had already partially separated."

I took a breath before going on. "Someone summoned fire—normally the purview of our dragons—a whole lot of it. Once it was fully ignited, they fed it with air until the resulting explosion created shock waves that ran the length and breadth of Midgard."

"I thought you said the spell was self-perpetuating," Jarle muttered.

"After the initial blast, it was," I clarified.

Jarle's forehead crinkled into a mass of lines. "But why? What was in it for this mysterious Celtic god?"

I shrugged. "Never was able to figure out that part. I have shadowed the woman, and I'm convinced she's as clueless as I am. She's another mystery. She has power—an enormous amount—yet she lives a hardscrabble existence along with witches who don't have a hundredth of her ability."

"Maybe her kinsmen kicked her out of the pantheon," Jarle suggested.

It had occurred to me, but I'd discarded it out of hand. I'd never heard of a banished Celtic god—except the Morrigan.

Usually, they kept their squabbles in-house. "I don't think so," I said.

"Have you talked with Odin?"

I shook my head.

"Why not," Jarle pressed.

"He's there almost every night," I mumbled. "Surely, he can figure things out for himself."

A cunning expression flickered behind Jarle's hazel eyes. "It's the woman. You don't want Odin's eyes on her."

I winced. "You know me far too well."

"Surely, you're not worried she'll fall into his arms. Not when he's leading the Hunt and appears as a half-rotted corpse to blend in with the other Riders." When I didn't answer, he kept talking. "Have you told anyone? Perhaps some of the other gods in Asgard?"

I shook my head again.

"Do you mind if I do?"

"Aye." The reply shot off my tongue. "This discussion is private, and if you wish to maintain our friendship, it will remain so."

"I see." Jarle frowned. "All right. I shall honor your request. For now."

I made a grab for his wrist. "If you ever decide to break that vow, you will tell me before you talk with anyone."

"I can do that, but why?"

"By then, I may know more than I do right now. Things are scarcely static in Midgard. I've done what I can to undermine the fragments of Celtic power that are still pumping out chaos. Meanwhile, other problems have developed."

"Like what?" On the heels of his question, I heard Jarle mutter he didn't really want to know.

I told him anyway. "The current blend of magics has proven perfect for sorcery to flourish. All manner of wicked creatures have invaded Midgard, and they're running wild. The balance point I mentioned earlier has become seriously skewed. If someone doesn't take a stand and begin herding them back to the holes they crawled out of, Midgard will be lost. And then we'll be down to eight worlds. Who knows how things will go without Midgard? It's always been a neutralizing element."

"Apparently, not anymore," Jarle mumbled.

I wasn't sure what to say next, so I opted for silence. I'd given my instructor a lot to chew on. He understood brute power. Standing solid like a tree and mowing through whatever rose against him. The intricacies of strategizing against a magical enemy weren't exactly up his alley.

A miniature wind tunnel formed. I looked up in time to see one of the elder dragons, a massive fellow with tarnished golden scales heading right for us. To be on the safe side, I tossed a ward around Jarle and myself. The damned dragons were so big, they sometimes misjudged their trajectory. I'd had one land on me a time or two. It wasn't pleasant.

I culled through my memory for the dragon's name. They never forgot our names, and they took it as an insult if we didn't greet them by name. Title too, if they had one.

Clouds of dust wafted high into the air as the dragon thumped down. Only a dragon's perpetual heat could dry the wet earth on contact. Too late to see if Jarle remembered the dragon's name.

I tried harder.

It took the beast a while to get its wings folded and lumber around so he faced us. His tail swung about, but slow enough Jarle and I were able to step over it.

At what felt like the last possible moment, the right neurons connected in my brain, and the dragon's name was just there. Relief streamed through me. The beast obviously wanted to talk with us. He'd gone to a fair amount of trouble to drag his bulk out of the air. He'd be annoyed if we didn't greet him warmly.

I hadn't spent all that much time with the dragons who shared Vanaheim with us. They had a rather large colony at the base of the distant mountains. Not that they lived in Vanaheim, but it provided a gateway to their actual home on a world called Fire Mountain.

I'd been there once. Hot. Dry. Sandy. Ringed by active volcanoes. It was probably perfect for dragons, but I'd been pretty uncomfortable. Twin suns baked anyone who stood beneath them. Keeping my clothes on, I'd turned into a sweat-soaked mess—until my body ran out of liquid. Removing my garments would have been out of the question. Even magic wouldn't have saved me from turning into a well-done roast.

The dragon, Nidhogg, had finally settled across from us. Jarle and I had risen to our feet to greet him properly. I bowed my head as a sign of deference.

"Welcome, Nidhogg, Elder Dragon," I said. "Your presence humbles us. How may we serve you?" Next to me, I felt Jarle stiffen. He bowed to no one. Not man. Not dragon. He wasn't red-hot about service, either.

"I am the Norse Dragon in addition to being one of the Elders." The dragon towered above us. He must have stood nearly three meters. Up close like this, I could see how his scales fit against one another and feel heat pouring off him.

Should I congratulate him on what sounded like a promotion? Nah. Maybe he'd always carried that title and I just hadn't known about it.

He turned his head and lazily directed a stream of fire at a pile of moss-covered rocks. Our world was wet enough, I wasn't especially worried about spontaneous combustion.

"I heard your discussion about Midgard," he rumbled, punctuating his words with smoke.

I waited. Nidhogg would get to the point eventually. He was one of twelve Elders. Exactly what that meant was shrouded in secrecy, but I assumed they were the first dragons, and that all others had come from them. Regardless, the beast sitting a meter away had enormous power. Magic sheeted from him, right along with heat.

What I wouldn't give to have a hundredth of his ability. A thought hit me so hard I swayed on my feet. Dragons could put Midgard to rights. They could kill off the griffons and gnomes and trolls— I clamped down on my mental wanderings. Nidhogg was probably monitoring them. Jarle's too, but I wouldn't tell my old friend.

It would annoy the crap out of him. And make him wretchedly uncomfortable.

The dragon was looking at me. I made the mistake of looking back and got snared in his whirling eyes. At first I thought they were gold, like him, but they shaded to green and then silver. I suspected I wouldn't be able to look away until he released me, but I didn't test my theory.

Next to me, Jarle growled, "Stop that."

He must have fallen into the dragon's hypnotic eyes, absent magic to counteract their pull.

I felt a sharp rebound as the magical thread holding Jarle released. It wasn't gentle. He staggered and might have fallen on his ass. I didn't know because I couldn't look at him.

"Ye shall depart," the dragon suggested in a deceptively silky tone.

When I checked with magic a few moments later, Jarle was gone.

"Good." Nidhogg dusted his talons together. They were long and sharp and bright red. "Ye are whom I wished to speak with."

I started to ask why, but decided it was impertinent.

"Can ye hold secrets, Bjorn?"

I nodded and hoped to hell whatever secret he was about to entrust didn't end up destroying me.

His eyes whirled faster, and I felt him drape magic around the two of us. Unlike my brand of power, his was uncomfortable. Rather like a vise had snapped me into its maw. I knew instinctively that fighting against the sensation would make it far worse.

"Above all, ye must not involve Odin," Nidhogg said. "Can ye give me your blood bound oath?"

I held up one hand, and he bent toward me. One of those sharp talons slashed across my fingertip. He snaked his tongue out and licked drops of blood that welled. Something like a cage clicked shut in my mind. I couldn't have told anyone anything about what Nidhogg wanted if I tried.

"What happens if I slip up?" My voice was thin, as if I hadn't used it in eons.

"What do ye believe will happen, wizard?"

"I will die."

"Excellent." He puffed steam until it formed clouds around us. Only then did he let go of my hand.

"The Nine Worlds exist in a delicate balance. Midgard failing is not an option. If it continues on its current trajectory, all the other worlds in our circle will break down as well. Yggdrasil will perish."

My throat went dry. I'd suspected we needed Midgard, but I'd assumed the other eight worlds could somehow limp along without it.

"We—I and other dragons—have tried to get Odin's attention, but he is sunk in greed, plundering what he can from Midgard." The steam turned to smoke and ash.

I coughed reflexively.

"The more time he spends with the Hunt," Nidhogg went on, "the less amenable he is to hearing reason."

"The damage to Midgard," I croaked, "can it be undone?"

"Och, ye mean what the meddling Celtic bitch did? Mayhap. 'Tis gone on far longer than I would have liked."

"What do you require of me?" The smoke had cleared, and it was easier to talk. Who was the Celt he'd referred to? Was it the woman masquerading as a witch?

"For now, exactly what ye've been doing. Spend time in

Midgard. Ensure the carnage from the miscast magic doesna worsen."

I wanted to protest such a task might be beyond my capabilities. Instead, I asked, "What if things slew sideways despite my best effort?"

"Call for me."

"Why can't you—?" I began and then stopped. He wasn't some minor god, one I could request favors from. Pulling Midgard out of the hole it had sunk into was an enormous undertaking.

He bent and dropped a foreleg on my shoulder. "I erased your companion's memories of me. It should ease your way since ye willna have to lie to him. Pay close attention to anything different within Midgard. No alteration is too insignificant to report."

Something liquid dropped from one of his eyes. When it hit the ground, it had become a creamy moonstone with a deep golden center. I'd heard about dragons' tears turning into gems, but I'd never found any lying about. I figured the dragons scooped up anything that smacked of hoard material.

"Keep the stone," Nidhogg instructed. "Whatever ye think or do whilst holding it will find its way to me quickly."

I opened my mouth to protest I hadn't agreed to a total loss of my privacy, but he must have anticipated me. Rather than the slow, cumbersome set of movements he'd used to drop out of the sky, power jetted from his open mouth. It painted a glowing gateway. In a movement that seemed impossible given his bulk, he leapt through the portal.

It winked shut behind him, leaving me staring gape-mouthed. The moonstone bounded up from where it lay in the dirt and ended up in a pocket of my leather trousers where it pulsed warmly.

Feeling like I'd wakened from a particularly rough night, I stared around me bleary-eyed. Nothing had changed. Dragons still soared overhead. Flocks of sharp-beaked birds cawed. A pair of squirrels chased one another up a nearby tree.

Vanaheim might not have changed, but I had. I'd rather enjoyed my stealthy trips into Midgard. But that was before I'd been drafted as a spy. Jarle would have relished the role, but not me. I didn't have a single drop of warrior's blood in my entire makeup.

I shook myself from head to toe. The dragon wasn't asking me to change stripes. The ancient beast was canny enough to have simply piggybacked onto who I already was. A curious wizard who'd always been fascinated by magic. To avoid running into anyone and having to stammer through an explanation of why I looked so out of sorts, I drew magic and teleported to my abode.

Once its humble stone walls had closed around me, I started to prepare my evening meal. When I was barely midway through cooking up a pot of grain, the moonstone kicked up a fuss, vibrating like a live thing. I hadn't exactly forgotten about it, but it was clearly reminding me I had work to do.

Apparently, cooking my supper wasn't on the bill of fare. I dragged the stone out of my pocket. It was so hot, it singed my fingers. I tried to drop it on the table, but it clung to my hand.

"Fine," I told it, feeling like a fool. Who the hell spoke to rocks? "I'm leaving. Right after I eat."

That seemed to do it. The moonstone dove back into my pocket. I checked my rice dish. It wasn't quite done, but I dug in anyway. I understood perfectly. I was eating on borrowed time.

The dragon's talisman wouldn't rest until I was back in Midgard. I cleared my mind of everything. Damn dragon had me right where he wanted me. My new goal was to be so good, so compliant, that someday my life would be my own again. If that didn't work, I'd have to batter my way free.

Brave words from a wizard, but I refused to spend the rest of my life bowing and groveling and doing Nidhogg's bidding.

CHAPTER FOUR, ROWAN

J woke almost more weary than when I'd gone to bed. Of all things, I'd dreamed of dragons. Flights of them in gold and silver and red and blue and green. They were gorgeous, but they wanted something from me too. Toward the end, a blood-red female had chased me, wings spread and casting long shadows. I was pretty certain she had to be Dewi, the Celtic dragon goddess, but all she'd done was to paint long tracks of fire on either side of me.

It's not a well-known fact, but you can die in dreams. Mortals can, anyway. I could be trapped in the dream world, though, and I couldn't afford a lengthy absence. Not right now.

The witches needed me.

"Mrrooowwww." The long, wailing squeal was followed by Mort, my black cat. He was linked to me in ways I'd never understood, but it allowed him to waltz right through my wards. He'd singled me out years ago when he was a skin-

and-bones kitten. Like a bat coming in for the kill, he'd jumped on my shoulder, and that had been that. He'd been with me ever since. Mort stalked up my body and dropped a dead mouse on my chest, looking inordinately pleased with himself.

I stroked his head and scratched behind his ears. "Thanks for breakfast," I told him. He purred madly, thrilled I'd noticed the still-twitching rodent—and the fact he hadn't eaten it himself.

No more sleep. Not for me. Not today. I moved the cat off to one side and placed the mouse on a small table that sat next to my sleeping pallet. I'd gut and skin it and add it to the community breakfast pot. We'd moved past our antipathy for eating rats and mice a long while back. Meat was meat.

If my plan worked, the one I'd hatched yesterday, we'd be able to grow vegetables again. I'd have to kick it around with the witches. It would mean being up-front about who I really was, but most of them had known I wasn't like them from the moment I showed up at their coven's lodge.

Like most buildings in the UK, the lodge had been a casualty of the Breaking. Not many structures could have withstood the rolling earthquakes, torrential electrical storms, and hurricanes that had battered Earth. It had taken months before the worst of them blew through. By then, very little remained.

At the time, I'd marveled at how thin the veneer of human society really was. How little it had taken to bring it to its knees. Mortals would have been better served to remain in caves without all their fancy fossil-fuel-driven contraptions and electronic crap. Even in the throes of the

Breaking, I'd overheard humans bemoaning the loss of the Internet. And their bloody phones.

There had been too many of them—people, not phones. At least that little problem was solved.

A soft tap sounded on my door. Mort skinned his lips back from his teeth and hissed, doing a decent feline imitation of a guard dog. For some reason, the comparison amused me.

A quick scan told me Tansy stood on the far side of the door. I reeled in my warding and said, "Come in."

Leather hangings that served to close off the entry point to my small room fluttered as Tansy slipped through. She looked just as undernourished as she had last night, but something had changed. The vulnerable air that had dogged her was gone. She bowed her head but straightened quickly.

"I was afraid I'd wake you," she said.

"Mort beat you to it." I rolled into a sit and planted my feet on the floor. It left my knees bent at an awkward angle since my pallet was so low.

Tansy walked closer to the cat. "Good kitty. You went hunting."

After one more hiss, Mort slithered beneath Tansy's extended hand. He acted tough, but he was an attention whore at heart, although he picked and chose who he allowed to pet him.

"Did you sleep well?" I asked as I got to my feet. I hadn't ever undressed last night. Made my morning preparations simpler. I smoothed my woolen leggings into place and pulled my streaked-and-spotted tunic low on my hips. Time to wash it, but not today.

Crap. I hadn't even gotten around to taking off my lace-up boots. No wonder dragons had dogged my dreams.

"Not particularly," Tansy muttered in response to my query about how she'd slept. "It's all right, though. I'm sure tonight will be better."

I wasn't, but I kept my mouth shut. Running up against the Hunt changed a person. Not that Tansy, young as she was, didn't realize evil existed in the world, but knowing it and seeing it were two different things.

She looked up from petting Mort. A quick glance that took me in from head to toe. "I am so glad you're all right. The Hunt. They let you go?"

"Yes and no. It's a long story, and I'll talk with everyone at breakfast."

"We're all in the common room," she told me. "I, uh, told them." Before I could rebuke her for not minding my instructions, she hurried on. "I know you said to keep my mouth shut, but I was crying. Hilda came to me and tried to comfort me. When her spell didn't work, she looked into my mind."

"It's all right." I gave Tansy a quick hug. Hilda was the girl's aunt. Shared blood made mind reading possible for witches. Tansy's mother was dead. She'd made it through childbirth, but nursing had depleted what few reserves she had left.

"No. It isn't," Tansy said. "You saved my life. I—"

I gripped her shoulder to stem the flow of words. "The main reason I told you to remain silent was I didn't want any of the others coming after me in a misplaced bid to help.

Witch magic is no match for Odin and his Riders." I stopped before adding I had enough on my conscience.

Mort slithered between the skins and out the door. I grabbed my hairbrush, something I'd crafted myself from boar bristles from the last wild pig we'd managed to catch, and worked on my hair. It had tangles on top of tangles.

"I'll do the back, but you need to sit so I can reach it." Tansy pried the brush out of my hands. Witch magic settled around me as she worked on my unruly locks, braiding sections as she finished with them.

"Thanks." I stood and picked up the mouse. "Shall we join the others for breakfast?"

Tansy nodded. I was touched she'd waited to eat to check on me. The witches were fair. They'd have saved her portion. And mine. Enough of us had faded away from starvation and illness, we'd lost a third of our numbers.

I kicked the jewelry I'd discarded the previous night into a corner before I followed her out of the room.

We made our way down branching corridors deeper into the cave system. I'd led our band to this place. I'd known about it from Celtic history. Ben Nevis had been a sacred spot since the British Isles had risen out of the North and Irish Seas. As I'd hoped, the caverns had kept the witches safe, offered us a place to live where earthquakes couldn't touch us.

No one had questioned how I'd found this spot. Almost as if they hadn't wanted to force me into a lie. It wasn't the type of place I'd have stumbled upon. The primary entrance was so well hidden, no one who didn't know about it could have found it.

The witches called out greetings as we ducked beneath the low lintel and into the common room. A peat fire burned smokily in a hearth at the far end of the space. One of my distant ancestors had built that hearth—and vented it. More likely, he (or she) had located the hearth beneath an existing flue leading somewhere no one would notice smoke.

"Go and get your breakfast." I gave Tansy a small shove and pulled my belt knife, intent on gutting and skinning the mouse.

"I'll take that," Patrick said. "I had cooking duty this morning." Short with thinning blond hair and blue eyes, he held the same ragged, half-starved look as the rest of us. Frayed woolen breeks hung off his slim hips, and he wore a patched flannel shirt that had once been a green plaid. I handed over the mouse and tucked my knife away.

Tansy brought me a bowl before getting another for herself.

I spooned some of the gruel mixture into my mouth. Wild grains, roots, and bits of a stringy squirrel, it was better fare than we usually had. Once my dish was empty, I set it aside and walked to the front of the common room. There was no way to ease into what I had to say, so I dove in. Worst that would happen was they'd kick me out of the coven, but I didn't believe they'd do that, not after all the years I'd bided with them.

I scanned the room. Maybe fifty witches remained. Mostly women, but there were still a dozen men. "I have things to tell you," I began. "You may have questions. Many of you will feel I've wronged you, but please let me get through what I have to say."

Murmurs of assent swept through the room.

"All of you figured out I wasn't a witch a long time ago," I said. "You were kind enough not to pry. I am a Celt. Ceridwen is my mother. I have no idea who my da was."

The murmurs changed in tone and timbre. At least I had everyone's undivided attention. "Last night, Tansy and I ran into the Hunt. I bargained for her freedom, and Odin allowed her to return here on the condition I showed back up out on the moors.

"When I did so, two Valkyries jumped me. I killed one. The other surrendered. I'll spare you the details, but Odin and my mother were in cahoots. Once he realized who I was, he sent me on a bogus journey to locate her. It was stupid since he knew where she was all along.

"She'd offered him a bounty for locating me because she was too lazy to show up on Earth and hunt me down herself. Or maybe too proud. It doesn't matter which. Anyway, I met her in what's left of Inverlochy Castle. Back in the day, it was the Celts' primary domicile, and it's still standing."

I took a deep breath and blew it out before continuing, "I propose we go take a look at it. Much like this cave system, it's shrouded by magic. Unlike the cave, it offers courtyards where we could grow grain and vegetables."

A muted cheer rippled through the witches. Hilda stood. Short with steel-gray hair, she had keen blue eyes and a no-nonsense demeanor. A colorful skirt fell to the ground, and she'd wrapped a black woolen cape around her upper body. "When can we go visit it?"

"As soon as I'm done." I swallowed around a thick spot in

my throat. This next was tough, but I'd be damned if I'd cover for my mother. Not with the knowledge I had.

"One more thing," I went on. My voice had a harsh, raspy edge, but I didn't bother modulating it. "The Breaking was my fault. Mother apparently thought I'd get over my 'witch fascination' and return to her and the other Celts. When it didn't happen, she set a spell in play to hurry me along.

"I have no idea if she expected it to be so extensive or so destructive, but she's never given two fucks about mortals. In her mind, whatever damage she did to Earth was collateral and totally justified if it achieved what she wanted."

Breath steamed through my teeth. "Nearly done here. Last night, she made a bid for me to return. I threw her offer back in her face. Before, my exile was voluntary, but I bet it's permanent now."

I uncurled hands I didn't realize I'd fisted and dropped my habitual glamour. "No reason to hide what I am any longer."

Already on her feet, Hilda hustled to me and threw her arms around me. "Och, you poor child," she said.

I hugged her back, touched by her caring.

One by one, every witch in the room came to me and either touched me, kissed me, or gripped my hand.

"You are one of us," Patrick announced. "We wouldn't have it any other way." A chorus of *yesses* and *we agrees* rose around me.

I blinked back tears, grateful for every single witch. How different they were from the Celts I'd grown up with. "Shall we go take a peek at Inverlochy Castle? It's not far from here."

"We know, lass," Patrick said. "All of us do not need to come. Perhaps ten or so. We'll gather in the lee of the entrance."

Wise of him. We'd be exposed to goddess only knew what as we walked the few kilometers north of Fort William proper. Or what was left of it. I made my way to the meeting point. Mort materialized and jumped onto my shoulder. He probably hadn't liked it that I'd been gone last evening, and was doing his best to ensure I didn't give him the slip again.

Like all cats, he only pretended to be independent.

Nine of us began the trek across the moorlands. I tried to dislodge Mort, but he dug his claws into my shoulders, so I relented. I draped the best ward I could dredge up around our group. My magic was still depleted from the previous night and my nearly nonexistent amount of sleep.

Where had the dragons come from? I'd had dragon dreams before, but nothing as vivid as last night's visitation.

I kept my magical antennae extended, searching for any sign of threats. It was early enough in the day, I didn't sense anything out of the ordinary. There was a time when the bad things didn't come out until after dark, but I'd met everything from Vampires to Furies to Trolls in broad daylight. Guess it depended on how hungry they were.

The Vamps had surprised me. I always thought they reverted to being dead as soon as the sun came up, but maybe the Breaking had altered enough in the warp and weft of Earth's harmonics, sunlight wasn't a deterrent any longer.

It might have taken us an hour to cross to the ruins of

Inverlochy Castle. It sat on the banks of the river Lochy. Hilda stared at the piles of stones and looked at me. "Is there a secret way inside?"

I stood next to her. "If you look through your third eye, what do you see?"

I felt her power kindle and flare around her. "More of an outline of what used to be here, but I still don't see a doorway."

I walked to the perimeter of what had once been the castle walls and placed the flat of my palm on it. A rapid intake of breath from Hilda told me my magic made a difference.

"Hold on a moment," I said to the witches. While I saw the castle quite clearly, and it was simple for me to duck through the illusion holding its secrets, that was probably because I had matching magic.

The trick that made Inverlochy look like nothing beyond piles of tumbled stones had been forged by Celtic enchantment. I hadn't counted on it requiring the same power to unlock it, but apparently it did.

Could I dismantle it? If I did, would every passerby view the castle as a prime target to raid? I had an idea, and I moved back from the walls. I crooked a finger at everyone and said, "I'm not sure this will work, but if it does, it's easier —and far less risky—than me taking down the wards that render this place invisible."

I led the witches around to the back of the castle. An extensive graveyard peppered with family crypts spread around us. Many had probably caved in during the Breaking, but the larger ones had sported underground passageways into the castle, so the wealthiest families could visit their dead undisturbed.

"Fan out and check the crypts," I told everyone.

"What are we looking for?" Tansy asked.

"Passageways into the castle proper," Patrick answered her.

We'd been at it for maybe half an hour when I stumbled across exactly what I'd hoped to find. It hadn't been obvious. No. But I'd been searching with magic in addition to my eyes and hands. One of the back walls in the MacLinn crypt didn't feel right to me, so I cleared away debris. Sure enough, I spied a rounded passageway. Iron staves blocked my way, but the metal had rusted through and a stout kick sent the pieces clattering to the dirt floor.

I stuck two fingers into my mouth and whistled. It was safer than deploying more magic. As it was, I was amazed our combined power hadn't drawn a flock of curious sprites or faeries.

Or something far more malevolent.

Once the witches were crowded in around me, I stepped to one side and motioned them through the rounded corridor. I wanted to make certain they could get inside this way without my magic greasing the way. It wouldn't do much good for us to unearth a better lair if no one could enter.

Or leave.

I followed them through a winding passageway. We had to clear cave-ins in two spots, but neither was too serious. Finally, we stood in the lower hall. "Smells like Celts in here," Patrick muttered.

I took a long, deep sniff. It did, indeed, but very faintly to my nose.

"Are we certain your, um, kin, won't be returning?" Hilda asked.

"No. I'm not certain," I admitted, "but they haven't used this place since they left right after the Breaking. Earth isn't very pleasant these days, so I don't know why they'd return."

"If they did, we could go back to the place we are now," Patrick said.

I didn't have the heart to tell him it had once been a Celtic stronghold as well. If my kin were feeling territorial, they might well lay claim to both places. My memory of the Celts was that they might not have strong feelings about a particular item—until they thought someone else wanted it.

Then the gloves came off.

The witches had scattered, each intent on exploring what Inverlochy Castle might have to offer. I wandered outside into the extensive courtyards that had once been gardens. They were near enough to the river, we could rig up watering systems, and if we were smart about things, we could plant in raised beds that would maximize our yield.

My mouth flooded with saliva at the prospect of spinach or lettuce or carrots or radishes. Surely, we could locate seeds in the wreckage of one of several garden shops in Fort William.

Patrick and Hilda and Tansy found me hunkered next to a broken planter box running my fingers through rich dirt. I got to my feet and faced them. "What do you think?" I asked.

"We like it," Hilda said.

"Very much." Tansy smiled, soft and shy. After last night, I was delighted she still could smile.

A muted *wahoo* sounded from within.

"What is it?" Hilda cupped her hands around her mouth.

"Clothing chests. Lots of them. And boots. And cloaks."

"Is it all right for us to appropriate Celtic possessions?" Patrick screwed his face into a concerned expression.

I took my time answering. Finally, I said, "If my kin never return, obviously, there is no problem. If they do, however, you're bound to run into someone who's out for blood because you took their favorite cape."

"We could give it back," Tansy said.

"They wouldn't accept it," I told her. "The Celts can be petty bastards, and at that point they'd be more invested in making you pay for transgressing than in seeing reason."

"How did your mother seem last night?" Hilda asked.

The question surprised me. "Worse than usual," I replied. "She doesn't like it when she believes she's been thwarted."

"Mmph. How likely is she to return anytime soon?" Patrick narrowed his eyes to slits.

I considered it. "I honestly don't know. Given how many years it's been since the Breaking without her making an appearance—and how angry she is with me—I'm not expecting her back period. But I could be wrong."

The other witches drifted in from wherever they'd been exploring. One carried a pair of well-worn leather boots. Another had a warm, woolen cloak draped over her shoulders.

Should I tell them to return the spoils? Something in me rebelled. The Celts probably had no idea what they'd even left here. No reason for the items not to see some use.

"We will return and hold a whole coven meeting," Patrick said. "Everyone will vote on how they would like us to proceed. I believe this place is goddess sent. Perhaps Ceridwen's unexpected appearance had a secondary purpose."

While I followed his line of reasoning—witches didn't believe in coincidences—still I had a tough time believing Mother's untimely visit was linked to jarring my memory about these halls.

Mort was still draped around my neck, and he began to purr. The deep, throaty rumble soothed me as I crawled through the tunnel and back out into daylight. A spot of engineering work would make getting into and out of Inverlochy simpler.

A small frisson of unease filled me. This was my idea. What if the witches jumped on it and it blew up in their faces? I walked faster. I'd be part of the meeting, and I would make certain everyone knew Inverlochy Castle wasn't a risk-free venture.

Neither was our current location. In all fairness, I'd have to provide a full disclosure about it as well.

My breath formed clouds around me in the chilly air. By the end of the afternoon, we'd have a direction. I said a quick prayer to Danu we'd pick a path that would keep us all alive. And then I chided myself. I'd live no matter what, but I didn't want another witch death on my conscience.

I'd stood by while one after another had slipped away.

Weakened by short rations, disease had picked them off. Sometimes my magic had made a difference. More often, it hadn't.

I still couldn't believe Mother was behind the Breaking. Every time I thought about it, my vision hazed red and I wanted to kill her.

Not productive, I lectured myself. *Focus on today.*

It was how I'd lived since the Breaking, by dealing with what was in front of me. I'd done it for a long time, and I would keep doing it until things got better and I could risk letting my guard down for a while.

We went our separate ways once we returned. Patrick said he'd gather everyone in the common room in an hour. Since I had a spot of time, I picked up my discarded jewelry, dropped the items back in the wooden box, and tossed the whole mess down one of the many shafts dotting the caves beneath Ben Nevis.

It might be stupid and shortsighted on my part because the amulet concentrated my power, but I didn't care. If I never touched anything Celtic again, it would be too soon. Once I'd rid myself of the last remnants I had from Mother, I changed my clothes and headed for the common room.

I would have liked to have eaten more, but before I was halfway through my supper, the moonstone started acting up again. Travel between the Nine Worlds is straightforward. Yggdrasil extends to all of them, and it is climbable, but that's quite a waste of time. Those of us with strong magic use Bifrost, the Rainbow Bridge. Myths would have you believe only the gods can use the bridge, but it simply isn't true.

Long ago, I leveraged my power to travel to many worlds outside our realm, but I never found reason to remain. My exploratory jaunts grew shorter, and finally I retired to my stone hut with my lore books and my spells. Other than sparring matches with Jarle to maintain at least a semblance of physical conditioning, I lead a rather lonely life.

Except it doesn't feel that way to me. Magic has its own draw, and it's filled every nook and cranny in my heart and soul. I've worked diligently to develop my skills until my ability is stronger than some of the gods. Not that I would ever tell them—or anyone else—that little tidbit. What better way to have Odin smite me with lightning or Thor with his hammer?

I had some time to think about things over my rather truncated meal. Nidhogg had chosen me specifically. He'd said he overheard my conversation with Jarle, but I understand dragons. No matter what he'd overheard, he'd never have deigned to land unless he had a plan in mind.

One he'd been working on for a while. Dragons are deep thinkers. No off-the-cuff, spur-of-the-moment decisions for them. Beyond that, his comments about Midgard told me he'd been watching me for a while. When Odin ignored the dragon's concerns, he went looking for another emissary, one who might be a bit more malleable.

I bit back a laugh. That would be almost anyone except Odin. He and Thor and their cohorts who wandered through Asgard answered to no one. And wasted huge amounts of magic bickering among themselves.

I tossed on a jacket. Night was falling, and while Vanaheim was usually warm, Midgard had seasons. Right now, it was winter in the Scottish Highlands, which meant short days and long nights. One of my dirty little secrets was I'd spent a few years living in Midgard before the Breaking.

More than a few.

I liked humans, and it was a simple enough matter to pass as one. What finally drove me back to Vanaheim was it hurt watching mortals make choices I knew full well would create problems for them. Naturally, I hadn't anticipated the Breaking, but even I could see that unchecked breeding would eventually strain finite resources.

Beyond that, mortals had no idea Midgard was part of the Nine Worlds. They assumed their world, their Earth, was its own entity. When things they did to it caused Midgard pain, her unhappiness rippled through to the other worlds. I tried to make a difference, but there were limits to what I could do without revealing what I was.

Even if I had, no one would have accepted my words. Men had stopped believing in magic at least a century ago. Most of them, anyway. And now none of it mattered. So many were dead, I rarely saw them anymore.

Colors washed over me as I transited the bridge. Timing was everything with Bifrost. It was easy to overshoot or undershoot my destination. Tonight, though, I was paying close attention. I had no idea what the moonstone would do if I misjudged, and I didn't particularly want to find out.

One of my first tasks once I returned would be figuring out how the bloody thing was linked to me and loosening its ties. I assumed I could do that, but maybe I was wrong.

The chill damp of Midgard closed around me. It was pitch dark because clouds occluded both moon and stars. A fine sleet drizzled down on me. Normally, I made my scouting runs in daylight, but the dragon's gem clearly had a plan for me. I opened my magic to it, hoping it would tell me where it wanted me to go.

Sure enough, a route formed in my mind, although it was on the creepy side to be controlled like that. If I hadn't linked to it, the infernal thing probably would have zapped me every time I took a wrong turn. Better this way. Following a hunch, I probed a certain way and thought I sensed dragon energy hovering.

But maybe I was wrong. I've always had a hell of an imagination. It's a prerequisite to wield power since I have to visualize the outcome I want before it happens.

Bypassing the moonstone, I scanned empty fields stretching around me. Tonight, I was in Scotland, but it was where I usually went. For one thing, it was where the Celtic casting that had broken the world still pulsed weakly. Someone—not me—had done their best to defuse the spell.

I searched for magic. For anything out of the ordinary. For something I could report back to Nidhogg, so the dragon didn't label me a slacker. Sticking to my moonstone-approved route, I covered the ground between me and where a coven of witches lived. They'd taken up residence in an old Celtic citadel beneath Ben Nevis, although they'd been damned lucky to find it in the midst of the Breaking.

Witch magic was weak, but the occasional practitioner pulled off a miracle.

A flicker of something dark pinged the edges of my seeking spell. I turned toward it and fed more magic into that particular sector. Nothing too obvious, but I wanted to see if anything was really out there.

I stilled my breathing, blended into the darkness, and let clues flow to me. The stone must have augmented my ability because I wasn't working as hard as usual. Goblins were about, along with one troll.

I may have mentioned, I'm far from a warrior. Normally, I'd have teleported far from the wicked creatures. Nothing good ever came from trafficking with such persons. But tonight was the beginning of a different life. I edged away from where I'd sensed the goblins to see what would happen.

The moonstone stabbed me hard enough I nearly yelped.

If I hadn't known better, I'd have thought one of Nidhogg's claws was in my pocket. "If you want to know what's going on so badly," I muttered, "you should be here yourself."

I waited to be struck down by dragonfire, but it never happened. The goblins were on the move. I couldn't find the troll anymore. One of the many lochs dotting the Highlands seemed to be where they were headed. I split my seeking spell and understanding kicked me in the gut.

Humans had taken up residence in crumbling ruins that had once been row houses. They'd make a tasty meal for the goblins, who preferred human flesh above all else. I remembered the dragon's instructions. He'd said to call for him if need arose, but would a dragon show himself in Midgard?

That part wasn't my problem. I'd been tasked to observe and call in help if it was needed. While I'd dillydallied, the goblins had nearly reached the human encampment. Gripping the moonstone, I used telepathy to alert the dragon.

I started toward where the mortals were, intent on at least warning them, when a roaring filled my ears. I checked the stone still clutched in my hand, but for once it wasn't ordering me about. It wasn't even warm. I fought an inane desire to chuck it as far away from me as I could, but a slight pulse brought me back to my senses.

The roaring turned into a cacophony of noise and the sky

lit as a hole ripped in the ether. Nidhogg—or some other golden dragon that looked just like him—leapt through, fire hissing from his open jaws. Beneath him, the goblins were lit up clearly. Easily double the number I'd sensed, so they must have been masking their foul magic.

Something about the dragon immobilized the creatures. I expected them to flee. Instead, they stared upward. The troll I'd lost track of lumbered into view and screeched something at the goblins in a language I'd never heard. Whatever it was, it got through, and they scattered.

The dragon bugled and painted crazy paths of fire between the goblins, cutting off their retreat. They'd run in one direction and hit a line of fire. Turning and going the other didn't yield any better results. It dawned on me the dragon was playing with his victims.

Making them miserable before he finally killed them.

The troll bellowed and shook his fists skyward. He was made of stone, so fire couldn't harm him, but if he was caught outside in daylight, he'd become inert like the standing stones that peppered moors all through the British Isles. They'd all been trolls once.

The dragon didn't need me. He had this well in hand. When I tested walking away this time, the moonstone sent waves of approval washing through me. Nice to have its support. I wasn't paying much attention to where I was going, so I was surprised when I ended up a stone's throw from Ben Nevis and the witches' lair.

I heard raised voices from within, followed by a woman saying, "I'll see what's wrong. The rest of you remain here unless I call for aid."

On the heels of her words, the Celt burst into the open. I wasn't surprised to see her, but I'd never viewed her like this. Oh I'd known she employed a glamour, but I'd never expended magic to pry beneath it. I assumed she shielded her real appearance for a reason. Never in my wildest imaginings did I suspect she'd hidden herself because she was beautiful enough to lure men to their deaths.

Not that she hadn't been stunning before, but now she shone with an inner light. Magic spilled from her as she sought the source of the disturbance that had drawn her out of doors. Her hair was the same. Brilliant red shot with gold. But her face held the unmistakable stamp of the Celtic gods. High forehead, sculpted cheeks, full lips, and golden eyes.

She was taller than I'd thought, and strongly built. Slender, but muscular. I'd run into more than a few of the Celts over the long years of my life, and she was a dead ringer for Ceridwen. Was this the Mother Goddess of the world? I risked a small bit of magic, checking.

Two things happened so fast, they shocked me. The woman must have felt my probe because she pelted toward me at top speed. Meanwhile, my seeking spell told me the woman wasn't Ceridwen. Far from it. Mixed in with her Celtic origins, she carried dragon blood.

A lot of dragon blood.

How was that even possible? Dragons almost never mated outside their own kind. I was almost positive it was forbidden, and the very few falls from grace had all been Norse-dragon pairings.

Living, breathing proof I was wrong was nearly upon me.

She stopped about a meter away; magic flashed and flared from her raised hands. "Who are you?" she demanded. "And why are you spying on us?" Her voice was low and lyrical. I could have listened to her read the dictionary and been captivated.

I knew I was staring, but I couldn't tear my eyes off her. Meanwhile, the damned moonstone was practically purring, almost as if it recognized the woman standing before me. A skirt that looked as if had been sewn from rags hit her at knee level, and a black woolen cloak with many holes swathed her upper body. She hadn't bothered with shoes.

"Either you answer my questions, or I'll trap you where you stand until you do." She took a step closer, and I felt magic seep from her and begin to form a circle around me.

I could have defeated her spell easily enough, but I didn't want to alarm her. "My name is Bjorn," I said adding a smattering of a calming spell to my words.

"All right, *Bjorn*"—she paused after my name for emphasis—"what the fuck are you doing here?" She slitted her golden eyes. "While we're at it, what are you? You have the stink of a Norseman."

"Aye, lady, and you smell of the Celts," I countered, less than pleased about her slur aimed at my kinsmen. I wasn't overly fond of Odin or Thor, but I'd defend them to the death from insults.

She twisted her mouth into a disgusted expression. "Fine. Odin sent you." She waved a hand skyward. "Where's the Hunt? I thought only dead things visited Earth."

"Odin did not send me," I protested. About that time, Nidhogg chose to overfly where we stood. He must have polished off the goblins—and the troll. He didn't remain long, just cut through the sky once before he turned around, presumably heading back to the gateway he'd used before.

The woman stared upward. "Fuck me. A dragon."

It would have been a perfect opportunity for me to escape, but I didn't want to leave. "Have you not seen one before?" I asked.

"Yes, but not since I was a child." Her chin was still tilted, and she twisted her head back and forth. The flow of her magic was directed at where Nidhogg had been flying as she sought information.

The Celts had their own dragon named Dewi. I considered asking if that was who she'd seen, but we'd barely met. She lived with witches. Maybe she hid her dragon and Celtic natures.

Why else would she have covered up all her charms with a glamour that made her look far more ordinary?

Finally, she glanced at me once again. "If you were a threat, you'd have tried to jump me. How about if you just leave? I have enough problems without figuring you out." A weary undernote lay beneath her words.

"I gave you my name," I pointed out.

She rolled her eyes. "I'm Rowan."

Somehow, it didn't quite fit. "Has that always been your name?" I winced. "Sorry. It's none of my affair."

"You're right. It's not." Her nostrils flared. "Something is burning. Crap. What did the dragon do?"

Before she took off running, I said, "It's all right. I located goblins and a troll intent on a group of humans. The dragon took care of them. I assume the goblins are what you smell.

The troll may be immobilized. If so, daylight will finish him off."

As I'd been talking, she'd folded her arms beneath her breasts. "What are you doing here?" she asked again. "We've never had a spot of aid from any quarter since the Breaking. Why you? And why now?"

I didn't have the answers to either question. Not really. And I had no idea how much she knew—or didn't—about either her Celtic side or her dragon one. She did admit to having seen a dragon before, which likely meant she knew full well what she was. But why hide out with a coven? She could be with the other Celts—wherever they'd run off to.

"Rowan?" a man's voice called from a few meters away.

"I'm all right," she called back.

I peered around her and funneled magic to see who was there. I didn't like the idea of a man being interested in her wellbeing. Was she married? To a witch? Why hadn't she aimed higher?

I cut my train of thought off cold. What she was or wasn't, and what she'd done or not done marriage-wise was absolutely none of my affair. I was here to spy for Nidhogg, nothing more and nothing less.

I hadn't been paying close attention, so I wasn't prepared when she tossed a truth spell over me. I tried to slice through it, but the weave was quite fine. Not that I couldn't have defeated it with magic of my own, but it would take me a while. And force me to reveal just how much power simmered within me.

"Do you know who the dragon was?" she demanded.

Trapped between her spell and the moonstone, I opted

for silence. I was certain the stone wouldn't approve of me telling her much of anything at all. Contrary to my expectations, it warmed, almost as if it were urging me to say something.

"I believe so," I replied.

"What does that mean?"

"I'm here on the ground just like you. What I saw was a large, male golden dragon. It could have been one of several candidates."

She absorbed what I'd said for a moment before she muttered, "So there's more than one of them. Where are you from, Bjorn?"

The weave of her spell tightened. So far, the moonstone hadn't done much more than warm and pulse pleasantly. "Not here."

An exasperated breath whistled through what sounded like clenched teeth. "I'm neither stupid nor as young as I appear. When I ask you something, I expect information. Not here doesn't cut it."

The man who'd spoken to her hadn't left. He moved forward until the light sheeting from Rowan illuminated him. I sucked in an involuntary gasp of air. Of all the wretched luck, I knew him. He'd been one of those I'd hung about with before the Breaking.

He clearly came to the same conclusion because he extended an arm, index finger pointing right at me. "You. Where the hell have you been these past fifty years?"

Rowan turned to look at Patrick. "You know him?"

"I do, indeed. His name is Bjorn. He showed up out of the blue maybe a hundred years back and drifted in and out of my dry goods store—when I still had one. Over time, we became friends, and we'd often stand one another a pint and a game of pool at the local pub."

"And then one day I wasn't there anymore," I cut in. "I had my reasons."

Rowan ignored me. "What is he?" she asked Patrick. "I sense Norse, but it's faint."

Patrick grunted. "When I knew him, he convinced me he was a witch, albeit a damned weak one."

Rowan flapped a hand my way. "Not a witch."

Since neither one of them were paying any attention to me, I started a surreptitious teleport spell. No way I could win here, so the best thing was for me to leave.

The moonstone wasn't having any of it. Where it had augmented my power when I faced goblins, this time it did the opposite and power frittered through my fingers. Or maybe Rowan's truth spell was getting in the way.

I felt the full brunt of her focus once again. "You understand how to circumvent truth spells. Not here is true enough, yet it tells me less than nothing. You will accompany us within."

I pushed my shoulders back and stood tall. Before, I'd used a bit of my own glamour to appear less than what I am, but I needed Rowan and Patrick to take me seriously. I wasn't some minor magician they could push around.

"It's time for me to be on my way. I'm scarcely your prisoner. I've done nothing to justify you holding me against my will." I considered adding they should thank me for wiping out a herd of goblins, but that might be laying it on too thick. Besides, the wiping out had actually been the dragon, not me.

Raising a hand, I cut through the webbing of Rowan's truth spell and turned. No one called after me or tried to stop me as I strode into the night.

After I'd gone fifty paces, I called up an entry to Bifrost and traversed the Rainbow Bridge. After making its desires known earlier, the moonstone had reverted to stone like inertness.

Even after I was back in Vanaheim, I couldn't escape Rowan's image. Her scent clung to me, amber and mint and vanilla. Leaving Midgard had been difficult. I hadn't wanted to leave her, but neither did I want other coven members dredging up the many memories they had of me.

Groups of witches formed and reformed as years passed. While I knew about the witches beneath Ben Nevis, I hadn't paid close attention to individuals within the coven. Were there others besides Patrick who'd remember me? If so, what exactly would they recall?

My ears weren't exactly burning. How could they be with layers of the Nine Worlds between us? But I didn't fancy anyone recounting tales to Rowan. I'd been a bit of a philanderer in those days. Witches made willing partners. It wasn't as if I were stepping out on a mate of my own. I've never had one, but some of the witches I dallied with did.

I always figured with all those festivals of theirs, fertility rites like Beltane, no one would get too upset about who had sex with whom.

I'd reached my house. Instead of going inside, I settled on

my haunches in the dirt. The sky had developed the gray-pink aspect that told me dawn wasn't far off. I had plenty to do. Spells in various stages of completion required my oversight.

But the only thing I wanted was to return to Midgard.

"Get over yourself," I muttered just before I stood and shambled inside. I hadn't made a particularly stellar showing. Besides, Rowan—or whatever her name really was—was a goddess.

And a dragon.

She'd have less than no use for a poor sod like me.

I fumed as I watched Bjorn walk away. He'd given me less than nothing in response to my questions. Only his name. I wanted to shout a power word to stop him in his tracks. It would have worked, but I'd never shown anywhere near the full scope of my power to the witches. Granted I'd finally fessed up about what I was, but them hearing it and seeing the evidence might yield different reactions.

The way things stood, I was still one of them. A full on display of my magical ability could change all that. Much as I did not want Bjorn to leave, I also didn't want to risk alienating the only family I'd ever known. Mother didn't count with her tempers and her self-serving ways. Her go-to place was what was in it for her. Our recent exchange was a potent reminder nothing about that had altered in the least.

Patrick stood by my side not saying a word. Indecision must have been rolling off me in waves, but he knew better than to mine for information. Bjorn was easily the best-looking man I'd ever run across with his ice-blond hair and eyes the shade of a sun-dappled ocean. His square chin, broad forehead, and hawk's beak of a nose were rugged, but they fit together nicely.

His hair had been caught up in small bits of leather. Not exactly braided, but tucked out of the way. Judging from how far down his body it fell, I assumed it was as long as my own. Leather garments had hugged his rangy frame. A wee bit taller than me, his build was muscular but not broad. As in the muscles arranged themselves pleasingly across his shoulders and down his arms. I hadn't examined his legs. I would have had to move past his groin to do that. A risky action given how attracted I was to him.

His power was different from mine, but strong. I'd sensed him masking his ability, and I wanted to unwrap him, strip all his layers away until the man beneath stood before me. The image was so sensual and so graphic, my body vibrated with need.

It had been a long while since I'd taken a man to bed, so long I barely remembered the mechanics of lovemaking. I rarely thought of men in that way, so why the hell was I swimming through a sea of heat and hunger and lust? Nothing had passed between Bjorn and me, yet I was attracted to him. More than attracted, I craved him with a singlemindedness I'd have to bury ten leagues under.

I had a lot to deal with. I did not need to add to my problems.

"Rowan?" Patrick touched my arm, and I startled.

"I'm all right," I muttered for the second time that evening. "You know him?"

Patrick nodded. "Of a time, I did. It was long ago, well before the Breaking. As I think on it, he likely hid much of his true nature because the man who just walked into the night carried himself very differently from the one I recall."

"How so?" I turned to face my old friend. Witches were far from immortal, but many were very long-lived, lasting centuries. Patrick was one of the old ones.

"He made us believe he was one of us," Patrick replied and held up a hand. "Aye, I know how tough that is to swallow, but he concealed a lot of what shone through tonight. He'd romp with us during festivals, fade in and out of coven life. Back then, none of us minded."

I absorbed what he'd told me. Before the Breaking, everyone was more accepting, more trusting. "What kind of man parlays with dragons?" I asked.

"Legend has it dragons and Norsemen are connected." He exhaled noisily. "I'm not being impertinent, but how much of your Celtic background did you absorb before you left?"

"Some. Living with them day in and day out, I figured out who was who." I licked at lips that had gone dry. "I, uh, I've never exactly admitted this, but Mother didn't show me off. To anyone. I lived in her rooms in the Celts' castle for many years before I broke free."

"Do you mean to say, she hid you away?" At my nod, Patrick drew his brows into a thin, unhappy line. "Do you know why?"

"No. I always figured it was because she'd dallied with

someone she was ashamed of and feared the other Celts would throw it in her face if the result—me—was too visible."

"Aye, but she could have rid herself of a child she didn't want." He focused blue eyes filled with compassion on me.

"Do. Not. Feel. Sorry. For. Me," I hissed.

"There's a difference between support and sympathy," he reminded me in a brusque tone. "Back to your Celtic roots. How much of your history do you know?"

"Not much," I admitted. "The Celts have our own dragon god, but there was only one of them. I believe Dewi was female. She kept to herself, and I only caught the odd glimpse of her. Mother told me she had a foul temper and to steer well clear of her."

"Interesting. What do you know about the Norse pantheon?"

I had no idea where he was going with this. Sooner or later someone else would come outside to see what had happened to us. "About as much as I know about the Celts." I shrugged. "Odin and his stupid Hunt. Thor and his hammer. Asgard. Valhalla."

The corners of Patrick's mouth twitched, and he told me, "The Hunt is but one small aspect of Odin's power."

I crooked two fingers his way, not in the mood to play guessing games where I had to keep feeding him questions.

He understood. "My take is Bjorn is from somewhere in the Nine Worlds. They're all linked together by Yggdrasil, the One Tree. It's an enormous ash and a key part of all Norse legends."

"Go on. I've heard of the tree, but I figured it was a metaphor for something else."

Patrick shook his head. "No. The tree is real. I've seen it." He stopped for a moment before going on. "This"—he stooped and patted the dirt—"is one of the Nine Worlds. What we call Earth is named Midgard by the Norsemen."

I thought about it. "So if they're right, and everything is linked together, did the Breaking impact the other eight worlds?"

"I have no idea."

"There are a whole lot of worlds out there," I murmured. "Hundreds of borderworlds. Maybe thousands. Most of them don't support life."

"I suppose you'd have to teleport to get there." Patrick sounded wistful. That type of magic was well beyond witch-linked ability.

"Yeah. But it's not pleasant. The place between worlds has no air. If you guess wrong and hit a world that also has no air, it can be nerve-wracking."

Something occurred to me. "If you've seen Yggdrasil, the Norse worlds are close."

"Aye. Mortals are denied access to most all of them. Our place is here."

"But you've snuck into some, haven't you?" I raised a brow.

Patrick nodded. "I have, and I wasn't apprehended. Fortune smiled on me because my life would have been forfeit had my incursions been discovered."

I gave him a quick hug. "You must have been very curious."

"Och, I was. Also very young. And rash enough to return many times."

I was still thinking about Bjorn. How long had he been traveling back and forth between wherever he lived in the Nine Worlds and Earth? Had tonight's visit been coincidence? Was he an actual god? If so, which one?

But most important was whether or not he'd return.

I scraped my teeth together. I was being stupid. What difference would his presence make? He was easy on the eyes, and he'd probably be a great addition to my bed, but the very last thing I needed was to get mixed up with any more deities.

It was bad enough that dragons had invaded my dreams. One question I hadn't picked over was whether my dragon dreams from last night had anything to do with the dragon who'd just flown over my head. I had an odd feeling the answer was yes, but I didn't see the connection.

"The others will wonder what became of us," Patrick said.

"I'm surprised they're not out here *en masse* already," I retorted. "How about if you go back inside."

"Where are you going?"

"To see what's burning. I'll be quick about it."

"I'll send Mort after you." He turned to trot back toward the well-hidden entrance to the caves beneath Ben Nevis.

"Thanks," I called. The cat was good company. Not precisely a familiar, but near enough. If the need arose, I was certain he'd share his feline magic with me.

I summoned a mage light to illuminate my way and loped toward the smell of smoke. It wasn't long before I saw flames and counted five pyres. The troll Bjorn had mentioned stood like a sentinel between the burning piles.

When I probed him with my power, I found life within, but it was already beginning to ebb.

Sure enough, dawn was breaking.

A quick search yielded humans, still safe in their rubble pile. I couldn't imagine what they'd lived through. Absent magic, I'd have thrown in the towel long since. I tilted my head and stared at the sky. The thick cloud cover from earlier had receded, and a few stars twinkled in the velvet darkness above me.

I wanted the dragon to return, but I had the oddest feeling the beast was linked to Bjorn in some unknown way. Reading between the lines of his description, they'd worked together tonight. Did it mean the witches and I weren't alone any longer? Or was the goblin massacre an isolated incident?

I cursed Ceridwen nine ways from Faery. She could have taught me far more than she had. Most of what I'd learned I'd picked up from context or from poring over her books and scrolls. She would have rebuked me sharply for treading on forbidden ground, but she never consulted her old source materials. If she wanted something, she bent over her cauldron.

I'd hated that kettle with a passion when I was a child. It got all the attention I'd craved. If Mother was communing with her darling, I had to wait. And if that damned thing bubbled or snorted or puffed steam or smoke, Mother came running. I could be crying my eyes out, and she ignored me.

"Oh for the love of Andromeda, stop it," I told myself, talking out loud so I'd be certain to take my own advice.

Whatever Ceridwen was—or wasn't—it wasn't my fault, nor did I have control over any of it. Lots of kids drew rotten hands. I didn't have a corner on that market, and feeling sorry for myself was a dead-end road. It wouldn't buy me anything but the icky, uncomfortable feeling if I only turned over enough rocks I'd figure things out.

There weren't enough rocks in the universe. Or enough time.

A low purring growl told me Mort had found me. Sure enough, he launched himself to my shoulders and curled around my neck. I stroked his ratty fur, happy for his simple, uncomplicated presence.

I needed to get back to the witches' meeting. At the point the dragon's magic—or maybe Bjorn's—had drawn me outside, they'd nearly decided to move to Inverlochy Castle. The discussion when I left was about whether to split our forces and maintain both locations.

I could see arguments on each side of that coin. The primary one for picking one locale or the other was there weren't all that many of us, and we were stronger together. The best rationale for separating was that each spot had specific advantages. I hadn't yet told them I was still keeping an eye on the magic that had spawned the Breaking.

If it got away from me, we'd be far better served beneath Ben Nevis. Who knew what impact runaway Celtic magic would have on Inverlochy Castle? The place might not have been originally constructed with Celt power, but it may as well have been. Once we took it over, we redid all its moorings.

I pushed my shoulders back from their slumped position. Yeah. Lots to think about. A bunch of responsibility. If I guessed wrong, or my power faltered for some unknown reason, witches might die. I didn't want even one more witch death on my conscience. Not that I hadn't done all I could for the witches who'd faded away, but my best wasn't good enough.

It rankled.

What hurt even more was it would have cost Ceridwen almost nothing to have helped. No need to reveal her spell was the culprit that had unraveled the world. She could have rustled up Gwydion or Arawn or Arianrhod or Bran. Or even Andraste, although that one would have been truly out of her element tending to the sick and wounded. And not just witches. Mortals had died in droves. Piles of bodies had rotted to nothing but bones.

I shook myself so hard, Mort yowled and dragged me out of my funk. I couldn't go backward. Nothing to be done about the devastation that had already occurred.

The sky had lightened with the dawn. A quick little gasp from the troll told me he was gone. Good riddance. He'd do far more for the landscape as a standing stone.

I turned back toward Ben Nevis with Mort purring up a storm. Time for a stern lecture. From me. To me. Usually, I did better than this holding my disenchantment at bay. And my anger. Why had I chosen now to throw myself a pity party? Mother wasn't any different than she'd ever been. I had to accept it and move on. She might be annoyed I hadn't tossed myself at her feet begging forgiveness for unknown sins, but she and I were done.

"No." I was back to talking out loud. "We were finished almost the day I was born. I just didn't know it back then."

For some reason, acknowledging the truth made me feel

better. I'd done all right on my own. I hadn't faltered for lack of maternal hovering. Mort traded off purring for licking my neck with his rough tongue. Almost as if he divined my thoughts and was trying to make up for the mothering I'd never received.

Together, we covered the distance to the witches' lair and ducked inside. A quick trip down the central passageway spit us out in the common room.

Tansy ran to me, light on her feet. Tonight her fair hair was loose, and it fluffed around her head and upper body lending her an angelic appearance. "You're back. We were just getting worried about you."

I gave her a quick hug. "Of course, I'm back."

"Are all the goblins dead?" someone called.

"Yes, and a single troll. We have a handsome new standing stone down by the small loch." I made my way to the front of the common room and asked, "What did you decide?"

No need to elaborate. They'd understand what I meant.

"Is it acceptable if I speak for the coven?" Patrick asked.

After a sea of yesses and ayes, he went on. "We believe it best to split our forces. Initially, only a few of us will make the move to Inverlochy. We will plant seeds and tend them and see how it goes. We do have a request of you, Rowan."

It surprised me since the witches had never asked me to for anything before. "Of course. What is it?"

"Since you can teleport, and travel between the two locations will be risky, we hope you'll agree to spend time in both places."

"I'd planned to do that anyway," I told the witches. This

was as good a lead-in as I was likely to get for my other revelation, so I went for it. "You'll recall I told you Ceridwen's magic was behind the Breaking. By the time I discovered the spot she'd loosed her destruction, it had mostly played itself out.

"I've done my best to oversee it since then, to make certain it's not boobytrapped in some unknown way and biding its time before it surges to life again. So far, I've done all right, but magic is slippery, and there could come a time when my efforts fail." I stopped without telling them about Mother's legendary temper. After our last go-round, if there was a way to stoke the remains of her spell back to life, she'd do it to get back at me.

"We appreciate what you've done." Hilda stood up in the middle of the room. "Before this, you've worked alone. We understand why. You didn't want to reveal your magic to us, but now that we know, we're standing ready to assist."

"Aye, tell us what you need," rose from several quarters.

Their unstinting support and belief in me thickened my throat, and I felt the hot bite of tears behind my lids. Mort upped the ante on his purring.

"Thank you," I told the witches. "I appreciate it, and there may well be a place for magic that's different from mine. Since I realized it was Mother's magic that caused the Breaking, I've been considering how I can neutralize it and give Earth a fighting chance to rebuild. The earthquakes and storms have lessened enough, we might have a chance."

"That's a broad topic, and we've covered enough ground for tonight," Patrick said. "Tomorrow, we'll firm up who will go to Inverlochy. When I asked for volunteers earlier, nearly everyone raised their hand. I'm delighted by your enthusiasm, but what we're looking for will be a mix of magics. So those who are there have a chance of defending themselves."

"Worst thing that would happen," I murmured, "is a stray Celt might show up, but when I was there a couple of nights back, the place hadn't been disturbed in a long time."

"What's the best approach if that happens?" Hilda asked.

I beat back a grin. "Blame it on me. Ceridwen's errant spawn. Apologize and leave. I truly don't believe we have much to worry about. This place"—I spread my arms wide—"was shaped by Celtic magic too. It's how I knew about it. Not that I'd ever seen it before, but I felt the pulse of its power."

"You're full of surprises," Patrick said and angled a speculative glance my way.

I shrugged. "'Fraid I've about run out of them. The Celts don't have ties here. They've settled on a borderworld, and, from the looks of things, they seem fine there."

"Any chance your mother might rustle them up to undo some of the harm she—?"

"None." I cut Wendell off. Another of the elder witches, he was angular and thin to the point of emaciation. White hair fell around his bony shoulders and patched clothing.

"What Mother did was forbidden," I told them. Harsh words, but the witches deserved the truth. "Part of the covenant that governs those with strong magic is we will not strike the first blow against humans."

"How could they not know what Ceridwen did?" Patrick asked.

"They probably do and have looked the other way, but it doesn't mean any of her kinfolk would aid her if she proposed further harm." I reached up, detached Mort from my shoulders, and cradled him in my arms. "A little bit ago, you said this was enough for tonight."

"It is. I'll see everyone tomorrow when we break our fast," Patrick said.

I scuttled out of the room before anyone could hit me up with any more "what-ifs." A lot had happened, and I was tired. Would the dragons visit my dreams again? A corner of my soul—one I didn't recognize—made a bid for dragons.

Lots of them.

I should have been frightened. Instead, a fine edge of anticipation tightened in my chest.

I'd have liked it better if I understood why.

CHAPTER SEVEN, BJORN

I overslept, something I rarely do. By the time I was up and moving and had slopped down my morning tea, the sun was well on its way to its zenith. No one had come knocking this morning, also an unusual occurrence. It was rare no one wanted potions or poultices or a special tea.

Something to strengthen their magic. Or weaken someone else's.

I held secrets. Lots of them. But I was careful not to provide anything that would weaponize anyone's magic. I might tell them a particular powder or herb would have specific effects when it was far more benign than what they'd requested.

So far, I hadn't been caught, and I probably never would be since my magic was more robust than anyone's seeking my services.

I'd dreamed of Rowan. And of dragons. If my dreams

were a bellwether, I'd been correct about Rowan not being her true name. Another golden dragon—not Nidhogg—had told me her name was Runa and that it meant shining secret. The small discordant ping I'd gotten off Rowan dissipated when I heard her named Runa.

It was a fine, old Norse name.

Why did she hide it away? Did she even know about it?

I tightened the cord that held my trousers in place and tossed on a shirt. The previous day and evening had been so surreal, I checked in my pocket for the moonstone. Sure enough, it hadn't moved.

Ha. Wishful thinking. Where would it have gone?

I withdrew it and held it in the palm of my right hand. Light filtered through my single window and bounced off the stone, turning its white and gold to violets and blues. I wanted to return to Midgard, but the stone didn't seem to have any opinions one way or the other about how I spent my day.

Guess I couldn't use it for an excuse to shirk my other duties, ones I'd had long before Nidhogg tasked me with reporting back to him about Midgard.

I was due—actually overdue—for my monthly visit to Alfheim, home of the Elves. They're almost a forgotten race, but they are linked to the Vanir, the gods who rule Vanaheim. I suppose you could say I answer to them, but I don't. Not really. They haven't paid any attention at all to me since they handed off Alfheim.

I always figured they felt guilty about ducking out from under their geas, but likely it was more of an out-of-sight, out-of-mind progression. Particularly after the Breaking, the Vanir have had a rough go of things.

I do my best to keep a low profile and stay out of political maneuverings. No one listens to me anyway, since I'm not a god. Makes it simpler to fly beneath everyone's gunsights. Historically, the Vanir were responsible for human and agricultural fertility. It goes without saying, that's pretty much taken a serious nosedive since the Breaking.

The humans who are left aren't doing much breeding, and the fields lie fallow. Too much dark magic wandering about to make farming worthwhile. Not if a gnome picks you off while you're checking on your watering system, or harvesting your crop.

I've overheard a few arguments between my local gods, like Frey and Freya, and the Asgard crew. They haven't been pretty. Meanwhile, I suspect Yggdrasil has problems of its own. The One Tree isn't my responsibility, so I haven't looked too closely since the Breaking.

Everybody's been into mudslinging, and I figured if I was the bearer of bad news about Yggdrasil, the gods would blame me for the problem I was trying to highlight. Rather an arbitrary bunch, the Norse gods.

Odin used to do a better job ruling things, but he's been immersed in doing all the plundering he can, right along with leading the Hunt. Funny thing, the Wild Hunt. Anyone who spends too much time with them ends up not quite right in the head. I'm not suggesting Odin isn't powerful enough to keep the dead from eating up his sanity, but he hasn't been acting like his old self, either.

He used to be more interested in drinking and wenching and chewing the fat as he relived his glory days.

Like I said, I keep my head down and do my job.

No time like the present for my long-neglected visit to Alfheim. Half the day was already spent. I headed out the door, intent on making my way to Bifrost so I could at least poke my nose in and see how the Elves were faring.

Maybe no one would be sick or need anything in the way of magic from me. That would free me up to return to Midgard with a clear conscience. I knew exactly why I wanted to be there. It should have bothered me, set off a phalanx of alarms, but it didn't.

Rowan—Runa—fascinated me. I wanted to know more about her. Aw hell, I wanted to know everything. It was convenient to have the dragon's orders as a fallback—in case anyone gave me grief for being gone.

I made it through one of many entrances to Bifrost and jumped on its shining surface. When it became clear I wasn't heading for Midgard, the moonstone sent hideous waves of cold into my leg. It was easier to take than when it had jabbed me last night, but it was still damned unpleasant. Like I said, I'd passed beneath the lintel and was on the bridge. It's not the kind of place where I could have stopped and had a heart-to-heart with my new pocket-mate.

Once I access Bifrost, I can't turn around, nor can I leave until I reach the destination I keyed into its harmonics when I tapped into its particular magical frequency. Spells are like that. Once cast, they don't "uncast" easily. Now I might miss my get-off point. It only meant I'd have to cycle through the worlds once again to reach it. I gripped the stone, but all it did was freeze my hand.

"Now look here," I tried for stern, "I will return to Midgard as soon as possible."

If anything, the cold grew worse. Did the stone know I couldn't reverse paths? Or was it only steeped in instructions from its dragon lord? I suspected the latter. Bypassing the moonstone, I raised my mind voice.

"Nidhogg. I must stop by Alfheim. As soon as I'm finished, I'll go back to Midgard."

I waited, wondering if I'd ever regain the use of my right hand. It was so cold I couldn't uncurl my fingers from the stone. They'd frozen in place. It wasn't immediate, but by the time I got near my exit point—and believe me, I was paying very close attention—the infernal cold had retreated a few degrees. And then a few more.

Alfheim has heated pools where steaming water bubbles up. My hand was better, but my first stop once I stepped off Bifrost was a nearby tarn. I was soaking my hand, luxuriating in the return of blood to my poor fingers, when I heard movement behind me.

"Bjorn. It's so good to see you."

I didn't have to turn around to know Mirie had found me. She was kind of a combination grandmother and busybody who knew everything that was going on in Alfheim. About a meter tall with pointy ears and gobs of rainbow-shaded hair that fell to her feet, she peered over my shoulder and asked, "Are you all right?"

"I am now," I told her. Before she could dig for details, I added, "I had a small run in with a dragonstone."

Her mouth rounded into an *oh*, and she murmured, "I see." Her eyes were dark, expressive pools. Like most of her kin, she wore a long, sashed cream-colored tunic woven from a combination of sheep and goat wool. Alfheim wasn't as warm as Vanaheim. A chilly breeze crept into every gap in my garments and made me wish I'd tossed a cloak over my shirt.

"How is everything?" I asked. "Seems as if you might have been waiting for me."

"Och, I was..."

I listened as she rattled on about an elf in the midst of a difficult labor, an aging elf whose magic was fading, and concerns about Yggdrasil. Apparently, the tree root that touched Alfheim had retreated a few centimeters. I shook water off my hand and straightened.

We set off to deal with the elf in labor with Mirie chattering a mile a minute. Elves are the gossips of the Norse world. If I ever wanted to know what everyone in the eight worlds occupied by Norse magic was up to, all I had to do was visit Alfheim.

Obviously, the elves would have done fine without me, but they took comfort from my presence. My power is different from theirs, less earth and more air and fire. It's a good blend, or I wouldn't have been so quick to agree to caretake them.

I HADN'T MEANT to spend quite so long in Alfheim, but

Mirie insisted I take a peek at Yggdrasil's root before I leave. It didn't look any different to me, so I did my best to reassure her. The baby elf—a boy—was healthy, and I'd eased the aged warrior into Valhalla. All in all, a satisfying day. My trips to Alfheim didn't always go quite that well.

I was tired. And hungry. But the stone had taken up its incessant nagging again. I'd have to speak with Nidhogg and see if he couldn't tone it down a bit. Despite my eagerness to see Rowan, I'd have stopped by home to grab a quick bite before traveling to Midgard.

The damned moonstone would have a nervous breakdown—or kill me outright—if I tarried, though. So I boarded Bifrost with a clear image of Midgard in my mind. The human world was quite shy on rations, so it would be a while before I was able to eat. As I moved from one level to another, I wished I'd had more than a cup of tea before leaving home.

I walked out into Midgard in nearly the same spot I'd left it the previous night. Residual smoke from the goblins still marred the horizon. At least it wasn't raining, but clouds covered the gray sky from end to end. I checked the angle of the sun. It would be dark soon. Days were quite short in Midgard this time of year.

The dragon had instructed me to do what I usually did in Midgard, so I headed for the spot responsible for the Breaking. It was quite a way from where I'd emerged, so I called up a teleport spell to take me to the flat plain just south of Loch Lomond.

Once, it had been a busy area, and quite a collection of rusted cars and trucks were parked at odd angles. Some off to the side, but others in the center of the road. They'd been abandoned during one of many violent earthquakes. Huge craters had broken the asphalt, making further progress impossible in a vehicle.

I did a quick scan, keeping my power subdued, to see if anyone remained in the assortment of deserted buildings. I checked every time, but never found a soul. Not like last night where there'd been a small herd of humans next to a loch.

Had they been there all along, and I'd missed their presence? It was possible since I'd never focused much attention in that area. No reason to. It was magic I was on the hunt for. I'd never fancied myself a savior for mortals.

I could see where a more pastoral setting would be preferable to living here, though. Castle Balloch had been reduced to a rubble heap. The new Castle Balloch, mind you. The original one crumbled around 1300. This one wasn't built until the early years of the nineteenth century. Both were right on the shores of Loch Lomond, a lovely setting at one time.

Not anymore.

Something about the Celtic spell that spawned the Breaking had opened channels deep in the earth. Toxic gasses and fumes had billowed out and killed most of the trees and shrubs and grasses. They'd probably not been easy on any mortals in the area, either.

By the time I located this spot, there weren't any dead lying about. Not because no one had died here—some of their shades still roamed—but because human flesh is prized as a delectable treat by every wicked thing that walks the

Nine Worlds. As if Midgard sensed my bleak thoughts, it added chilly rain to the weather mix. It was cold enough, once full dark fell the rain would turn to snow.

My scan came back clean. Nothing anywhere near. But then, there never was. I could have gotten away with doing nothing, not bothering to check my surroundings, but it wasn't my bent to be sloppy. Sloppy caught you off-guard, and it could get you killed. I am long-lived, but far from immortal. If someone was determined, they could drain my essence quicker than I could replace it with magic. The Nine Worlds were full of those with magic. I've never understood why mine was stronger than most. Part of it is I've worked hard to master spellcraft, but I had the raw material to begin with. If I didn't, all the elbow grease in the universe wouldn't have mattered a twit.

I hurried to the shores of the loch and squatted next to it. The water looked clearer to me, and I hoped the fish who'd survived were doing better than they had been. A few years back, I'd worried they'd all die out. A school swam toward me, silver-orange scales gleaming beneath the water's surface. Probably, they retained some archetypal memory of humans feeding them.

If I'd had food, I'd have eaten it myself. The gift I could —and did—give them was not snaring any of them to make myself a meal. I stood and hustled to the spot that had spawned the Breaking. The magic clinging to it made my skin crawl, so I drew power of my own, cloaking myself with it to reduce the sting of Celtic enchantment.

Usually Celt power has a clean feel, but not this spell. Whoever had done this knew full well they'd done wrong.

The stink of guilt hugged places where the spell had burst forth, fully formed. Maybe guilt isn't quite right. Whoever had done this hadn't given a good goddamn who they hurt. They'd wanted something.

I drew back from the jagged edges of what was left of the spell.

What the hell could a Celt have wanted with Midgard? Granted, they had a small presence here in the ruins of Inverlochy Castle, but I'd always seen it as a portal to some borderworld that suited them better. Kind of like what Underhill was to the Fae: a spot to bide separated from humans, yet still with a toehold in this world.

Back when men believed in magic, their adulation strengthened us. Those days are long gone.

I stood, head cocked to one side, and regarded the remains of the Breaking spell through my third eye. I hadn't employed my psychic view lately, and it might yield new information. Slowly, I titrated power into the rift, urging it to cough up its secrets.

The scents I've always associated with Celts, mint, vanilla, and amber, wafted from somewhere. Had my magic loosened them from the residual spell? I switched back to my earth eyes in time to see Rowan striding purposefully toward me.

"You! What are you doing here?" she shouted and skidded to a stop, hands raised to draw power. Magic arced between her raised palms.

"Keeping an eye on the spell that caused the Breaking." I kept my voice mild to conceal my roiling inner landscape. I'd wanted to see her again, and here she was, but why the hell was she so angry? It wasn't as if she owned this misshapen place. Unless—

An ugly thought pushed through and took over. Her magic wasn't an exact match for the Breaking spell, but it wasn't all that far off, either. I slapped a truth spell over her. "Did you do this?" My tone wasn't gentle, but I hadn't meant it to be. This was serious business. Before all the gods, if she'd set this spell in motion, I'd find out why and see justice done.

My attraction withered on the vine as I waited for her answer. I couldn't afford to have even a single positive thought. Not if she'd sundered this world.

Angry darts shot from her eyes, and she batted at the obvious weave of my truth spell. "I could break this."

"Really? Try it." I challenged. Fury added to her allure, but I'd still see her punished if she'd done this. Not that I would be the determining factor, but I'd drag her in front of Odin—or Thor—and let them take over.

For a scant moment, her eyes took on the whirling aspect of a dragon's as that part of her nature pushed for ascendency. Or maybe I imagined it because it was gone quickly. The outrage bled out of her, and her shoulders slumped.

"It wasn't me, but Ceridwen, my mother, who crafted this abomination."

The revelation hit me like a sucker punch to the guts. No wonder Rowan had felt so much like Ceridwen. They shared blood. I must have been staring at her gape-mouthed because she said, "You didn't know."

"Of course, I didn't know," I sputtered. "About either

thing. I determined Celtic magic was behind the Breaking, but I had no idea who was responsible." I hooded my eyes, still unwilling to dismantle my truth spell. "How is it you know about this?"

She folded her arms beneath her breasts with a small return of her spirit. "How else? Mother confessed, but I only dragged the truth from her a few days ago. I found this spot long before that and have been watching it closely. Despite all my poking and prodding, I have no idea how to totally defuse the residual magic. And I was afraid to just go in slugging. What if I made it worse? Now that I know Mother was behind it, I may be able to finish dismantling the damned thing."

She stopped to suck in a ragged-sounding breath. "I've been afraid it would spiral out of control, that there were other hidden spells hanging about just waiting to spring."

Her words pinged sweetly off my spell. She'd told the truth. I reeled in my magic. "It's amazing I haven't run into you here because ever since I found this spot, I've been checking on it too."

"Not so amazing." She sounded weary but resolute. "I always scanned the area before I allowed myself to access it."

I'd done the same. No wonder we'd never crossed paths.

A frisson ran through me as she took my magical measure. It didn't alarm me because she didn't mean me harm. Her eyes widened, and she muttered, "Stronger than you appear."

I wasn't sure whether to take it as a compliment or a reproach. Or whether she simply expected everyone she met to be weaker than herself. I wanted to ask about her dragon side—since it was a dragon who'd commissioned me to spy on Midgard—but it wasn't the kind of thing you blurted out to a stranger.

She regarded me with wary eyes, and her tongue snaked over her lips. It told me how nervous she was. "Um, feel free to say no, but we could do more if we joined forces. That way, both of us would be keeping watch over the Breaking spot. Coordinating our efforts, as it were." She swept a hand toward the rift.

I took a step back. She'd just suggested we work together. I'd always flown solo with my magic. Never had a colleague, for a whole lot of reasons. I stole a glance at her, but her face didn't give anything away. She may as well have asked if we'd team up for a hunting venture.

I stood a little straighter. I could see advantages to each of us knowing what the other was doing, but I could see drawbacks too. What if our magic didn't mesh well? It was one of the reasons I flew solo. "I'm honored you trust me enough to suggest it..." I began.

"But?" She raised a russet brow.

"We need to test our power. See how it blends."

The tiny lines between her eyes smoothed. "Of course. That goes without saying. When would you like to start?"

A smile pushed its way through. I tried to stifle it, but it got away from me. "How about right now? You're here. I'm here." I didn't add she might change her mind even though it had been her suggestion. The specter of her being a wicked sorceress had been laid to rest, and I didn't want to risk letting her get away.

Working with anyone else opened you to them in a very

personal way. We'd be vulnerable to one another, know each other's strengths—and weaknesses. It could draw us closer. Or have the exact opposite effect.

After a short pause, she tilted her chin and said, "Right now would be perfect."

I drew power and began a cleansing incantation to hang on the remnants of the Breaking. It would keep me busy and not let me think too long nor too hard about changing my lifelong pattern of working by myself.

It had been her idea, but I'd accepted. Her magic probed the edges of my fledgling spell. I peeled back a corner to let her inside.

CHAPTER EIGHT, ROWAN

I have no fucking idea what got into me. Yeah, I was shocked to find Bjorn working magic at Mother's sandbox but thrilled to see him again too. This little jolt of absolute joy shot from my toes to my head. What in the Nine Hells was wrong with me? I should steer so far clear of him, all I ever saw was my dust as I loped away.

I could have done a whole bunch of things, but I ponied up the bright idea about us joining forces. Granted, it was a decent strategy.

From a purely magical point of view.

Before Mother fessed up, I was afraid of mucking about too deeply in the remains of the Breaking. What if I made things worse? Created a second Breaking that finished what the first had begun? I felt guilty I hadn't spent any time here untangling her casting, but there was always so much to do.

Moving the Coven's base of operations was one of them, and it took precedence now that we'd selected a cadre. They should be well on their way by now, if not actually there. It meant three spots for me to keep an eye on. The witches' original location, the new one, and where Mother broke the world.

There were many practical reasons Bjorn's help would come in handy. I had no idea what a magical powerhouse he was until a little bit ago. Granted, I got a taste of what he could do the night he and the dragon wiped out the goblins and the troll, but even that underplayed his ability by a good big bunch.

What was he?

Did he have dragon blood? Was that why power shimmered about him in iridescent bands? Not the kind of thing I could ask. We barely knew each other.

Would I have been so quick to float the idea of working together if I wasn't attracted to him? I'd like to believe the answer was yes, but I'm not certain. I've spent years avoiding complications. It was why I ditched Mother and the rest of the pantheon.

One of the reasons.

Her indifference had hurt me. When I'd hurt enough, I voted with my feet.

I felt Bjorn summon power. I was curious if we were well-suited to blend our magic. Sometimes my efforts flew in the face of witchy spells. I'd learned to keep my contributions low-key until I was certain I wouldn't cause something to run off the rails. It had happened a time or two and made me cautious.

No need to do anything but run wide open with Bjorn. It was the first time since I walked away from the Celts I'd met someone I didn't have to pussyfoot around. The specter of throwing caution aside was heady. I pushed a few jots of power against the perimeter of his casting. It was a purging spell aimed at what remained of the Breaking. Not precisely how I'd have cast it, but elegant in its simplicity.

The hard truth was I hadn't had the nerve to attack the remnants so directly. Once I'd discovered Mother was behind it, I'd have been bolder. Maybe. The stakes were high, and I didn't trust Ceridwen. Mercurial as fuck, it would be just like her to add a backdoor trap that would lock me away forever.

The thought was sobering, and I started to tell Bjorn to be careful, but I didn't want him to think I didn't trust his ability to sort things out on his own. Instead, I pushed harder at the edges of his casting. Maybe he hadn't felt me the first time. Or maybe he'd been busy. Complicated magic is structured into layers. If you lay the foundations well, the upper parts take care of themselves.

He peeled back a corner of his working, and I slid into it. At first, I was delighted he wasn't simply planning a demonstration of his own ability, but when my magic blended with his, I felt a jolt all the way to my feet.

Like nothing I'd ever experienced before, it was similar to an arcane key finally finding the lock it was meant for after searching for centuries. That comparison was a wee bit overblown. More than a wee bit. I was starstruck by him, and I needed to get over my infatuation fast. I shouldn't have, but I couldn't resist sneaking a glance his way to see if I'd imagined what I felt. The "where have you been all my life" sensation. He looked as flummoxed as I felt, but he covered it well.

Only a raised brow and a twitch at the corner of his mouth gave away his surprise.

No going back.

Not now. I was firmly entrenched in his spell. It should have worried me, but I leapt forward. The rich scents of Norse power—the briny touch of a restless ocean and the baked clay essence of dragon fire—eddied around me. I couldn't help myself. I sucked the smells into my lungs like a starving urchin. As if Bjorn's magic could save me from every evil that stalked the many worlds.

I gave myself a sharp mental shake. I was being stupid. The luxury of relying on anyone but myself had come to an end long before the day I finally walked away from the Celts. I focused on Bjorn's developing spell, locating weak places and shoring them up with my own magic.

We had different ways of attacking the same problem, but it took very little output from me to turn his—no, our—casting into a virtual storm of power. The jagged edges left from Mother's hideous ploy to force me back to her side took on a shining aspect, becoming far more visible.

I'd never viewed them this clearly before, and the specter was chilling. Even spent as it was, her magic had sent its roots deep into the underpinnings holding Earth together. She'd picked a spot where the plates above this world's liquid center were weak and had capitalized on their instability.

"This isn't good," Bjorn mumbled. A wave of his hand sent an object auguring into the area beneath us. It began with a vertical trajectory and then turned so it sat parallel to the dirt beneath our feet, not unlike the English letter L. Power drained from me as if he'd opened a spigot, and I must have gasped a little.

He turned eyes darkened to midnight on me. "Can you stand a little more?"

Out of energy for anything beyond nodding, I met his direct stare. His mouth had taken on grim lines. "Even with both our power, I can't repair the damage, but with your help, I can stabilize it better than it is."

"Don't talk," I gritted. "Finish it."

The next moments lasted years. I held myself open to him when every instinct I had for self-preservation screamed at me to run as far and as fast as I could from Bjorn. I was trusting him with my most precious possession.

My magic.

I wasn't just weak. I was vulnerable. If he wanted, he could truss what was left of me like a Christmas goose and barricade me in a tower. Or a cellar. Or a cavern. The L-thing glowed first red and then white as he leached residual evil into it.

I swayed on my feet and pried my eyes open. I had no idea I'd closed them. Three shimmering L-shapes had joined the first one. Spaced at maybe half-meter intervals, they made a difference. The pulsing, living Celtic magic had dulled to a faint throb. Somehow, Bjorn had transferred it into the glistening containers. If I hadn't known the Breaking spot was there, I might have walked right by.

A barrier fell, severing my linkage with Bjorn. I doubt I could have reeled my magic in. It didn't exactly bounce back in my face. Nope. It fell around me with all the élan of a limp dishrag. The swaying worsened.

Was I about to pitch facedown into the dirt?

Bjorn ran to me and wrapped a steadying arm around my shoulders. I leaned into him, mostly because it was either that or crumple to the rock-strewn mud. He was breathing hard. I wasn't the only one the spell had taken a toll on. We stood like that for quite a while.

Finally, he let go and repositioned himself so he faced me. "I'm sorry. I didn't know it would take so much magic, but once I had the spell in hand, if I'd let it go—"

"I know," I broke in. "Neither of us would have had enough juice for a second go. Not today."

He nodded somberly. "Aye, and if this casting is sentient, as I believe it might be, in the space of time it would have taken before we gave it another try, it might have strengthened itself in some way." He stopped to take a measured breath. "As it is, I barely got my precautionary measures in place."

I turned my head and looked through my third eye. Sure enough, the stanchions, or whatever they were, glowed brightly. Their lower arms had levered into the dirt. "How long will they last?"

"Not all that long. They'll contain the worst of things for now, but we need a permanent solution, and that will require study. Consultation with those older and wiser than me."

I shook my way out from beneath his hands. It was hard because I wanted him to keep on touching me in the worst way. To reduce the temptation to reach for him, I folded my arms beneath my breasts and said, "Not Odin."

To my surprise, Bjorn laughed.

It annoyed me. "What's so fucking funny?"

"I'd never ask Odin for anything. He barely acknowledges my existence."

Mmph. That was a relief. After Odin's little sleight of hand with Mother, he was the last one I wanted anywhere near me. For all I knew, he'd cooked up some new scheme with my mother. All she had to do was make good on the coin she owed him, and he'd whore for her.

"If not Odin, then whom?" I persisted. I didn't know zip shit about the Norse gods beyond a few of their names, but I'd be damned if I'd admit it to a Norseman. It would be akin to telling a mortal I'd never heard of Christ or Mary Magdalene or the Holy Ghost.

"I'm not sure yet."

I closed my teeth over my lower lip. "You're hedging."

He nodded. "I am. I'll start with the Norse dragon god and move down the ranks from there. Nidhogg is ancient beyond reckoning. If he doesn't hold the answers I seek, I have no idea who would."

An odd sensation, heat prickles but with sharp edges, jabbed me unpleasantly. The push-pull of fascination married to disbelief was unsettling. Rather like the other night when I'd rushed outside only to find a dragon whipping through the sky.

I'd heard of Nidhogg. Just like I'd heard of Odin and Thor and a few of the rest of them. But why should the sound of his name spoken aloud make me shiver with anticipation?

To center my restless thoughts, I asked, "What do you want to know that the dragon might have answers for?"

Bjorn pointed at the spot Mother's spell had been. "That casting isn't normal magic. It reaches beyond this world, but I was unable to trace its roots. In that way, it reminded me of Yggdrasil, the One Tree, whose roots support the Nine Worlds."

"Yeah, but isn't Yggdrasil pure of heart?"

"Not exactly. It just is. Were it to fail, the Nine Worlds would wither along with it, so it plays a critical role, but Yggdrasil is neither intrinsically good nor intrinsically bad. Which makes it very different from your"—he stumbled before saying—"mother's complicated weaving.

"The reason we had such a hard time with even the small working we managed today is that her spell draws its essence from places beyond the Nine Worlds. It makes her casting challenging, and it also makes me certain she's not monitoring it."

The chill I'd felt earlier about the dragon changed pace and tempo. The fascination aspect departed fast. Before terror dug its claws in too deep, I stood straighter and dropped my arms to my sides.

"I can trace her spell."

A corner of his mouth turned downward. "Not today, you won't."

I slitted my eyes at him. "That sounded dangerously like an order. We're barely partners—although we haven't talked about that part yet. Partners presumes equal standing, and—"

Bjorn sliced a hand downward. "Stop it. I'm not

planning on expending any more magic today, either. We don't have much left."

I opened my mouth to tell him to speak for himself but shut it fast. I was running on fumes. To suggest otherwise would be lying. Worse, he'd know it. I mumbled something incomprehensible to avoid apologizing. We seemed to be done for today.

Maybe we were done with each other, although not blending our magic ever again seemed like a crime of the highest nature. Our power was meant to work together. I was certain of it, but uncomfortable too. He hadn't said anything about being taken aback by how seamlessly we'd blended our abilities.

Had I imagined it because I was so taken with him?

Weary, confused, I turned away and stumbled toward a clearing far enough from Mother's perfidy to set a teleport spell in motion.

Bjorn loped after me. "Wait. Where are you—?"

Before he got more words out, a roaring filled my ears. Gale force winds blew up out of nowhere and drove me to my knees. I was a heartbeat too late throwing a ward into place—or the one I cobbled together was too weak. I felt rather than saw a whirling vortex form right in front of me, its pull too potent to deny.

"Nooooo!" Bjorn shouted and dove right for me. He gripped me hard, and both of us were sucked into the maelstrom.

"You stupid, stupid man. Why'd you do that?" I cried.

We spun, turning end over end, as the whirlwind tossed

us this way and that. "I'm saving you," he informed me tartly, but humor edged his words.

"If I'd wanted a knight errant, I'd have ordered one up." By now, he had both arms around my body and was hanging on. I did my very best to ignore the hard planes of muscle pressed against me. I could fight my own battles. I'd been doing it for so long, I'd forgotten there was any other way.

Magic hummed around us. Bjorn's, not Mother's slimy touch. We might have the same magic, but hers felt dirty to me. What was he up to? I would have asked, but I didn't want to tip Mother off. She had to be the one who'd tripped the vortex.

Maybe I'd been off base about thinking the Breaking was booby-trapped. It appeared the snare was right next door—and had my name stenciled all over it. The trap might have done the same to anyone who'd mucked about in Ceridwen's casting, but I didn't think so.

Bjorn's working thickened around us. We stopped tumbling end over end, but the vortex still crashed around us. "Better," he said. "At least I can think." His nostrils twitched. "This has Ceridwen's touch, but not only hers."

"Whose, then?"

"Not sure."

I sharpened my own antennae and dug into the pulsing mass that swirled around us. We had to be in the space between worlds, except I could breathe. Either the vortex had trapped enough air to keep me comfortable. Or I was wrong about our location.

If not the airless void, though, then where were we?

"Good question." Bjorn's deep voice rumbled near my

ear. "Sorry. I helped myself to your thoughts. We would be in the void had I not placed constraints on the magic that created the Breaking."

"Does that mean you know where we are? Or how to return us to where we were?"

"No to both."

He went back to chanting low and urgent. I did what I'd done before and pressed the pathetic amount of magic left to me into his spell. He sucked it up but didn't keep drawing on my slender reserves. Almost as if he'd figured out last time how quickly he could turn me into an empty husk.

His concern reassured me. If he'd meant me harm, I was in a precarious spot. Too depleted to fight back. Hell, I was almost too weak to care what happened next. But I wouldn't always be. Mother had declared war on me, and I wouldn't rest until I took her down.

Big thoughts from her half-Celtic spawn, but I'd figure something out.

"Hang on," Bjorn told me. "This next part won't be pleasant."

Before I could ask what he was doing, a blast of destructive power, red with golden edges, burst from him. The vortex shattered, leaving us in the familiar airless nothingness. If I'd had more warning, I'd have harbored air in my lungs. They seized and seized again. Breathing was a reflex. It never went away. My chest burned. My vision developed gray edges.

"*Not much longer.*" Bjorn switched to telepathy.

I barely heard him before pressure built in my chest, and the world went black.

When I came to, I was shivering, but there was air, blessed air. Frosty darkness surrounded us, and Bjorn still held me in his arms. "Thank all the gods that worked."

I wanted to ask what had worked, but my brain was still disconnected from the moving parts of my body. When I found words, my first ones were, "Why is it so cold?"

"Because we're in Niflheim."

I squeezed my eyes shut trying to remember what it was. Norse something. Obviously one of the Nine Worlds.

"It means world of fog," Bjorn explained. "What it really is, though, is our primordial world of mist and ice. It's a counterpart to Muspelheim, the world of fire."

I cut to the chase. "Are we safe here?"

The corners of his mouth twitched. "From Ceridwen's meddling, yes. From the Frost Giants, perhaps."

I didn't ask what they were or how likely to strike. "How can we leave?"

"We can't. Not until our magic has replenished itself. I've been here before. I didn't exactly hit my goal, but there's a cave not too far from here where we can wait things out."

"For how long?" Alarm filled me. I had to get back to Earth. To the witches. They were counting on me, especially now that I'd shown them how to breach the illusion surrounding Inverlochy Castle.

"As long as it takes. I will get us out of here as soon as I can."

Not liking his answer, I reached for my own magic, intent on dredging a teleport spell out of it. Ha! What a joke. I'd never been quite this worn-out. I was useless until I rested and ate.

"Do you trust me?" he asked.

My teeth began to chatter as I answered, "Not really. Goes against my nature to trust anyone."

"I understand because I'm the same way, but for now, Rowan, we are forced into an alliance."

"Why did you say my name that way?"

"What way?" He hustled us across crackling ice, through fog so thick it penetrated every pore.

"You're hedging. You understood me perfectly." Fascinating I could shiver and pant at the same time.

Bjorn didn't even break stride when he said, "If your name sounded odd rolling off my tongue, it's because it isn't really your name. I'm a truth speaker among other things, and such things are noticeable coming from me."

"Of course, it's my name," I sputtered. Of all the possible answers, what he'd said had been damned low on the list of what I'd expected.

He didn't answer, just kept loping along. When I slipped and slid on the ice-crusted ground, he caught me. He'd said the cave was close. Maybe it was to him, but I was stumbling from cold and exhaustion by the time we ducked into its darkness.

At least it offered protection from the icy wind. I was so miserable, I hadn't exactly noticed the chilly gusts until I was out of them.

"Here." He kindled a feeble mage light and led me to a pile of skins in a corner. "You're cold. Get under them."

I looked around, but there weren't any other skins scattered on the dirt floor. "There are enough to share," I said and dove beneath them. It would be a long while before I stopped shaking.

"Thank you, but I'm leaving."

"What?" My voice held a frantic note that made me look weak and pathetic.

He knelt next to me. "We need food. I shall return once I've secured something for us to eat."

I wanted to drag him under the skins next to me. What if he was lying and had no intention of returning? What if something about this world meant my magic would never recover? I was too tapped out to read his mind. Apparently, he'd retained more magic than me because he said, "Have a little faith. I'll be back soon enough."

Embarrassment swamped me. Would the next thing out of my mouth be I was afraid of the dark? Curling into a ball, I willed the return of warmth. Maybe by the time he got back, we'd have enough magic between us to leave this frozen wasteland.

Footsteps plodded away from my makeshift pallet, and I shut my eyes. I'd lived through worse than this. I just hoped the witches wouldn't launch a search party when I didn't show up. They were safest out of sight.

Nothing I could do about it if they did, though.

Nothing I could do about anything until my magic came back online. Funny thing, the electronic age was just as dead as the mortals who'd cherished it, but the lingo lived on in my tired brain.

CHAPTER NINE, BJORN

I'd been shocked when Rowan showed up, and totally flummoxed by how well our magic slotted together. When it happened the first time, I'd figured it was a fluke, but flukes didn't happen twice.

Not that way.

The more time I spent with her, the surer I was she had no idea about the dragon blood pulsing through her veins. She'd told the truth when she'd owned her name. She truly believed it was Rowan. As I moved through Niflheim's murk, intent on finding at least a winter hare or two we could cook and eat, I thought about what it all meant.

The only way she could have remained ignorant of the circumstances of her birth was because Ceridwen—the parent she knew about—had made certain she remained clueless.

After half an hour with not so much as a whiff of game, I broke a few rules and paid out bits of magic—not that I had enough left to sneeze at—and lured animals across my path. Two rabbits and a vole-like creature later, I headed back to the cavern where I'd left Rowan. I'd been trapped in this frozen world centuries ago and had stumbled onto the cave.

Or been led there.

Hel's realm shares walls with Niflheim, and I'd always believed the goddess of the dead had shown me the way. She was probably the one responsible for leaving the pile of skins there. They didn't belong to any creatures endemic to this world, which meant she'd imported them from elsewhere.

For all I knew, Hel entertained the occasional lover. The warriors who ended up here were the ones who'd been found lacking, who didn't deserve Valhalla's glory. No wonder she'd keep her dalliances brief and oh-so-private, if she'd sunk to having sex with her charges.

I yanked my ungracious thoughts out by the roots. First off, I had no idea who she'd shared those skins with. Even if I did, who was I to judge anyone? I'd checked out of any relationships more complicated than my sword practice with Jarle long since. Easier that way. Plus most of the women in the Nine Worlds were goddesses or Valkyries or elves. Goddesses expected me to be at their beck and call. Valkyries wanted to kill me if I so much as looked at them. Elves appeared so childlike, they were off the table when it came to anything of a romantic nature.

Women aside, what I really needed was a heart-to-heart with Nidhogg. The dragon knew about Rowan. I'd bet my last beaker of alchemy experiments on it. It could well be why he'd sent me to Midgard. To keep an eye on her. As I turned it over, I was certain he knew about her connection to Ceridwen. And the source of the Breaking.

Was he Rowan's father?

The thought rattled around in my head. If that were true, I'd have to tread very carefully. He'd broken several rules mating outside dragonkind and would have every reason to hide his faux pas. After all its energetic antics earlier, the stone in my pocket might as well have been a random rock I'd picked up off the ground.

Poor Rowan. Saddled with two parents who had multiple motives to deny her existence. Assuming I was right about Nidhogg, he'd done a fine job of ignoring his spawn for centuries. If he was going to pick up the parental reins, why wouldn't he have done so when Rowan first left the Celts? Or after the Breaking?

There had to be a whole lot I didn't know.

Balls in play that were well above my pay grade.

I grinned at the human slang that jumped into my mind from time to time. I'd enjoyed my time living among mortals. Midgard was poorer for the Breaking that had wiped out so many. And turned the ones who were left into a bunch of scarred husks.

I felt sorry for them, but pity only reached so far. Saving humanity was not only above my pay grade, it wasn't my job. I had my hands full as the *de facto* sorcerer for the Nine Worlds. Not that the gods viewed me in that light, or the dragons, but most everyone else did.

I was close to the cave now. Spreading magic in an arc, I checked for danger. Mostly, Hel kept good order through her realms, but Frost Giants were an unpredictable lot. They lived in Jotunheim, another of the Nine Worlds, but they adored the cold here. A type of overgrown serpent with two heads was another potential problem. Loosely related to the dragons, they lacked wings.

I'd left a blood trail from my kills, but so far it hadn't come round to bite me. Not that I hadn't been careful, but fresh meat has a particular stink about it. I didn't exactly leave a crimson path, but anything with a nose could have tracked me.

Ducking into the cave, I kindled a mage light. It wavered and flickered but managed to shed enough light for me to see Rowan huddled beneath the pelts. She'd fallen into an exhausted sleep, and her brilliant hair fluffed around her still form. She had the most beautiful hair. Like silky dragonfire, it reflected gold and ruby from my light.

Power shimmered around her, visible to another with magic. Good that she'd had the presence of mind to ward herself, and also encouraging she'd had enough magic left to fashion protections.

I battled a ridiculous desire to run my fingers through her hair. Before I gave in to the urge to touch her—assuming I could reach through her wards—I rustled my way over to a hearth vented up one end of the cavern. I wasn't trying for quiet. Before I got a fire well and truly going, she yawned and made a purring, mewling sound that was tough to resist.

"I found food." My voice was gruff. I couldn't afford to give in to the attraction I felt for her. She hadn't presented me with even the smallest indication she viewed me as anything beyond a nuisance, and we had far more important issues facing us.

Like escaping Niflheim.

It wasn't the easiest place to leave. The longer you stayed, the less you cared about going anywhere.

"Can I help?" Rowan was on her feet. She'd wrapped one of the warm skins around herself and walked to where I stood coaxing fire out of a few bits of frozen wood. Somewhere between her impromptu bed and my side, she'd dismantled her ward.

I blew on the fledgling flames and pointed to where I'd laid the animals on the cave's floor. "Sure. Help is always welcome."

She nodded and reached beneath her clothing. When her hand reappeared, she held a wicked-looking dirk with a ten-centimeter blade. Squatting next to the rabbits and vole, she worked quickly and methodically skinning and gutting them.

My fire had finally moved from a smoky mess to something that put out heat, and I laid our dinner over the coals.

"Thanks for hunting food for us." Her voice was low and lyrical. She bent and cleaned her blade with dirt before tucking it back away.

"I'm lucky I found anything. I have no idea what happened down here, but these animals didn't exactly fall into my lap." I took a measured breath. "As soon as we're done eating, we need to try to leave."

She crinkled her forehead into a mass of lines. "I want to get going too, but there's something you're not exactly telling me."

I offered her kudos for shrewdness. "This world shares many elements with Hel—"

"That's the same as our underworld, right?" She raked curved fingers through her tangles to move her hair out of her face.

"Yes. The important part, though, is the goddess who runs Hel utilizes enchantments to keep the dead in line, It's a sort of forgetfulness casting. The longer anyone remains here, the dimmer their memories become about the life they had before."

"I see. And the less anxious they are to find their way out." Rowan's mouth twisted into a sour expression. "It's already working on me. I'm far less worried than I was when I arrived here. I hate to admit it, but I can visualize myself, uh, settling in,"

She fisted a hand and punched the air. "That cannot happen. The witches need me. They're vulnerable, and I just set them up in Inverlochy Castle, or what's left of it, so we have a prayer of growing enough food we won't starve."

I turned the meat over. "The Celts' old stomping grounds?" At her nod, I went on, "I thought it was naught but ruins."

"That's how it appears when people look at it, but if you gaze through your psychic vision, you'll see it still stands in most of its former glory. My kin abandoned it when they moved to a borderworld right around the time of the Breaking. I believe the witches are fairly safe, but if one of the Celts decides to revisit the place, they'll be most put out to find it occupied."

I moved the smaller pieces of meat to warm stones around my firepit and asked, "What do you think they'd do?"

Rowan looked askance at me. "Depends who finds them. Some of my erstwhile kin are more compassionate than others. Best case, they'd chase them out."

"And worst?" I quirked one brow.

"They'd kill them for trespassing."

It was about what I'd expected. The Norse deities weren't any more forgiving when it came to human incursions into places they felt belonged to them.

She picked up a small bit of rabbit and popped it into her mouth. The smells of cooking meat were rich and delectable. I plucked a bite for myself. Soon we were eating the moment meat came off the coals. I was sorry I hadn't killed double the number. Winter hares weren't very big once they were skinned out.

"I hate to take the time, but I can get more," I said around my last bite.

Rowan shook her head. "Not a good idea. I'm full enough. My magic is coming back around. I'm not anywhere near my complete strength yet, but what I have should be good enough to teleport. How's yours doing?"

A quick assessment told me I might have enough to encourage Bifrost to open to my command, but not enough to teleport. Whatever we did, I wanted us to remain together, but perhaps it wouldn't be possible.

I wiped grease from my fingers with a combination of dirt and rubbing them together. "You should go as soon as you can," I told Rowan.

She leveled a glance my way. "You never did answer me. What about you?"

I stood straighter. Last thing I wanted was for her to feel sorry for me—or view me as a magical inferior. "I'll be along. I want to run Hel down before I leave."

Her expression had been open, unguarded. At my words, she smoothed it into neutral lines. "As you wish," she said, not adding anything about believing we were partners.

I might not have wanted her pity, but neither could I let her believe I didn't value the way our magic wove together into an amazingly viable whole. "There is a magic-imbued passageway running through the Nine Worlds. I have sufficient power to utilize it, but not yet enough to teleport." Anticipating her next question, I added, "The passageway is actually forbidden to any but the Norse gods. No one ever complains when I use it, though."

A corner of her mouth quirked into half a smile. "But they'd notice me, huh?"

"You bet they would. Celt magic sticks out like a sore thumb here." I didn't mention her dragon blood would provide a clarion call of its own. It was possible our blended magic would be enough to transport both of us to Midgard, but I wasn't positive.

And I wasn't willing to chance it.

Rowan had far more pressing reasons than I did to return quickly. If we gambled—and lost—she'd be stuck in Niflheim right along with me until we built up our power stores again.

"It's fine," I told her. "Go ahead. I'm sure we'll run into one another back at the Breaking sooner rather than later."

Her half smile deepened into a full one. It softened the

lines of her face, and her beauty shone through even more brilliantly than it usually did. "I'll look forward to it." Power bubbled around her, filling the air with the scents of Celtic magic. Mint. Amber. Vanilla.

I stood for long moments, fixated by the spot where she'd vanished. Whatever drew me to her, I had it bad, and I needed to find a different focus. As if on cue, the dragonstone warmed and throbbed where it sat in a pocket. I hadn't forgotten about it, but neither had it been in the forefront of my mind.

"What?" I mumbled and hoped to hell it didn't switch up to emitting its previous waves of cold. Niflheim was chilly enough without add-ons from Nidhogg's gift. I rolled my eyes. Not a gift. He'd given me the stone as a way to keep tabs on my whereabouts. And to push me in directions that met his needs.

Free will was a joke. Just because the gods had left me alone most of the long years of my life was no reason to believe they couldn't exert their sovereignty over me whenever they chose.

I turned to leave. Before the stone got riled enough to do more than vibrate. I'd walked about twenty paces from the mouth of the cave where we'd sheltered when Hel glided out of the mist. She hadn't bothered with a glamour. No reason to. She and I were well acquainted. Half the bones of her body were exposed. She'd been born that way, and I always suspected it was why she'd ended up queen of the underworld. Her appearance was unsettling.

Long black hair shielded some of her exposed skeleton, and she regarded me out of dark eyes. Hel was at least half a meter taller than me, but her mother had been a giant, so I was surprised she hadn't turned out bigger than she was.

"Visiting?" she inquired archly.

I understood exactly what she craved. News of the world above. She wasn't exactly a prisoner in Hel and Niflheim, but when she left her magic gradually faded. Worse, the dead grew unruly. If she was absent too long, they migrated away from her realm, angering both Odin and Thor.

"Not precisely," I replied. "This was the closest place for me to transport us once I broke us free of Ceridwen's spell."

Hel craned her long, bony neck around. "Us? I see only you."

"I was with a woman who is half Celt and half dragon. She's Ceridwen's daughter."

"Ooooh, there's a story behind all that." She strode closer. "Tell me."

I've always liked Hel and felt a little sorry for her. So I hit the high points of what had happened prior to our ending up in her lands.

Long before I was done, she slitted her eyes. Whenever she does that, she looks so much like her father, Loki, it makes me cringe. I've come to loathe him because his presence always bodes ill for everyone nearby. Her two serpents slithered to her side. Long, black, and deadly, their forked tongues flicked in and out as they scented the cold, damp air.

Hel crouched and stroked their scaled heads as if they'd been dogs or cats. When she straightened, she said, "I must go. Please. Visit more often."

"I will try." It had been a long while since my last

sojourn to Niflheim, and I didn't want to raise false hopes. "The other worlds keep me busy, but if you ever have need of a sorcerer—"

She rolled her dark eyes and waved me to silence. "I will never put you to work, Bjorn. Consider my realm a place you can be invisible for a bit. Betimes, such is useful."

"Thank you, Goddess." I bowed my head. When I looked up, she and the snakes were gone.

A quick scan told me I had enough magic to teleport, but I headed for Bifrost. It was just as fast and required zero expenditure of effort on my part. The stone had upped the ante. Still warm, it was vibrating faster. Left to my own devices, I'd have headed for my humble stone cottage to clean up and regroup. I was still hungry, and I had food there.

Deciding to test the waters, I exited the bridge in Vanaheim. The stone wasn't happy, but it was only a stone. There were limited ways it could express its displeasure. As I hastened to my home, I raised my mind voice. "*Nidhogg. If you're available, we need to talk. If not now, please let me know when might work better for you.*"

I blew out a breath. Maybe my plea would work. I hadn't requested anything beyond an audience. At the dragon's convenience. I'd moved beyond the mists shrouding the rainbow bridge and located the track that would lead me home. A few twists and turns later, I noticed the dragonstone had turned back into an inert lump.

What did it mean? Was it done bothering me? I hoped so. Beyond taking care of my own needs, I was certain work had piled up. People left me notes—magical and otherwise—

when they required my services. Normally, I was almost always at home. That I'd been gone for well beyond a day didn't bode well.

Head bent in thought, I wasn't paying close attention until the unmistakable baked clay smell of dragon hit me broadside. My head snapped up. Sure enough, Nidhogg sat in front of my cottage, golden wings folded behind his back, whirling eyes staring right at me.

I stopped a meter away, remembered my manners, and bowed my head while murmuring, "Thank you so very much for—"

"What did ye want to talk about?" The dragon didn't sound overly annoyed, but neither did he sound happy. Or I could have read him all wrong. It's not as if I've spent much time in the company of wyrms.

Questions danced in my head. He probably knew them all. Dragons were adept mind readers, but Nidhogg just stared at me. He wasn't going to make this easy by plucking queries from me at random.

I wanted to invite him inside, but he wouldn't fit through the door. With my head still partially bowed, I murmured, "I would very much appreciate more information about why you wish my presence in Midgard."

I longed to ask about Rowan but didn't. Just because I asked something was no reason for Nidhogg to answer me, so I stuck with a general question and hoped for the best.

Smoke and ash puffed from his open jaws. "What ye really wish to know is why ye were caught up in a Celtic spell with Ceridwen's get. 'Tisn't a question I shall answer. Not yet."

I stole a glance at him and took a chance. "She has dragon blood. A lot of it."

The dragon nodded amidst ash and fire. "Astute of you."

"Anyone with enough magic would notice."

"Nay. Not anyone. Her origins are shrouded by spells."

I blew out a breath and stood straight. "Then why were they obvious to me?"

He tilted his great head, eyes whirling faster. "Because ye have power that's a direct complement to hers."

"How?" I sputtered, followed by, "Why?"

Rather than answering me, Nidhogg spread his wings and let the air currents carry him upward. It wasn't very breezy, and I didn't understand how he gained height and remained airborne. Not that I'm any expert on the habits of dragons, but it was obvious he was done talking with me.

I waved a hand skyward—a sign of respect and farewell—and strode into my house. For once, the dragonstone was inert. It didn't even protest when I removed it from a pocket and placed in on my table.

As I heated water and made a meal, two things were clear. Nidhogg not only knew about Rowan. He also recognized I had a connection to her, but he wasn't about to make anything simple.

I'd have to do some serious digging and figure things out on my own.

I smiled and tucked into a pot of grains I'd hurried up with magic. I was the original figure-it-out-myself guy, and Nidhogg has just handed me my favorite kind of puzzle.

CHAPTER TEN, ROWAN

I fretted and fussed and fumed during the time it took me to return to Earth and quest about with magic to figure out whether I should go to Inverlochy first or the witches' original lair beneath Ben Nevis. Many things were bothering me, not the least of which was running into the rough side of another of Mother's nasty spells.

Were more lying in wait for me?

An unsettling thought surfaced. Had she spirited me away to do damage to the witches who'd sheltered me and become my family? It was very like something she'd do. Hurt those she knew were dear to me. I added a healthy shot of magic and teleported to Inverlochy, heart in my throat.

A good, deep sniff reassured me no Celts had been here since my ill-timed visit with my mother and Odin. Damn! Who could I appeal to? Mother was as close to the top of the pantheon as anyone. I couldn't come up with a soul who'd bring her to heel.

None of them knew me well at all, so I didn't expect Bran or Gwydion or Arianrhod or Arawn to take up my cause. One of the downsides of living forever was relationships went full circle. From lovey-dovey to full-blown ire and back again. Rinse and repeat, endlessly.

They'd see Mother's bad behavior as a phase, pat me on the head, and reassure me she'd get past it. Well, it had been a very long time, and she wasn't anywhere near past it yet. In truth, things seemed to be getting worse. As if she'd nursed a grudge since the Breaking and was only interested in forcing my hand.

Chivvying me back to her side, so she could ignore me.

"There you are!" Patrick's raspy voice rang from somewhere above. I'd aimed for the courtyard on purpose, in order to plot a strategy if I needed one. "Where were you?" he asked as he joined me. His sparse blond hair was even rattier than normal, and his blue eyes had circles beneath them. He'd traded his usual breeks and flannel shirt for a long black-and-green tartan layered over a frayed linen shirt.

"It's a long story. Is everyone all right?"

He angled a pointed look my way. "Yes. We even arranged a foray into town and brought back seeds. One of the garden shops had a cellar that hadn't been discovered—or disturbed. Is there any particular reason you're worried about us?"

I couldn't not tell him. "Mother is on the warpath. Everyone needs to be extra careful."

"Was that what happened to you?" He added narrowed eyes to his already-pointed expression.

"Yeah. I ended up in Niflheim."

A shocked look crossed his face. "'Tisn't good news. You escaped. How?"

"I was with Bjorn, and—"

"The Norseman from the other night, right? The one who pretended he was a witch long ago."

I nodded. "The same. He got swept up in the casting, and he's why we ended up where we did. I have no idea if I could have broken free of Mother's spell without him. Or where I would have landed once I finally extricated myself from it."

"Were you over by the Breaking site?"

I nodded again. "Got to keep an eye on it. Turns out Bjorn has been doing the same thing. I'm surprised we haven't run into one another, but both of us have been extremely cautious, leaving at the first hint anyone else might be near there."

"Mmph."

"What does that mean?" I asked.

"Not sure I meant anything by it." Patrick exhaled noisily. "We're all here. All who were planning to move. We can set wards—"

"Don't. Anything you do that disturbs the feel of this place from the outside might alert my kinsmen."

He curled a hand around my upper arm. "Are you certain this is a good idea, lass?"

I shut my eyes for a moment. They felt hot and dry and gritty. "No. But I don't have any better ones. We need to be able to grow food. Right now, we can't. This is as protected a spot as we're likely to come across."

"We might try one of the deserted fields."

"No. All the bad things are still out there. They'd figure out quick enough we need to tend to whatever we're growing, and they'd ambush us."

"Aye. Same reasons we're not doing it now," he mumbled.

More witches clattered down the stairs. Hilda and a couple of other women gave me a quick hug. Walking around us, they picked up an assortment of garden tools and a bag of seeds that sat off to one side. I motioned to Patrick to follow me outside.

Once we exited through the crypt, I turned to him. "Be sure to let everyone know to be cautious. If you can hurry a crop along with magic, do it. We don't need to remain here forever. Just until we can harvest enough to dry or preserve by canning. Then we'll go back to our spot beneath Ben Nevis until we need to plant again."

"Safer there," he agreed.

"And more defensible. Speaking of which, I'm going there now to check on everyone else. Mort will give me hell for being gone. Once I've mollified him, I'm going to eat and sleep."

Patrick wrapped an arm around my shoulders and squeezed. "Take care of yourself." He hesitated before adding, "You don't have to remain with us, yet you do. We very much appreciate your help."

I squirmed out from under his arm. "Eh, you did the same for me. You took me in without a bunch of questions, and you've treated fairly with me. Blood doesn't make family. Actions do."

Before he could thank me again, I pulled magic and

teleported to the cave at the base of Ben Nevis. It took longer than I expected, which told me my reserves were still pretty thin. If I'd been paying closer attention, I'd have understood how tapped out I was.

I hustled through the complex, avoiding much beyond "hello" or "good to see you." Someone had thoughtfully placed a dish of gruel in my tiny room. I ate mindlessly, touched almost to tears by the small kindness. A strident *mrowwww* announced Mort seconds before he launched himself into my lap and proceeded to dig sharp claws into my threadbare clothing as he climbed my body to the spot he preferred draped across my shoulder blades.

He did his damnedest to remain aloof, but after the first purr leaked out, I knew he'd forgiven me. Reaching up, I stroked his matted fur, and the purrs intensified.

"Missed you too," I murmured and wished human interactions could be this simple. I hadn't thought about Bjorn on purpose. Something about him called to me at a soul-deep level. I had no idea what it was. I also didn't understand why our magic worked so well together. Back during my days with the Celts, my power had never blended quite so seamlessly.

With anyone else's.

I hadn't been offered a chance to share power very often, but my memories of the few occasions weren't pretty. Once Arianrhod had turned her odd eyes—one silver, one gold—on me, cursed me roundly, and chased me from her studio. She'd been making magical arrows for her mighty yew bow at the time, and I'd asked if I could help. I wanted my own power-imbued arrows, so I'd been curious what she did to strengthen hers.

If Arianrhod's ill-temper wasn't enough, when I next ran into Mother, she'd rebuked me for bothering the other Celts.

I guess I was hoping she might have apologized for Arianrhod's abruptness. Softened the rejection by explaining it away. That incident was quite a while before I gave up and left. Funny how long it takes to abandon the dream of a normal childhood and a mother who actually cared about me.

I washed my dinner down with water and moved to my pallet, Mort still curled around my neck. He licked me with his rough tongue, probably because I tasted salty from sweat. After relocating the cat to one side, I plopped down on my back and folded my hands beneath my head.

Bjorn was an enigma, and a damned attractive one. If he'd been short and squat and swarthy, my life would have been a whole lot simpler. His blond locks begged to be touched. They had a way of escaping his braids and the leather thongs he tied them into place with.

I muffled a snort. His hair might look as if it needed a woman's smoothing hand, but he was abrupt and snappish. He'd had a graceful moment or two after he decided to play Sir Galahad and rescue me from Mother's perfidy, but it hadn't lasted long. By the time we were ready to leave Niflheim, he'd all but chased me away.

He'd made an offhand comment about maybe running into one another again at the Breaking site. I should have nodded and left, but I must have appeared quite the fool when I told him how much I'd look forward to it.

Arawn's balls but I was a prime idiot. Bjorn hadn't given me even one flicker of an indication he wanted to see me again. Given his almost total lack of interest, I suppose I was lucky he'd taken pity on me and latched onto my body when it was clear if he didn't, I'd be sucked into a funnel leading goddess only knew where.

"Fine," I mumbled. "He has a chivalrous side. He'd have aided any woman in dire straits."

Mort meowed a time or two, as if he totally agreed with me.

I shook my head to clear it. My exhaustion hadn't gone away, and my magic was still on the low side. I'd caught Bjorn looking me over a couple of times when he thought my attention was elsewhere. Not that I've had many men in my life, but I know the difference between an appraising glance that leads to a seduction attempt and the other kind.

The Celts used to spear me with the other kind frequently. As if they were trying to figure out what type of interesting bug I was. As I rolled that particular memory over in my head, it wasn't all that different from the way Bjorn had looked at me.

As if he were trying to figure something out.

Breath hissed through my teeth. My magic was strong. What else was there to determine? The cat moved from lying next to me to perching on my belly. Between his rumbly purring and everything else that had happened, I drifted downward. Not quite asleep, but not exactly awake, either.

Damn, it felt good to just lie here. No one needed anything. I was safe. If Mother had been determined to roust me from the center of the coven, she'd have done so long ago. I suppose her stumbling block was pride. Like a jilted suitor, she wanted me to want her for her, not because she'd shattered the world and made everyone's existence a living nightmare.

A large scaled form with outstretched wings flew across the darkness behind my closed lids. "Go away," I mumbled.

The dragon veered and flew back across my visual field. Lit from within, it glowed golden. Or maybe copper. I tried again. "Go away."

I should have ignored the fucking thing. It landed and folded its wings behind its back. Squatting on huge haunches, the beast stared at me through large, liquid eyes that spun like pinwheels. They shaded from silver to green to dark, and back again.

I knew instinctively not to look right into his eyes. Or maybe it was a her. Did dragons even come in genders? I assumed they had to, or there'd never be any new dragons. Fully committed to being awake, I pried my eyes open as I pondered whether something that was immortal even needed to reproduce.

The dragon didn't go away.

I blinked hard and rubbed my eyes. The creature hadn't moved. Smoke plumed from its nostrils and rose toward the ceiling of my chamber.

"All right. You're real. Why are you here?"

It didn't answer. I asked the same question in mind speech. And then in Gaelic and several of the elder tongues. The cat still curled on my tummy, oblivious to our visitor.

Some cats make decent watch animals. Mort was

halfway in that camp, and he should have at least reacted to the dragon's presence. That he didn't suggested perhaps I was the only one aware of the wyrm. Or the illusion that had formed in the shape of a wyrm.

That train of thought sent me bolt upright. Breath caught in my throat, and I sent a veritable cascade of seeking magic shooting outward, intent on deterring whatever shared my bedchamber.

Steam joined the smoke puffing from my uninvited guest. The dragon's mouth opened in what might have been a grin. Or maybe I was anthropomorphizing the fuck out of whatever it was feeling. Since I couldn't get rid of the dragon, I trolled for Celtic power.

Once I determined the dragon illusion wasn't Mother or one of her spies, my breathing rate lowered from panic mode to slightly above normal. There were many wicked things in the world, but I'd take a troll or a goblin or a sprite or a gnome—or a dragon—any old day over my Celtic kin.

During my momentary panic, I'd looked right into its eyes, but it hadn't snared me. Did that mean the old tales about dragon eyes capturing your soul weren't accurate?

Unfamiliar magic swept from the crown of my head to my feet, warm and probing but not unpleasant or threatening. "What do you want?" The question burst from me, but the dragon didn't answer it any more than he'd answered why he was here.

I kept returning to "he," so maybe that part was right. Perhaps my caller was male. Oblivious to my turmoil, Mort slept on. Tail tucked around his body, his purring was a soothing counterpart to the dragon's quiet presence. A small whoosh snapped my head around in time to see Tansy poke her nose through the hangings that formed a door to my room.

I fully expected her to take one gander at the dragon and run screaming back the way she'd come. Instead she walked toward me, a soft smile on her face. "Do you want more to eat?" she asked, and then added, "We hoped you'd be asleep. I told everyone I'd come check on you."

I shook my head. Apparently, the dragon, still puffing ashy smoke in a corner of my room, was visible only to me. "I'm all right," I told Tansy. "Thank you for making certain I was fed."

Color suffused her thin cheeks, and she bowed her head for a moment. "You saved my life, Ro. It's not something I'll ever forget. Is Mort bothering you?"

"Not at all." I opened my arms. Tansy all but dove into them, and I hugged her tight. It's good to be loved. No matter how tough I think I am, having Tansy in my arms and my cat next to me were a good reminder to focus on what I had. I'd been sunk in self-pity over what was missing.

No matter what I did, Ceridwen wouldn't be any different. Neither would Bjorn. The Breaking wouldn't reverse itself without a whole lot of planning and effort—and maybe not even then.

Tansy brushed a thin finger across one of my cheeks. "You're crying."

So I was. "I'm just overtired. I'll be better once I've rested."

She scooted off the bed. "I'll make you some tea and spell it to relax you."

I smiled. "That would be lovely. Thank you."

When I angled a glance at the dragon, he wasn't there anymore. Tendrils of smoke danced near the ceiling, but the beast was gone. Had he ever been there? Or was my weary mind playing tricks on me. Another possibility surfaced. I'd been thinking about Bjorn. He was linked in some unknown fashion to the dragon who'd been with him killing goblins.

Was Bjorn a dragon? To put a finer point on it, was the dragon who'd just been here the same as the one I'd seen in the air the previous night? Oftentimes, magical creatures had animal familiars or another form they could morph into. Had Bjorn paid me a visit in dragon form to check if I was all right? I might be impossibly far off base, but the idea soothed me, so I clung to it.

By the time Tansy brought me a mug of steaming tea, I was more settled. She sat with me and combed my tangled hair with magic and her fingers as I drank the comforting beverage. It had a mildly alcoholic undernote and tasted of wildflowers I hadn't seen since the Breaking.

"How did you make this?" I asked.

She ducked her head, looking pleased by my question. "I found patches of dried flowers near the shores of the closest lake and gathered them."

"But it's not safe," I protested. "That's where Bjorn and the dragon killed all those goblins. And the troll."

She patted my shoulder. "This was a long time ago. I'd forgotten about the flowers but came across them when I was helping Hilda and them get items together to move to Inverlochy Castle. Most blossoms would have turned to dust after all this time, but not these, so I put them in a spot in the kitchen for us to use."

Tansy sat with me a while longer. I shut my eyes and quieted my breathing so she could get back to her other work. All of us had more to do than we had hours in the day. The time she'd stolen to nurture me was time she'd have to make up.

After a whispered, "I love you," she tiptoed out of my chamber.

For the second time since her visit, I fought the hot sting of tears. Patrick had said how lucky the coven was to have me. It cut both ways. They'd saved me from a solitary existence where I would have had no one.

It might have maybe made me stronger, but it also would have turned me into an embittered crone. Caring for the witches made me vulnerable—but I'd chosen wisely the day I'd shown up on their doorstep.

I'd struggled with my decision. The only way I'd made myself knock on their door was I'd promised myself I wouldn't remain long. Only until I'd patched myself up. I was raw from Mother's indifference and fearful I'd end up back within the velvet-lined trap of the Celtic pantheon. Loneliness rode my shoulders like a deranged hag, sometimes screaming, sometimes cajoling, but the message was always the same. Go home because I'd never make it alone and on my own.

I doubled up a fist and punched the air. It hadn't been my imagination. Nor had it been a crazy old woman. The incessant messages to return to the Celts had all come from

Mother. She was more than capable of that type of projection and compulsion.

Why had I been so dense I'd never realized it before now?

One more reason to hate her should have kept me awake fuming. Instead, the rest that had been so elusive swallowed me whole. When I woke would be soon enough to deal with everything. Bad mothers. Imaginary dragons. A man who didn't want me the way I wanted him.

Except maybe I was wrong about that last. If my visitor had been Bjorn, wearing his dragon form, maybe he cared more about me than I realized.

I hadn't even finished eating when a cavalcade of visitors began. I'd assumed people would leave me notes and let me triage my work as I thought best, but it had been wishful thinking. I wanted to return to Midgard, make certain Rowan had returned safely, but between broken wings, broken magic, twisted spells, and a magic wand that had turned on its owner, hours passed.

For the first time ever, I longed for a closed sign, similar to ones I'd seen in many Midgard shops before the Breaking. Humans had the right idea. They weren't always available.

The next problem was a chalice that was suddenly producing sour wine. Its owner, one of the smaller giants, was worried it might be poison. "I can live with sour," he grumbled, "but not if it makes me sick."

He was too big to sit on any of my chairs, so he stood hunched by the side of the room as he waited for me to pronounce his precious cup could be salvaged. Patchy dark hair sprang in erratic clumps from his otherwise bald head. Close-set dark eyes, swarthy skin, and a perpetually befuddled expression were par for the course for giants.

Some of their women are stunning. I have no idea what happened to the men.

Giants don't have a well-developed sense of smell when it comes to things like toxins. They're spot on locating mortals, though, since they like to eat them. I suppose it's always like that with predators and prey. It makes sense you'd figure out how to locate your favorite foods. After trying a few simple cleansing spells—all of which failed—I asked my client if he wanted me to dispose of the chalice safely.

The tarnished brass cup with intricate carvings covering its surface chose that moment to vomit a stream of cherry-colored death right at its owner. He moved fast for such a big man, and so the poison only sliced through the edges of his leather breeches. Before I could restate my offer to destroy the thing, he snatched it up and raced out of my cottage.

I considered locking the door, but there's never been a lock that kept determined magic-wielders out. Besides, they'd complain to Odin, perhaps go so far as to suggest he appoint a different master sorcerer.

Right about now, I'd welcome being fired.

Gah. Politics are such a grind, and I've never been any good navigating those waters. When I realized I'd been holding my breath, wondering who the hell was going to show up next, I exhaled long and loud.

No one else seemed inclined to darken my doorway. I cast a quick spell to neutralize spills from where the chalice had left smoking spots on my stone floor. They might have burned themselves out, but since I hadn't figured out what was powering the thing, better safe than sorry. If I'd let them be, I might have returned to naught but foundation stones.

The cottage might not be much, but it was mine.

It wasn't wise to tempt fortune, so I hustled out of my house, intent on catching a ride on the rainbow bridge. I hadn't made it fifty paces when a low keening whistle snagged me, drawing me back.

The bloody stone. I'd gone off without it, and it was reminding me in its inimitable nagging way to go back and fetch it.

How far did its influence reach?

Could I move beyond its scope?

In the spirit of scientific experimentation, I kept right on walking. And it got harder and harder to move forward. My limbs may as well have been mired in quicksand for all the progress I made.

"All right," I shouted, grateful no one else was about, "I give up." I turned around and the stone zinged through the air, ending up in the hand I extended to catch it.

Interesting. I hadn't actually had to return. All I'd needed to do was acknowledge its superiority over me. I filed that little tidbit away for future reference and continued toward the nearest spot I could grab a lift on the bridge. I had no idea what I'd do in Midgard. Not that I didn't visit there periodically, but I'd just been there.

After I chased Rowan down, I'd have no other reason to remain. The magical vessels I'd crafted to contain the worst of the Breaking's residual darkness should hold for another few days. Perhaps as much as two weeks—if I were fortunate. During that time, I'd make a point of asking Nidhogg if he had a more permanent solution.

Even if he didn't, the worst that could happen would be the remains of the Breaking would go back to how they'd been before my attempt to permanently defuse them. I blew out a thoughtful breath. The problem extended much deeper than the bits of Celtic magic clinging to the edges of the Breaking site. What I'd done was superficial, probably a waste of time and magic.

I hadn't yet reached Bifrost, and I slowed my pace until I wasn't moving at all. I could still return home and consult my lore scrolls and books about how to address the insidious darkness I'd felt pulsing beneath the Breaking. My haste was ridiculous. It certainly wasn't fueled by me caring about Midgard. No, it was all about my unholy fascination with Rowan.

Damn. Each time I called her that, I cringed. The name was just wrong. Should I tell her about her true name, Runa? I took a few mental steps backward. Maybe I shouldn't seek her out at all.

Once I'd reassured myself she'd returned to Midgard.

I had to do that. I wouldn't rest easy until I knew she was safe, but there was no reason to reveal any more about my obsession with her than she might already have guessed. The more I thought about it, the surer I was that a quick trip to Midgard was the proper course of action for me. I'd use magic to check on her, and then slip away.

We would run into each other when we checked on the Breaking, but not immediately. I'd agreed to work with her on securing its foul magic, but neither of us had tacked down a time frame. Besides, she'd be busy helping the witches with their crop project within the illusion that was once Inverlochy Castle. Meanwhile, I could slide in and out of the Breaking site without attracting attention.

Same thing I'd been doing for years.

After its hissy fit when I forgot it, the stone had been quiescent. Until now. I wasn't certain if it was reacting because I'd stopped walking, or because of my train of thought. The one where I'd begun the process of snipping the strings that bound me to Runa.

Rowan, I corrected myself. If I didn't watch it, and called her by her true name, she was bound to react to it. True names were like that. They resonated deep in your soul. Rather like a puzzle piece that snapped into the spot meant just for it. Knowing her name had been withheld from her would add fuel to the hatred she felt for Ceridwen. Rowan hadn't said much, but she didn't need to. Her angst and pain and anger had bled through her words.

The stone zapped me again. Clearly, it wasn't going to let me be until I was well on my way to Midgard.

Not the stone, I reminded myself. The crystalline chunk was inert. The energy powering it was Nidhogg's desire. Win, lose, or draw, I was shackled to the Norse dragon at the hip for the foreseeable future.

A rather considerable part of me rebelled, but it was wasted energy. I might have magic to burn, but compared with a dragon, I was small potatoes to the max.

My feet had begun moving again. Before I could summon a portal for the bridge, one bloomed to life in front of me. Normally, something like that would have given me the creeps because it proved Nidhogg was hovering, watching my every move. So much for my assumption about being invisible to the gods.

I leapt over the lintel, through the gateway, and onto the bridge. I've called it a bridge, but Bifrost is a living part of the Nine Worlds. Linked to their energy, it moves where it's called. So my journey feels the same whether I'm going to Alfheim or Niflheim or Midgard. I have to pay attention, though. Markers are carved into Bifrost's surface. Runes denoting each world. If I wait too long, I'll miss my destination, and then I have to start over.

The worlds flashed by in their usual order. Not getting off in the proper spot would add considerably to my journey time. Not much chance of screwing things up this trip. The same portal that had opened for me in Vanaheim popped into being at just the right moment.

I didn't linger within Bifrost to question why I suddenly had my own personal gateway valet. Nidhogg wanted me in Midgard, and he wanted me there badly enough to make things as easy as possible. It should have worried me. Dragons never made things easy for anyone. Not even each other. It's survival of the toughest almost from the moment they hatch—if the lore is to be believed.

The dragonstone had settled into a comfortable buzzy hum. I was being compliant, so no more need to ride me. Rain cascaded from a dark-gray sky as soon as I was fully out of Bifrost. This particular cloak had no hood, and I was drenched in no time. Water ran down my face and my neck; I directed a thread of magic to counteract the worst of it.

When that didn't work very well, I settled for keeping it from running into my eyes. I peered around at an empty vista. I'd come out in an unfamiliar spot, but Midgard was a big place. A wee bit of power gave me rough coordinates. I was a few leagues from the lake where Nidhogg and I had tangled with the goblins.

Thinking about them brought me around fast. Rain aside —it was the least of my concerns—I scanned for threats.

And for the dragon.

Had he turned into my new best fighting buddy? Like I've said, I'm not much of a warrior. About the only reason I spar with Jarle is I feel guilty about my lack in that regard. Never in my wildest imaginings did I long be a soldier when I grew up. Hel's offer to lose myself in her domain was beginning to look a lot more attractive. A wave of cold from the stone told me that particular avenue wasn't open.

Not for me. And not right now.

Bits of unfamiliar magic pricked me. What was out there? Would I even recognize whatever it was by sight? We wizard types don't exactly go to school. We read lore books. At least that's how I honed my power. I was never particularly interested in Strange Magical Creatures 101. So I'd skipped over those morsels.

Woven in with the magic I couldn't identify, I thought I sensed Rowan. Maybe. My impressions that might have been her were fleeting. When I amplified them with magic, they frittered away altogether.

Likely, I'd been wrong about thinking she was near. A product of wishful thinking on my part.

It was raining harder, if that was even possible. I blinked

water out of my eyes. A staunch crackling presaged lightning that split the sky in two. Thunder followed so fast, the storm must have been right on top of me. I gave up any pretense of anything beyond clinging to survival mode.

I was still catching faint pulses of Runa's—Rowan's— energy. The more I felt, the surer I was it wasn't her. Someone was tossing out copycat emanations as bait. Another lightning bolt hit the soaked ground only about a meter away. What the fuck? I've heard about lightning striking the ground in Midgard. Never happens in Vanaheim.

We have plenty of thunder. Scarcely any lightning. The standing joke is the thunder is Odin and the rest of his ilk farting up a storm in Asgard.

I should have followed my instincts and run hard and fast at the first hint of that odd magic. Didn't matter which way, just so long as I was moving quickly enough not to turn into a target. I spun in a circle, watching as bolt after bolt of electrical power scribed a circle around me. The air thickened with static voltage until my hair, wet as it was, rose off my head.

The sensation was worse than eerie. Not much rattles me, but no time like the present to get moving. It beat turning into a conductor when one of those jagged shots of lightning finally hit me. It wouldn't kill me, but it would be damned unpleasant.

Reaching deep, I tried to teleport out of there, but something stood between me and summoning enough of the particular mix of magic I needed to leave. A deep booming that had nothing to do with the thunder crashing around me filled my ears. Beneath my feet, the ground began heaving and buckling.

What kind of bizarre weather pattern included earthquakes?

Except whatever was happening around me had nothing to do with anything so prosaic as weather gone awry. I was under attack. Worse, the dragon had plopped me here. He must have known what he was doing. Hell, he'd hustled me specifically to this spot. Why? Was he planning to kill me? I didn't think so. He'd gone to too much trouble shaping me into a tool to do his bidding.

The quake worsened and tossed me from side to side. Staying on my feet without an infusion of power became impossible.

A huge gash opened in the ground a few meters away. The dirt was so wet, it crumpled into the hole, but it didn't stave off the inevitable. A hairy arm with claws where fingers should have been reached through the opening. Not much point in waiting for the whole of whatever it was to emerge.

I might not be able to teleport, but there was nothing wrong with the rest of my magic. I funneled as hot a jolt as I could right at the exposed hand. Might have overdone it because the flesh caught fire, burning hot and fast. Bellows from beneath me made me fear for my perch. I did not want to fall into another hole in the ground.

The owner of the hand was down there. He'd rolled his blackened stump back and forth, but it still burned courtesy of my power. I'd instructed the spell to keep on going until nothing was left. If it obeyed me, the flames would auger into the rest of the bastard.

In the space between two breaths, all hell broke loose. Holes opened all around me. Some in the earth, some in the ether. Gnomes, trolls, ratty goblins with splotched faces. They must have been the odd energy I couldn't pigeonhole. They looked like someone had tried to breed them with something else and failed.

The dragonstone pulsed merrily in my pocket. The fucking fucker was enjoying the hell out of this.

"Whose side are you on?" I muttered and arced magic in every direction I could. There were so many bastards out there, I didn't have to bother aiming. That was the good part. The bad part was no matter how many I took out, more showed up.

I was yelling curses and charging from one side to the other like a crazed person. Damn, the enemy arrayed against me smelled horrible. Unwashed bodies and a generalized *eau de rotten*. Except the trolls. They're stone, and it doesn't stink. Why were they even moving? Daylight was a curse for them. Not that the sun was anywhere in sight. Bleak as it was, even a vampire might have gotten away with waltzing about.

And then I remembered light was no longer a deterrent for the undead.

My previous sense Rowan might be near departed. I'd been right about her scent being bait to keep me from leaving. I'm not immortal, and it was starting to look as if I might not make it out of this alive. A cudgel landed on my shoulder. Pain shot down my arm like a dose of liquid fire, but if I diverted magic to heal myself, there'd be less for defense.

A knife descended from out of nowhere and sliced my face from cheek to jaw. Compared with my shoulder, it didn't hurt much, but I smelled my own blood as it dripped onto my chest. I was more careful after that and rerouted enough magic to build a ward.

Brave was one thing. Stupid quite another. I should have warded myself from the beginning, but this whole fighting thing isn't second nature. I ducked and wove and leapt and feinted. I stopped paying attention to who crawled out of gateways and fought what was in front of me. When they fell, I moved to the next adversary.

My chest was tight. My lungs burned. Maybe I'd broken a rib in addition to everything else. In the time it had taken me to come up with a decent ward, I'd sustained a couple more direct hits.

I didn't understand why I hadn't fallen on my face, but I'd found a dynamic balance point. One where I could keep on slugging. Day was long gone. At some point, it had quit raining and the rolling, booming quakes had passed through. The sound of distant hunting horns blared, but I had to be imagining it.

Who the hell had such things?

And then my battered brain made the connection. It had to be Odin and the Hunt. Made sense. Naught but dead things lay around me. The Hunt liked 'em dead, but they'd have a little fun with the ones still on their feet swinging knives and cudgels and flails too.

I risked a glance upward. Sure enough, the Hunt's ghostly trail lit the night sky. When they got closer, the stink of horses and death would waft down. Bad as the Hunt smelled, they were better than what I'd been fighting. Whoops and cries rained from the sky.

One thing was clear. I wasn't needed here. Not anymore. If I remained, one of the Riders might take me out by mistake.

I don't understand why I even bothered trying to teleport again, but I visualized the Celtic lair beneath Ben Nevis. I've never viewed magic as a fickle bitch. There's always a reason if it doesn't work the way I want it to. My power may have failed me earlier, but this time everything clicked. The killing field dropped away, replaced by the solid rock of Ben Nevis's robust flanks.

I wasn't inside as I'd hoped, but close enough.

I sank into a crouch, still panting. My shoulder ached. My face felt stiff from congealed blood. My side was sore, but nothing jabbed when I took a deep breath, so maybe my ribs weren't broken after all.

What had just happened to me? Nidhogg had plopped me into the middle of a passel of bad guys. Why? What was he hoping for? Did he view my sparring matches with Jarle as wholly inadequate?

I choked on bitter laughter. Truer words were never spoken. What little I'd done by way of dancing about carting a broadsword was worse than inadequate. It was laughable. For one thing, magic was a far better weapon than any implement.

Not for Jarle, but for me. He took the lead in our sessions because he was the one with the military skills, and magic was far from his forte.

My eyes snapped open; I sucked in a tight breath. All the

time I'd wasted with Jarle, I could have been honing my magical combat ability—and imbuing weapons with magic. The possibilities were staggering. I could craft weapons specific to different enemies. Knives where a simple touch would kill a gnome.

Of course, I'd have to get near enough to use it. Blades were always an up-close-and-personal proposition. Maybe it wasn't such a grand idea as all that. I'd have to develop far better warding and be quicker on my feet.

The sky was growing lighter. It was past time to get moving. Soon the new day would be upon me.

I stumbled upright intent on checking on Rowan and then returning to Vanaheim to lick my wounds and focus power inward until I recovered. Nidhogg and I were due for another heart-to-heart. If he was behind this—and he damn near had to be—the least he could have done was show up and make sure I didn't get mowed under by gnomes and goblins.

They live in the earth. Rumor has it they stash their enemies in iron cages. They don't have much magic themselves, but the metal mutes their captives' ability, and—

"Stop," I muttered, not wanting to look back and replay might-have-beens. Somehow I'd come through mostly unscathed. Keeping things subtle, I felt for Rowan's presence. The distinctive texture of her magic settled around me. With it came a deep sense of relief. She was here, and she was all right. It was all I needed.

I turned to put some distance between here and a gateway to the bridge. No reason to open anything quite so near the witches' lair where one of them might stumble into my residual force field and thence onto the rainbow bridge. My kin might tolerate me, but they'd flay any witches who ventured into Norse territory.

"Bjorn!" Hearing my name on Rowan's tongue was alarming. I hadn't meant to disturb her, but she'd clearly sensed my magic, trotted outside, and seen me.

I turned very slowly and tried to cover the worst of my hurts with a glamour.

A muted gasp told me I hadn't done a very good job. "What the fuck happened to you?" she cried and ran to me. "You look like you went a million rounds with the Dark Fae. And lost."

I managed a sweeping mock bow. "*Au contraire, mademoiselle.* I won."

Rowan snorted. "Alrighty then, *winner.* Come inside so I can patch up the worst of your winning injuries."

I waved her aside. "I'm fine. Or I will be. I was heading home to heal myself."

She hooked a hand firmly around my arm. It was the same side where my shoulder had taken a beating, and I bit back a yelp. She angled a pointed look my way. "No more discussion. I'll take a shot at fixing you up first. Then you can go home."

I might have argued harder, but I liked the idea of her magic searching out my hurt places. More than liked it, I yearned for her touch. For the jolt of rightness as our magics married together.

She let go of me but then stood aside, apparently not sure I'd follow along if she didn't keep her eyes on me. I didn't trust myself to speak, so I nodded and trudged toward the entrance she'd come from. I followed her scent and her magic and felt her energy behind me.

There wasn't any place I'd rather be, and it scared me as much as facing the endless stream of wicked creatures on that muddy field. Over my long life, I've never needed anyone, and I wasn't about to start now.

"What did you run up against?" Rowan's question was low, fierce.

I told her as we ducked within the cave system, and she shook her head. "This is why we have to make Inverlochy Castle work," she said. "If we can't grow food there, we'll starve. We sure as hell can't plant anything outside."

I wanted to say I'd help. That between us, if we leveraged joined magic, we should be able to outwit her Celtic kin and keep the witches at Inverlochy well hidden. I held silence. The more time I spent with her, the more we combined our magic, the harder it would be to be alone again.

Better not to open that door.

As I followed her deeper beneath Ben Nevis, I felt small and petty. So what if I was smitten by her. The witches were in trouble. I couldn't stand by and let them fade because it was easier for me. Rowan and I made a hell of a team. The coven was important to her, and the witches had been kind to me.

She led me into what looked like a dining room and sat me at a table. "I'm going to get hot water and bandages," she said.

"What can I do?"

"Take off that jacket and tunic."

"Are you always this pushy when you want to see a man naked?" I quirked a tired brow.

"You take them off, or I'll cut them off. Your choice."

I chucked as I watched her departing back and began to gingerly divest my upper body of its coverings. When she returned, I'd offer my assistance with her crop project.

I'd forgotten about the dragonstone until it began humming softly from my pocket. Clearly, it approved of my decision, which meant Nidhogg was still behind the scenes orchestrating my every move.

"It would be a whole lot simpler if you just told me what you wanted," I mumbled telepathically.

"Ye doona listen well. I already did." The dragon's immediate response in his deep, raspy voice told me I'd been spot on about him hovering in the wings. Out of sight, but near enough to keep right on pulling my puppet strings.

I should have been outraged. Instead, I was just tired and looking forward to the touch of Rowan's magic.

I'd been dreaming of dragons—again—when something jolted me from sleep. In this dream, I'd been a dragon, swooping and riding the air currents high above the wasteland Earth had become. The sensation was heady, mesmerizing, and the wonder I'd felt at spreading wings of my own defied attempts to resurrect it.

Other dragons had been in the air. No one had talked with me, but I'd felt a sense of community, of belonging to something greater than myself. It was how I'd always hoped things would be with the Celtic gods.

Except they never were.

A hasty scan told me Bjorn was right outside the cave system. He must have been searching for me, and his magic had shaken me from sleep. It was nearly dawn, so I'd rested enough. I rubbed sleep from my eyes and then jumped to my feet when I understood he was leaving.

What the hell?

He'd only come to make sure I was here, but hadn't planned to pop in long enough to say hello? Granted, it was a bit on the early side, but I'd have been glad to see him.

I winced. Too glad.

Maybe I should let him trot into the breaking day. No maybe about it. I should definitely do just that.

My traitorous feet weren't listening to reason, though. They made the decision for me, and I hustled out of my chamber and down the corridor leading outside. Bjorn was, indeed, striding purposefully away. I called his name, and he turned. Not eagerly, as I would have wished, but slowly, painfully. As if laying eyes on me was at the bottom of his list.

Hot words hit the back of my throat. I was about to tell him to go fuck himself. That sneaking about like a thief in a grocery shop was unacceptable. Either he accepted me as a friend, and treated me as such, or he could damn well remain in Vanaheim. Forever.

I understood full well I was hurt, and my wounded feelings were far easier to tolerate when they manifested as anger. Insight didn't make my rage any more manageable, unfortunately. My stomach twisted into a hot, sour knot.

Once Bjorn turned enough so I could actually see him, I was grateful I'd held my ire within. My pride might be trashed, but it paled in comparison to his body. I didn't care what he thought about me when I ran to him.

Damn. The whole side of his face was a bloody pulp. One shoulder sat stiffly, and his back slumped with weariness. I smelled magical residue all over him, but I had him tell me what happened, rather than guessing whom he'd fought.

I should have let him retreat and funnel his power into patching himself together, but I couldn't. Worse, I cheated and added a subtle dash of compulsion when I nudged him into remaining long enough for me to at least assess the worst of his injuries.

Pretty self-serving on my part, but it was for a good cause. Something about the way our magic fit together felt bigger than both of us. As if we were destined to shape events neither of us could yet imagine. I kicked myself for what had to be a total flight of fancy and settled him in the common room. Breakfast, such as it was, wouldn't happen for at least an hour, so we'd have the place to ourselves.

I guess I'd been wrong about him being a dragon shifter. If he'd had access to a winged body, he wouldn't be so beat up, which meant the dragon in my chamber couldn't have been him.

But he was here now. Even injured as he was, he'd cared enough to check if I was all right. A small warm place bloomed in my chest, and I let myself enjoy evidence of his concern.

I'd have taken him to my chamber, but it felt presumptuous. He wouldn't be comfortable there, and his presence in my private space didn't fit somehow. I didn't work too hard to sort out why. I've always trusted my instincts.

When I returned with a kettle of hot water, a basin, and bandage material, he'd removed the garments from his upper torso. The sight of his body hit me like a one-two punch. He was beautiful. Stunning. Even bloody and bruised, his skin glowed with an inner light. Pale-gold illuminated his gracefully muscled chest, arms, and back. He was tall and elegantly built. Not slabbed with muscle like brawnier men, but delightful to look at.

He'd removed the bands from his hair, and it spilled around him, thick, shiny, and so blond it shimmered like fields of summer wheat. His eyes were shut, and pain had carved lines into his forehead and around his well-formed mouth.

For a scant half moment, I imagined what those lips would feel like crushed against mine, and then I scrubbed the image from my mind.

He shook himself gently and opened his eyes. Mysterious as the ocean, they had silvery flecks in them. "I may have drifted off," he murmured. "Sorry."

I set the kettle and basin down near him and poured steaming water from one to the other. A quick healing chant infused power into the water. As gently as I could, I sponged dried blood from his hurt places. Slowly, tentatively, he wove his magic in with mine.

Because we'd been joined before, I was intimately aware of how truncated his power was. The battle had been worse than he described it. "You might have died," I scolded, and then bit my lip hard. Why, oh why, couldn't I keep my mouth shut?

"Big difference between might have and didn't." His tone was sharp, and I accepted the rebuke. I deserved it.

"You could have called on me," I murmured.

"Maybe at the beginning," he agreed. "Before I knew

what I faced." He curved his fingers and raked them through his hair. When he looked up at me, his expression melded grim resolution with humility. "I haven't spent much of my life tilting after windmills, but this battle blew up in my face damned fast. So fast I was reacting rather than planning my next moves."

I nodded. I knew exactly what he meant. I'd been there. More than once. I chucked the bloody water in my basin into a nearby bucket, poured fresh, and moved to his back. A particularly nasty gash had dug in across his ribs. As I cleaned the wounds, I seeded them with healing energy.

He leaned into my touch. It took all my self-control not to wrap my arms around him and bury my face in his neck. Why was I so drawn to him? He might be beautiful, but I'd met pretty men before. Whatever it was ran far deeper than his looks.

I forced myself to take a step backward and cast a critical eye over my work. I'd done what I could, but I didn't want him to leave. I started to suggest he bide a while in one of the vacant chambers. We had many we rarely used within this warren of hidey holes. Instead, I said, "All done. The abrasions are clean. Our power is complementary, so the magic I threaded into your hurt places will gel with yours."

"Thank you." He got creakily to his feet and picked up his tunic. Once it had been creamy linen, but it was stained and stiff with his blood.

"I can get you a cleaner shirt," I offered and gave myself a sharp mental slap. Talk about transparent. I didn't want him to go, and I was grasping at pathetic excuses to hold onto him for a little while longer. Subterfuge wasn't my style at all, but neither was I willing to out and tell him how much I wanted him to remain here.

Crap. Next thing I knew, I'd be suggesting he move in. He had a life. In Vanaheim. And it didn't include me.

He cast a sidelong glance my way. I felt like a young woman dealing with her first infatuation. In other words, like a prime idiot. He shrugged into the stained garment and then slung his cloak over his shoulders. It was a dark shade, so the bloodstains didn't stick out like glowing beacons.

He offered me a wry grin and said, "It's all right. I learned how to wash my own clothes a long time ago."

I felt like I should say something, make plans for when we'd meet again. This time I was wise enough to remain silent. At least about that. I remembered how the feel of his magic had jolted me awake. "Were you checking on me earlier?"

His smile widened. "Of course. Had to know you got back safely from Niflheim. Exiting from there is harder than it looks."

Teleporting hadn't felt any different than it usually did, but rather than correct him, I said, "Thank you. It's good to be cared about. I was just thinking that earlier when one of the young witches was fussing over me."

His blue eyes darkened to an inscrutable midnight shade when they met mine. "I remind myself of that all the time." He touched his forehead as if doffing an invisible cap. Magic flashed around him, and then he was gone.

I stared stupidly at the place he'd stood, inhaling the scent of his power, and of him. Brine-drenched air mingled with hot baked stones. The latter reminded me of my dream of being a dragon. What did it mean? Was I freer than I imagined? Or was I reading too much into it?

Dreams didn't always mean things, but I had a feeling this one did. I gathered the bloody rags I'd used to clean Bjorn's hurt places and trotted one room over to a laundry kettle that hung over a perpetual fire. So long as I was up, I may as well get the morning meal going.

All the coven tasks were shared. Whoever got to them first did them. I suppose there were lazy witches, but I'd never met one. Even the old and sick pulled their weight. I brewed myself another cup of tea once I'd made a pot of thin gruel and left it to simmer on stones heated with magic.

A quick stop at my chamber for a cloak, and I headed outside intent on checking the battlefield. Bjorn had told me his impressions of being set upon, of the earth opening and disgorging deplorable evil, but I was determined to unearth more in the way of clues. I'd been living in the midst of the post-Breaking world for a long while, and some of his descriptions hadn't made sense to me.

Why send so many to attack one man? Granted, Bjorn had potent magic, but I'd never known any of the wicked creatures to rain wrath down on one person. The spell that had snapped shut around me near the Breaking was different. It had Ceridwen's signature stamped all over it.

An unsettling thought surfaced as I hustled out of the cave system. Had Ceridwen somehow discovered Bjorn was aligned with me? Working on the assumption that my enemy's friend is also my enemy, was Mother targeting him?

It didn't make a whole lot of sense. Ceridwen was powerful, but commanding ranks of goblins and trolls and gnomes was beneath her dignity. Even if she could force them to fall into line and do her bidding, I couldn't envision my goddess mother stooping quite that low.

The morning was gray and chill. I strode to where I'd met Bjorn. The feel of his power lingered in that spot. It should be easy enough to follow. He'd described the field where he'd fought, but locating it this way was more expedient.

Moments later, mists cleared around me. I stood in the center of an unnerving vista. Pockmarked earth spread in all directions. Dead bodies sprawled at every angle imaginable. At least a dozen new standing stones formed a bizarre line of sentinels where trolls had breathed their last.

Bjorn had mentioned the trolls, but I'd discounted them. Trolls can't operate when the sun is up, even if it doesn't strike them directly. From the looks of things, these trolls hadn't made the slightest effort to make a run for their underground dens. What I didn't understand was why.

I walked closer, intent on examining the pillars. It took time for their features to totally disappear, for the stone to smooth to nothingness. Sure enough, I could still make out faces and hair. I looked for mortal wounds. Something that would have kept them from seeking safety. All but one appeared intact.

Had Bjorn immobilized them with magic? Was that why they hadn't moved?

I made a mental note to ask him because if he hadn't, it meant magic was reshaping itself again. And not on my side of the tally sheet. If evil was growing stronger, it didn't bode well for any of the mortals still clinging to their lives by the thinnest of margins.

My heart hurt as I thought about the witches. So far, we'd avoided others with any type of power, but there had to be other decent magic-wielders left. Like the Sidhe, for example. Or the Fae. Granted the light and dark courts were perpetually at war, but when the chips were down, they'd battle evil before they fought one another.

At least I thought so. Most of my magical education had come from Mother's badly neglected lore books. On a tangent, I fleshed out my mental list of possible allies adding Druids and sprites to the list.

As I wandered among the standing stones, still searching for clues, I considered just how the Nine Worlds intersected with Earth. By Bjorn's telling, Earth was Midgard in that system. Did it mean we could count on protection from Odin? From Yggdrasil and its roots?

How about from the Norse dragon? It took me a moment to resurrect his name out of my memory banks. Nidhogg. Did he and Dewi know one another? It would make sense. Not many dragon gods out there.

A strident *mrowww* announced Mort had tracked me down. The cat couldn't have walked this far so quickly. I'd always suspected he had magic of his own, and here was a spot of proof. I held out my arms, and he jumped into them. From there, he clawed his way into place across my shoulders. It felt good to have him there. Warm and soft and purring.

I scanned the field. Assuming Bjorn had worked alone, he'd slaughtered hundreds. So much for his assessment about not being much of a warrior. I didn't know very many who wouldn't be proud of what he'd accomplished.

"Not much more to discover here," I told Mort. He meowed knowingly as if he understood me perfectly.

Perhaps he did.

Before I left, I sent power auguring into the earth. What lay beneath me? Had Bjorn stumbled on the goblins' home? Or the gnomes'? Or had they simply chosen this spot to launch their attack?

I was careful. I took my time. While I sensed residue from dark power all around me, including underneath my feet, I didn't find any more bad things. It argued they lived elsewhere. Too bad. I'd been hunting for Goblin Central for years. If I could locate their den, I could obliterate it.

The concept was so real to me, I dusted my hands together. Problem solved. At least for one adversary. All I had to do was find them.

I smelled dragon before I saw it. Maybe because I'd been sunk in dragon dreams, the scent of rocks baked under a sun far hotter than it ever got here didn't alarm me. In an odd way, it was like coming home.

I shook myself out of complacency in a hurry.

Dragons were fucking dangerous. It was sheer folly to romanticize them. Was it too late to leave? A hasty glance skyward suggested the answer to my question was yes.

Two dragons were winging their way through the sky. A golden one that looked a lot like the wyrm I'd seen the other night, and a smaller one in shades of brilliant blue. It was definitely too late to summon the amount of power I'd need to teleport, but maybe they hadn't seen me.

I pulled power up through the earth and shrouded myself with it. Mort quit purring. A muffled yelp told me how much he hated being snared in my spells. I reached up and soothed him as best I could with gentle fingers buried in his fur.

"Hush." I breathed the word and laced power in with it. On the very off chance the beasts above hadn't noticed me, I'd be damned if the cat gave us away.

I willed invisibility, willed the dragons to keep right on flying. They didn't belong in this world. Earth had never hosted their ilk. For a pathetically short while, I believed I might have pulled it off.

But then, amid trumpeting and smoke and fire, they wheeled and dropped lower in the sky. No avoiding it. They were headed right for me. Since I'd been discovered—or maybe they'd known about me all along—I dropped my ward and stood tall.

Cowering in front of enemies is the wrong thing to do.

They hadn't declared themselves hostile. Not yet, but it paid to prepare for the worst.

Happy again, Mort licked my neck. I hoped to hell the dragons wouldn't consider him as some kind of appetizer. The gold one touched down first, maybe two meters from me. Clods of wet, blood-saturated earth flew up from the spot he'd splatted down.

I guess when you're that big, elegant landings aren't a priority. He folded his wings and stared at me. Steam puffed through his partially open jaws. Meanwhile, the much smaller blue dragon settled to his right. Both the beasts had the same spinning eyes I remembered from Dewi.

Eyes like that sucked you in and didn't let you go—until the dragon was well and truly done with you. Except they didn't appear to have that effect on me.

I pushed my shoulders farther back, making myself as imposing as I could. Laughable in the face of creatures who stood better than two meters tall. Hell, the gold might be close to three. Angling my head to one side, I said, "Can I offer my assistance in any way? If not, I'll be leaving."

More steam billowed from both dragons until it swathed us in a warm, damp cloud. Far from disconcerting, it made me feel safe.

Yeah. Right. Don't be a bigger fool than you already are.

Batting the mist away, I repeated my query.

"Who are you?" the blue dragon asked in a lyrical voice that was damn near as mesmerizing as its eyes.

It was an odd question, but one I was willing to answer. Names offered power over people, but the dragons outstripped my paltry magic by so much, I wouldn't be offering them anything by way of an advantage.

"I am Rowan," I told the beast, and then added, "Ceridwen's daughter."

The gold shook his great head. "Not right," it intoned. "Ye are rightly Ceridwen's get, but that is not your name."

If this was going to turn into a game of twenty questions, I was at a serious disadvantage. "Apologies." I bowed my head briefly. "It is the only name my mother ever called me."

"Because she had reasons to hide your true one," the blue dragon said.

I flinched from the truth shining through his words and

waited, but neither beast said anything further until the gold announced, "We shall return,"

"Aye, by then ye will have found your name. Once ye know it, we can proceed." The blue dragon tilted its head until I gazed right into its spinning eyes.

"What do you mean, proceed?" It was a struggle to get the words out since I felt like I was falling headlong into a tornado.

"Once ye find your name, ye will know," the gold dragon replied. "It has been withheld from you for far too long. Ye are needed, but afore ye can do aught but get in the way, ye must—"

The other dragon trumpeted, effectively obliterating his companion's next words.

The two of them were talking in riddles. A harsh blast of magic reeking of dragon pushed me from one side of the patch of ground I stood upon to the other. Mort mewled his displeasure and dug his claws into my shoulder. By the time I detached him, the dragons were gone.

I blinked at steam and smoke still sifting through the air. If it weren't for the evidence of their presence, I'd have thought I imagined the whole exchange.

But then, I'd have seriously considered the possibility I was losing my mind. No time to dissect this. I was beyond late checking on the witches at Inverlochy Castle.

Had the dragons been some kind of ruse? A diversion to keep me away while the Celts slaughtered my family? I set Mort on the ground with firm instructions to return home. The set of his ears and tail told me he was angry, but he'd obey. To be on the safe side, I added a short blast of magic to speed him safely on his way.

Fear gripped me. Far more compelling than when I'd been confronted by the dragons, I rode it all the way through a rapid teleport to the castle's ruins on the river Lochy.

If moving my friends to Inverlochy Castle ended up bringing death and destruction, I'd have a hell of a hard time living with myself. The rest of the witches would forgive me, but I'd never be able to forgive myself.

CHAPTER THIRTEEN, BJORN

I'm not sure how I marshaled the strength to walk away from Runa—Rowan. The touch of her power lingered on my skin for hours after I returned to my cottage. Her scent tantalized me. Sleep came in dribs and drabs. In between, I washed the stink of blood and roadkill out of my shirt, cloak, and pants.

The cloak was heavy wool. It would take forever to dry, so I hung it over wooden racks near my hearth and selected another from my slender stores. One advantage of living long is I've had centuries to collect a motley wardrobe. Things do wear out, but there are always others to take their place.

The stone continued to vibrate merrily. I'd put on fresh trousers, and it had leapt into my pocket unbidden. Somewhere during our brief tenure as associates, it had come to associate my right front pocket as its territory. So long as it wasn't nagging me to do something I didn't want to, we got along fine.

I rolled my mental eyes. That statement was true of just about anyone. Not that the stone was a person, but it may as well be. It was sentient and channeled Nidhogg's will quite effectively. Thinking about the dragon was a reminder. He and I were overdue for a chat.

One where he shared more than he had our last go round.

The bar was low since he'd said almost less than nothing then.

I've always been a believer in getting unpleasant tasks over with. It solved a lot of problems. I didn't have to hang about worrying, for one thing. After finishing the last morsels from the meal I'd been working on for hours, I decided it would be prudent to position myself outside.

I couldn't talk with the dragon from within my abode. Well, I could—if I shouted through the walls or used telepathy. Even if he did show—and it was far from a given— I'd end up outside anyway. May as well just start there. I admit I was dragging my feet a bit. I was still stiff and sore and bleary-eyed from the battle he'd plonked me into.

Annoyed too.

I needed to ask why he'd chivvied me into Midgard in that particular spot. More importantly, was he planning to do it again? If so, I needed to be better prepared than I was right now. The magical weapons I'd flirted with designing would shoot to the top of my list. Maybe Odin could assign someone else to Alfheim and general sorcery tasks. At least for a while.

I moved to the pump handle over the sink and worked it until cold water filled my hands. I ducked my face into the chilly stream hoping the dousing would sharpen my fuzzy brain. Not much point in a conversation with Nidhogg if he refused to answer every question I posed.

Once I'd dried my face and hands, I plucked half a sheet of used vellum from my stores and started a list. That way, at least I'd have a reference point if the dragon's presence thwarted my reasoning ability.

I'd made it through why he'd dumped me into the middle of a battle and whether such events were about to become commonplace when the unmistakable reek of dragon told me I had a visitor. It wasn't that the beasts smelled unpleasant, but nothing else smelled quite like them, either.

I jumped up from the three-legged stool where I'd been perched and started out the door, returning when I realized I'd forgotten my fledgling list. Not that I couldn't remember two items. It was more of a security blanket. A promise to myself I wouldn't back down until I had something to work with.

I emerged into what looked like midafternoon, judging from the angle of sunlight, in time to see Nidhogg and a blue dragon I'd never met before land in my courtyard. Don't get me wrong, the beasts fly overhead more days than not, but it isn't as if we're on a first name basis or anything.

Dragons keep to themselves. I suppose they deign to chat with Odin and perhaps Thor or Loki, but, for most of us, they may as well not be there at all. I shuttered my mind. Nothing like labeling dragonkind as snobbish and worthless when the dust hadn't yet settled around the two standing nearby.

"Not looking too much the worse for the battle," Nidhogg rumbled, sounding pleased.

It was as good an opening as I was likely to get, so I jumped in with both feet. "Why did you—?"

"To test your mettle, lad. Why else?" he boomed before I'd even finished my question.

I balled my hands into fists, effectively crumpling the vellum. The stuff was expensive and hard to come by, but I didn't give a shit. "Why did my, erm, *mettle*, suddenly require testing?" I didn't even try to mute the acid in my tone, and I felt compelled to add, "I'm a sorcerer. A wizard. I deal in potions and spells. I am not a warrior."

"Ye dinna used to be a warrior," the blue dragon corrected smoothly.

I planted my feet shoulder width and turned to face him. "I'm Bjorn. To whom do I—"

"Stuff it." The dragon's eyes spun faster. "Ye're mad as hell at Nidhogg, but ye must needs get past that as well."

I waited. I'd given my name. Common decency demanded the dragon provide his.

"I am Ysien," he said after such a long pause I'd become certain he wasn't going to respond.

Nidhogg puffed fiery ash off to the side. "Ye did well. Better than I expected."

Coming from him, I suppose it was high praise, but I still felt used and out of sorts. I uncrumpled the vellum, and bits of it fluttered to the ground. "What would you have done if I'd performed less admirably?"

"I'm not sure," Nidhogg replied. "It dinna come to that, now did it?"

"Will you be plopping me into the midst of other battles?" I looked from one dragon to the other, but it bought me nothing. I was decent at reading men's faces, but dragons have scales and reptilian jaws. It would be rather akin to looking at an alligator and determining its mood from the set of its teeth.

A blast of flame scored the ground a few centimeters from my feet. I stood my ground and glared at Nidhogg. "If you find my attitude lacking, perhaps you'd be better served starting anew with another flunky."

"Silence," Nidhogg roared. Fire shot at least five meters upward in an impressive display.

"Stop feeling sorry for yourself," the blue dragon piped up like a poor rendition from a Greek chorus.

"I am not feeling sorry for myself." I spoke firmly. "I liked my life fine. I wasn't looking for any changes. I'm not the type who requires excitement at every turn."

"Aye, well, we might have wished the obvious choice was someone other than you," the blue dragon said in a voice dry enough to suck all the moisture out of my mouth, throat, and lungs.

"What makes me such an obvious choice?" The words curdled in my throat like rotten cream. Did I really want to know?

Rather than answering, Nidhogg growled, "We're stuck with one another—at least for the present. We must join forces because Midgard is in deep trouble. Evil cuts so deep that world is in danger of failing entirely."

My eyes widened. I'd had no idea the situation was anywhere near that dire. Before I could ask what impact

Midgard failing would have on the other eight worlds, Nidhogg began talking again.

"If any of the Nine Worlds fail, rot will spread to the rest through Yggdrasil's roots, so we must do what we can to avert disaster."

"We should have started long ago," Ysien mumbled, "but dragons do not involve themselves in the affairs of others."

"You didn't used to." I threw his words back in his face and smirked.

Fire blasted from the dragon's mouth, missing me by centimeters. The dragon might be half Nidhogg's size, but the fire was a potent reminder it was unwise to bait him.

I flirted with apologizing and decided against it. Dragons appreciate strength. Nidhogg hadn't apologized for nearly getting me killed. Folding my arms across my chest, I said, "I require a few things."

"Ye're scarcely in a negotiating position." Nidhogg regarded me with his eerie eyes.

"Perhaps not, but there are only so many hours in a day. If I'm to switch vocations, I must be relieved of my current duties."

"And they are?" The blue dragon raised a scaled brow.

Before I could list off my tasks, Nidhogg answered for me. "He's the chief sorcerer for all worlds except Midgard. It may keep him busy, but it's a cushy job and leaves most of his magical ability on the table."

Hearing my status tarnished like that grated, but I didn't debate his impression of my efforts. I didn't care for his opinion, but he was entitled to it. "If that part is settled," I said, "I have other questions."

"Ye are not in charge," the blue dragon reminded me.

"Never said I was." I kept my tone mild, which was a long way from matching my mood. "How long do we have to salvage Midgard?"

"Not the type of question I have an answer for," Nidhogg replied. "Time grows short, or I wouldn't have rallied my dragons. But we have no idea how short."

"Something is powering Midgard's demise," Ysien broke in. "After the Breaking, we assumed the mischief wrought by that Celtic bitch would repair itself. When it dinna, we grew concerned. If we could determine what—or who—is sabotaging Midgard, it would help."

"Surely, you must have an idea or two in that regard," I pressed.

"Unfortunately, we do not," Nidhogg told me.

"Do you suspect Ceridwen is waging a not-so-subtle war on Odin?" I floated the idea that made the most sense to me.

"We considered it," Ysien said. "The piece we couldn't determine was why. What would be in it for her? She'd gain nothing by unseating Odin."

"Never mind Hel and Loki would make her life a study in misery if she set foot in Asgard or Vanaheim," Nidhogg growled.

I was relieved the dragons were talking with me, but their lack of information was disconcerting. I'd always assumed the ancient beasts knew everything, when in truth they grasped about as much as I did. At least concerning this issue.

"How about Odin?" I asked, hoping perhaps he knew more than the dragons.

Nidhogg shrugged amid rattling scales. "He spends much of his time with the Hunt. It's his way of watching over Midgard, yet the cavalcade of dead horsemen hasn't made any difference at all."

"It may be making things worse," the blue dragon mumbled.

"We do not know that." Nidhogg corrected him sharply.

I blew out a tight breath and took a chance. A big one. "Where does Rowan figure into all this? Or does she?"

Nidhogg puffed fiery smoke until black pieces of ash rained down. "Astute of you to figure that out."

"Figure what out? You didn't answer my question."

"Nor are we going to," Ysien said. Something about his tone, supercilious and patronizing, made me want to punch him.

"Each of you has...tasks," Nidhogg told me. "Focus on yours. She will do the same."

"We hope," Ysien muttered.

Breath hissed from between my clenched teeth. "Fine. I'll ask her what you tasked her with when I see her next."

"Ye'll do no such thing." Nidhogg shook a talon my way. The shiny red, razor-sharp claw must have been ten centimeters long.

"Why not?"

"Her path is different from yours, requiring a different type of courage. She may refuse and leave the Nine Worlds altogether."

"She canna do that." Ysien sputtered smoke.

I thought it unlikely that she'd go anywhere, given her attachment to the witches, but why had the dragon suggested her egress was forbidden? Silence reigned; time dribbled by. I wasn't going to get any more out of the dragons, so I switched topics. "Will you deal with Odin about reassigning my current job to someone else?"

"Perhaps," Nidhogg replied.

"If our paths cross," the blue dragon chimed in.

I looked from one beast to the other. "What am I missing?" I asked, wondering why they hadn't left.

Nidhogg nodded his huge head. He'd understood me well enough. "We are still here because we are waiting."

"For?" I furled both brows and swallowed annoyance. Being chained to him required patience. At least the stone was quiet while he was here.

"For ye to get moving," Ysien prodded. "Ye were bellyaching about being overworked, yet naught has occurred in the time we've been here."

Because no one in their right mind would show up with a request for me while the two of you are in my yard.

I kept my thoughts to myself and retrieved my ruined vellum. A trip inside yielded a quill and ink. Squatting over a flat stone near my doorway, I created two columns. It didn't matter that pieces of skin had flaked off my paper. It was still usable for the list I planned.

I recorded weapons in the left-hand column and adversaries in the right. As an afterthought, I added a third column and delineated the magical mix I figured would work on each type of enemy.

Both dragons lumbered close enough to read over my shoulder. Damn, they put out a lot of heat. Sweat beaded across my forehead and rolled into my eyes. It stung, but I was busy.

"Add fire here." Nidhogg tapped the vampire line with a claw.

"Aye, almost all fire," Ysien concurred.

"And earth will work best for gnomes." Nidhogg tapped a couple of lines up.

I twisted to look at him. "Why? They live in caves. How could dirt be deadly for them?"

"Do ye wish to take advantage of dragon knowledge, or no?" Nidhogg stared back. His eyes had slowed to perhaps one revolution every thirty seconds or so.

Only an idiot would have told him no. I nodded. "Of course, I welcome your wisdom."

"Then doona question it." Ysien was back to the patronizing, singsong tone that affected me like fingernails on a chalkboard.

We worked together for perhaps another hour. The dragons added creatures I'd never heard of to my list, but I didn't tell them that. I scanned the work we'd done and said, "Recapping here, it appears I'll need two broadswords, a longsword, and any number of shorter blades."

"Look at this. And this." Nidhogg pointed to a couple of lines. "The magic required is very similar. Ye could use the same weapon in both instances."

So I could. On closer inspection, the same reasoning applied to three groups of dark creatures. I rocked back on my heels. "Thanks for pointing that out. It will make things simpler." I thought back to the previous night. "Magic first, and then weapons?"

"Not necessarily," Ysien answered me. "Every battle will be different. If ye canna get close enough to draw a blade, use magic."

"Can I use existing blades, or must they be forged anew?"

"Newly crafted is best," Nidhogg replied. "That way, ye can add magic to the metal while 'tis still liquid." His head tilted at an angle as if he were listening to something. "We must go. If ye have need of me, use the stone."

"One last thing." I stood and held up a hand.

"Aye. What?" Nidhogg sounded annoyed.

"The Breaking site. Using a blend of Rowan's and my magic, I managed to—"

"Waste of time," Nidhogg cut me off.

"Aye. Focus on the darkness beneath," Ysien concurred.

I'd skirted with the same conclusion, but it was a relief when they validated my suspicions. I was rather glad to see them spread their wings and leave. Not that I wasn't grateful for their assistance, but if it weren't for their insistence I had a role to play in the Midgard problem, I wouldn't have required anything from them at all.

Sure enough, the dragons hadn't been gone five minutes when everyone who'd held back during their visit approached where I stood gazing at the empty skies. I hastily folded the vellum and got to my feet. Before anyone launched into queries about my visitors, I held up a hand and said, "No dragon questions."

Grumbling spread through the group, which was growing rapidly.

At least a dozen people ranged around me with more arriving from all sides.

"Who is here for my magic?" I glanced around the expanding crowd and was nonplussed when nearly everyone raised their hands.

Usually, I offer private audiences, but there were so many gathered in my tiny yard, it would take until tomorrow go get through all of them. It required a little doing, but I managed to sort my customers into four basic groups. Once they realized they weren't going to receive their usual personal time with me, a few left. I considered it a win.

Others grew tired of waiting after the first hour or so. They drifted away as well. I still had at least half a dozen in the magic gone awry group, three in the spells not working correctly group, four in the magic not working at all group, and two in the magical objects no longer cooperating one.

In all the years I've worked magic, I hadn't had this many clients with problems. They're not customers in the sense that they pay me for my services. The gods see I'm provided for. I have a place to live, food to eat, and garments to wear. It's always been enough, and I've been willing to do what I can to ease people's suffering. Power can be unruly, and it packs quite a wallop when it runs off the rails.

It became abundantly clear as afternoon ceded to evening, and evening to midnight, I couldn't continue to be everyman's wizard. Not and meet my obligation to the dragons.

I almost couldn't believe it when I looked up and didn't find anyone else waiting. I was still stiff and sore and tired. Big surprise. When would I have had a chance to recover?

My magic hovered at a lower level than I liked. Worst of all, though, I hadn't done a single thing by way of running down one of the many smiths in Vanaheim to see if they'd be willing to make blades for me.

Unlike with my services, they'd demand payment. I'd turn the matter over to Nidhogg. Surely, he had a vault or a horde somewhere. I wasn't concerned about who'd pay the smith. A far more pressing problem shot to the forefront of my mind.

Why were so many inhabitants in the Nine Worlds having problems with their magic? Was this the leading edge of the disturbance created by Midgard disintegrating?

It made sense to me.

I tottered into my cottage and pulled the door shut behind me. I should spend time with my list and plans, but my brain was stuck reiterating the myriad problems I'd solved today. I always did that: replayed what I'd done for the folk who'd sought my services.

Sometimes I learned something. Usually, I became better at dealing with the same type of issue the next time it cropped up. I reheated the gruel I'd made earlier and ate it standing in front of my collection of lore books. I wasn't sure what I sought, but magical books had ways of giving me what I needed.

Even if I wasn't quite certain what it was.

I'd just plucked a scroll from its spot and blown dust off it when amber, mint, and vanilla surrounded me.

Rowan!

Heart beating triple time, I spun in time to see her shimmer into being just inside my door.

CHAPTER FOURTEEN, ROWAN

*I*nverlochy's courtyard formed around me.

Inverlochy's empty courtyard.

Heart in my throat, I opened my mouth to yell for Patrick and Hilda. And shut it just as fast. At the same time, I swathed myself in wards. If Mother had sent a cadre of monsters here, I'd be goddamned if I'd make things easy for them. Hidden within the folds of my ward, I drew power, holding it at the ready as I bolted up the stairs and into the castle proper.

No one had been in the garden area. Maybe they'd taken a break to eat, but not finding anyone fueled my worries until they blazed into an inferno of righteous anger. The Breaking was inexcusable. If Mother lifted so much as a finger to sow further mayhem, I wouldn't rest until I banished her to a spot she couldn't get out of.

Big words, but I meant every single one of them.

How I'd manage it was anyone's guess, but I was done

standing by while Mother's spoiled hissy fits dismantled everything I held dear.

I took the stairs three and four at a time. I'd have teleported to the top floor, but I didn't want to risk alerting anyone I was there. When I reached the top floor, the one with the Celts' meeting hall at the end of a long, wide corridor, I snaked out a thread of seeking magic, intent on assessing who was here.

I was breathing hard. Adrenaline coated my tongue and throat, tasting harsh and metallic. I located the witches easily. All of them were two floors down. Moments later, I ascertained we were alone.

Still sucking air like a bellows, I loosed my ward and sagged against a stone wall. I'd worked myself into a frenzy. For nothing. I'd have to do a better job of—

"No!" I slammed a fist into the wall. Better to overreact and have there be nothing than to underreact and put those I love in worse danger than they already were.

I waited until I had myself under somewhat better restraint. The witches counted on me, and I didn't want them to think I'd totally lost control of my faculties.

"Rowan? What are you doing up there?" Patrick's voice drifted along the crumbling stairwell.

I winced. Busted. Sort of. Maybe I could get away with not answering directly. I trotted down the risers and met him coming up. His blue eyes radiated concern. "Good. You're in one piece. We weren't certain where you came from. Or what was happening. Your magic blasted us from above." He jerked his chin upward for emphasis.

"It's all right," I aimed for an upbeat note. "I got worried when I didn't find any of you in the garden, so I warded myself and investigated."

He patted my shoulder, and we walked slowly down the remaining stairs to the second floor. The other witches had gathered on the landing, apprehension stamped into their faces. Patrick said, "All is well. Rowan worries too much."

I grinned ruefully. "You've got my number."

"I should," he retorted. "After all the years you've lived with us."

Everyone retreated to the lower chamber they'd designated as a common room. It had a hearth with stones to cook on and was large enough to accommodate everyone's sleeping pallets. They'd collected the best of those from the remainder of the castle. Most had been eaten to shreds by mice intent on securing nest materials.

"Look what we found." Hilda sounded excited as she tugged out several full grain cannisters. "Rice and millet and barley. There's even moldy wheat, but we can salvage it with magic."

"That's wonderful." I grinned. It was far from an endless supply, but it was a whole lot more than we had and would make larger meals possible.

"It is, indeed," she agreed.

"Aye, and we're far from done searching," Leif said. His thick dark hair was streaked with gray, and his brown eyes glowed warmly. Thin like all the rest of us, he'd once been a large man. He was still tall, but not much meat was left on his bones. Threadbare trousers were covered by an ancient fisherman's knit sweater. Once cream colored, now it was more of a dingy oatmeal shade.

Something about the word "searching" pinged a warning. "Probably best if I do the searching," I said. "Sometimes the Celts lay traps, and I'm less likely to spring them."

"So long as we get every scrap of whatever is here, I don't care how it happens," he said.

I felt the same. My kin had food aplenty on their borderworld. They had no need for what they'd left behind.

I shared a meal with the witches and listened to what progress they'd made. If what they'd planted cooperated, we could be out of the castle in a couple of months. This time around. Provided our strategy proved fruitful, we would repeat it again and again. It would ensure our survival.

By the time I readied myself to leave, I was as excited as the rest of them, and I promised to pass the word along to the others who'd remained beneath Ben Nevis. The first thing I heard before the walls of my chamber had fully formed around me was Mort.

He was still furious, and he meowed up a storm telling me what an ungrateful bitch I was for abandoning him. I crouched next to him; he turned his back on me. "I kept you safe," I told my feline friend. "I'd do the same again."

Tail held high, he stalked from the room, apparently not appeased by my justification.

I sank onto the edge of my mattress, too keyed up to think straight. My mind raced in tired circles as I considered the dragons' message. My name wasn't my name. I had to ferret out my real one.

Somehow.

My eyes snapped open; my stomach clenched. The food

I'd eaten formed an indigestible lump in my belly. Bjorn had asked about my name. He wouldn't have brought it up if he hadn't at least suspected I had a different one.

"Damn it, Mother," I snarled. "When will you be done fucking me over?"

I didn't have much of a plan, but my first stop had to be Bjorn. I'd ask him about my name, and I hoped to every deity who'd ever walked, he knew what it was. Maybe if he didn't, he'd help me figure things out.

He might not like me much, but he ate, lived, and breathed magic. This was a magical conundrum. Ergo, it should appeal to his wizardly spirit.

Grabbing a scrap of paper and a pencil, I sketched out the good news from Inverlochy and tacked it outside my doorway. Someone would see it. I didn't have time to run everyone down and initiate a general meeting.

I crafted an incantation. When it failed, I shelved that approach and started over. Traveling to a borderworld was a different proposition from crossing into the Nine Worlds, of which Earth was one. I'd never thought much about Norse real estate despite Earth being separated from Odin's realm by the thinnest of gossamer veils.

I knew where Niflheim was since I'd been there. It was the only one of the Nine Worlds I'd visited. Except Midgard, of course. It scarcely counted since I lived here. Bjorn had mentioned Bifrost, the rainbow bridge running through the worlds. He'd also intimated I'd be fried alive if I tried to use it. I'd been considering returning to Niflheim—since I knew the way—but I decided against it.

I didn't want to waste time and magic bouncing about

from place to place if my first efforts turned into dead ends. A headache throbbed behind one eye. I dropped my head into my hands and rubbed my temples as I sliced and diced my problem. Getting stuck in the wrong world wasn't the end of things, but then I'd have to start over. I could try the bridge and hope for the best. I could also attempt to find my way by scaling Yggdrasil's roots.

Assuming I could even locate the One Tree.

Out of all my potential solutions, that one was the worst. It might take me days to climb from world to world. The ash tree was enormous beyond comprehension.

When a truly simple answer splatted in front of me, I grabbed hold of it. Blood spells were foolproof. All I needed was a miniscule amount of Bjorn's blood, and I could teleport right to him. I'd dropped my bandage material in the wash kettle, but maybe I'd get lucky and find a drop or two of blood on the floor near where he'd been sitting.

I bolted to my feet and raced out the door, mumbling entreaties to whoever might be out there rooting for me. Ha! Like I'd ever been that fortunate. Skidding around a corner, I hustled into the common room. Mort was hunched over the floor near where Bjorn had sat, licking it feverishly.

"Mort. Stop!" I shouted. He kept on licking, so I immobilized him with magic. He might never forgive me, but I wouldn't leave him that way very long. Only until I reached him and scanned the floor for what I sought.

Excitement coursed through me once I got close enough to inspect the flagstones lining the floor. Mort hadn't been thorough. Not yet. Another couple of minutes, and the stones would have been shiny clean and slick with his saliva.

Maybe I had a guardian angel watching out for me after all. I bent and carefully lifted two large, congealed dollops of Bjorn's blood onto a blade I'd just drawn from the thigh sheath I habitually wore.

As soon as the precious goo was mine to command, I released the cat. He skinned back his lips and hissed at me. I eyed him and said, "I told you to stop. You didn't listen."

More hissing.

I balanced the blade on a nearby table and bent to his level. "I love you. You're an amazing creature. I apologize for raising magic to control you."

Slowly, the hackles along his back relaxed. He regarded me with his amber eyes as if wondering whether trusting me again would be his undoing. Ever so slowly, I extended a hand. When he didn't draw back—or bite me—I petted his head and scratched behind his ears.

He didn't exactly push into my touch, but neither did he stalk away as he'd done earlier. So long as we'd established an understanding, albeit a fragile one, I told him, "I'll be gone for a little bit. It's to another world, so I can't take you with me."

I stroked him for a few more minutes before I straightened, glad I hadn't completely destroyed the connection between us. He meowed plaintively and looked right at the remaining blood.

"Not yet," I said. "Once I'm gone, it means I had enough to do the job. Then you're welcome to whatever is left."

Sitting, he curled his tail around himself and watched me as if I was the most intriguing person on Earth, but I wasn't fooled. He was making certain I didn't remove any more blood than absolutely necessary.

The next part went fast. Like I said, blood castings are infallible. I could find anyone anywhere, so long as I had a drop of their blood. Not everyone has the seeking gift, but it runs strong in me.

Turned out the dollops on my knife were sufficient. I transferred them to my palm and summoned fire and air to activate them. Smoke shimmered around me, thick with the coppery smell of blood. Usually it has an acrid undertone, but not this time.

The walls of the common room glistened and liquefied before they vanished entirely. Too late, I worried about bothering Bjorn. It was the middle of the night, assuming time flowed the same in Vanaheim as it did on Earth. What if he was with a woman?

I smothered a groan. I'd cross that bridge if I had to. Maybe I could wait outside until daybreak? Not the most comfortable setup, but not impossible, either. I hoped me showing up out of the blue wouldn't piss him off, but then he'd done the same to me. More than once.

It wasn't quite the same. He'd traveled to Earth, but not specifically to see me. Until this last time after the battle. Then he'd sought me out.

To make certain I was safe.

Perhaps this would have a better outcome than I anticipated. Regardless, I'd find out damned soon. My transport spell was developing a transparency around the edges that told me I'd arrive within seconds.

He'd been standing with his back to the door when I

arrived, but he spun so fast I missed the transition. I did my best to read his expression. He looked surprised, but not angry, and set down the scroll he held. A relieved breath rattled from between my teeth.

"Apologies," I stammered and moved my gaze to the stone floor of his hut. "For disturbing you. It's not as easy as it might seem to get here, and I'd never have been able to locate you without the bits of blood you shed beneath Ben Nevis." I was blithering, but I kept right on. "If it's not a good time, I can wait outside. Or maybe not so close as that, but—"

"Rowan!"

Hearing my name, or not-my-name as the case might be, had the effect of shutting me up. Good thing. Goddess only knew what would spurt from my mouth next. I'd been staring at the floor, but now I looked at him. Impressions rolled through me. His cottage was one moderately sized room. Crowded, yet orderly. Everything seemed to have a place. The wall he'd been perusing held books and scrolls. More than I'd ever seen in one spot outside Mother's library. A wooden table with four chairs ranged around it sat in front of a hearth. One corner held his neatly made bed.

Lights crackling with magic were spaced at uneven intervals, and the fire burned with a will of its own. It must be powered with magic as well.

"Do ye approve?" he asked me in an old form of Norse.

My face heated. I was embarrassed my appraisal had been so obvious. I shook my head. "Not my intent," I managed. "I'm always curious about, well about everything."

"Aye, I've guessed as much."

He was even more beautiful than in my memory. His

face glowed in the flickering illumination from the many mage lights. They highlighted his sculpted cheekbones, regal forehead, and squared-off jaw. I tried not to look at his well-formed lips. It hadn't been very long since I'd fantasized what they'd feel like pressed against my own. A small frisson that had nothing to do with being cold ran down my spine.

He'd changed into fresh clothes that looked much the same as the trousers and shirt he'd worn into battle.

Bjorn moved to the far side of the cottage. I felt his power kindle as he dropped leaves that smelled delicious into thick ceramic mugs. Water followed, and I understood he was preparing tea.

"Do ye wish honey in your brew?" he asked, still speaking Norse.

"Maybe a splash of mead," I said. Hearing my voice reminded me I hadn't added anything to my earlier rambling account.

"Ye're in luck. I happen to have some." He reached to a shelf, retrieved a flask, and poured a healthy jot into both cups.

I strode across the room and asked, "Which is mine?"

"Either."

"Thank you." Picking up the nearest one, I took a tentative swallow to assess if it needed to cool. Somehow, he'd managed to brew perfect tea without making it so hot it burned my tongue. Magic came in handy for the little tasks too.

"Would you like to sit?" He angled his gaze at the table. I noted he'd returned to English.

Grateful for the invitation, I made my way to the table

and sat near the hearth. I looked to see if there were logs I could feed it with, but my initial impression—that the fire took care of itself—appeared to be accurate. For a while, we drank our spiked tea in a companionable silence.

A sidelong glance—or two since I couldn't seem to not look at him—told me he hadn't recovered much since he left Earth. Guilt smote me. "I'm keeping you from your rest."

He waved me to silence. "You already apologized. Whatever you want with me, it must be urgent, or you'd not have used a blood vector to locate me. That's one of the harder castings."

Not for me, it wasn't, but I didn't correct him. I set my cup down and placed my hands on the table on either side of it. "I have a problem."

"Only one? Consider yourself fortunate." A corner of his mouth twisted into a wry grin.

A snort blew past my lips. "Yeah, huh? I have problems aplenty, but after you left I visited the place where you fought."

He raised both blond brows in surprise. "You did? Why?"

"I wanted the feel of it for myself."

"What did you find?"

I grinned. "For starters, I'll never believe you again when you say you're not a warrior. Arawn's balls, there must have been three hundred dead. Perhaps more. I didn't take the time to count bodies."

His eyebrows shot up another notch. "That many, eh? It surprises me."

Now was a time to level up and be honest. "The whole

thing surprised me. It's why I went to the trouble to walk the battlefield. I know about gnomes and trolls and goblins, but they've never banded together to attack a single man before. They must have wanted you dead in the worst way."

"That part is true," he agreed. "They did want my head on a pikestaff, but it's not why I was there."

"You didn't show up on Earth to fight?"

He thinned his mouth into a grim line. "Not exactly."

I waited, but he stopped there. It seemed wrong to pry. His life. His business. If he'd wanted me to know more, he'd have told me.

I took a few more sips of tea. The mead was warm, comforting, and the tea had a minty licorice aspect that lingered on my tongue. When I set the cup down, I said, "I appreciate you not pressing me for what the hell I'm doing here in the middle of the night."

"I figured you'd tell me eventually." He drained his mug and plopped the flask on the table. I hadn't realized he'd brought it with him.

"I'll do you one better and stop beating about the bush. After I was done on the battlefield, I was preparing to leave when two dragons showed up. They'd teleported from somewhere because they don't live on Earth."

Bjorn's expression sharpened. I felt the subtle weave of a truth spell settle over me. It hurt my feelings, but I didn't blame him. For dragons to seek me out was improbable. I would have conjured a truth spell too. If I'd been in his place.

I took a breath to settle my nerves and blew it out before I started up again. "Anyway, the gist of what they wanted was to tell me I had to find my true name." The heat that had mostly left my face returned in a rush that swooshed over the top of my head.

"Why come to me?" His question was smooth, too smooth.

"Because you all but told me my name wasn't my own." I slapped my palms on the table and skewered him with my eyes. "Please. If you know my name, tell me what it is."

He cocked his head to one side. "And if I don't?"

"Then I shall have to hunt for it the old-fashioned way. It might take months. Years." I closed my teeth over my lower lip. "I can't exactly articulate why, but I'm pretty sure I don't have that kind of time."

"These dragons, did they mention what would happen after you unearthed your name?" Bjorn met my gaze unflinchingly.

"No, but both of them said everything would fall into place."

He laughed. It was so unexpected I pushed my chair back half a meter. "And this is funny, why?"

"Not funny, but typical of dragons. They might not live in Midgard, but plenty bide here."

I resurrected what he'd said so far, and he had not said he had no idea what my name was. I waited. I'd give this another few minutes. If he blew me off, I'd leave and figure things out another way.

Mother. She was the logical next stop.

I'd find her and jack her up until she answered me. Yeah, and I'd get Arianrhod and Bran and a few of the others involved. I'd tell them about the dragons and me not knowing my name. The other Celts might discount me, but they wouldn't distrust dragons. Now that I was warming to the idea, I might even involve Dewi. More than one way to skin a possum.

The corners of Bjorn's mouth twitched. "I can see I've moved from important to dispensable."

"Yes, but how—?" I slapped my forehead with the butt of one hand. The truth spell. It would have given him easy access to my thoughts.

He reached across the table and covered one of my hands with his. "The dragons told me to stay out of it, but I'll tell you what you wish to know. And then, both of us will pay your mother a visit."

"If I know my name, I won't need Mother," I said tartly and winced. I should be falling all over myself thanking Bjorn, not contradicting him.

He just looked at me, an unreadable expression on his face. I would have bet one of Mort's paws he understood full well that despite all my bravado, the last person I wanted to deal with was Ceridwen.

CHAPTER FIFTEEN, BJORN

I guessed why Rowan—Runa—had paid me an impromptu visit well before I netted her in a truth spell, and she stumbled about picking and choosing words. Once she got the bit in her teeth, though, she was pretty damned direct. Interesting the dragons—and I was certain it had to be Nidhogg and Ysien—had only focused on her name, not her dragon heritage.

Bloodlines are very important to dragons, and I was close to positive they had hers mapped down to every relevant ancestor. Had they not known of her existence? Or were they biding their time, waiting for her to have a reason to embrace the wyrm half of her birthright?

Ceridwen might have had reasons for hiding her dalliance with a dragon, but the dragon in question wouldn't have been any more forthcoming. They didn't breed outside the fold any more than the Celts did. Not that the Celts weren't notorious for seducing mortals, but they made double damn certain their stray sperm—or eggs—didn't result in progeny.

"Well?" Rowan leaned back in her chair and kept right on boring a hole in me with her golden eyes. She was incredible. Perfect. Her scent hadn't fully faded from when she nursed my hurt places. It eddied about me, and I yearned to hold her, stroke her unruly hair back from her comely forehead.

I thought I'd moved past my body responding unbidden, but my cock thickened, pressing uncomfortably against the front of my trousers. I wanted to shove it to a better position, but I couldn't. Not with her staring at me.

She narrowed her eyes. "Um, look. I probably came off way too pushy. If my request crossed some lines, breached some rules I don't know about—"

I held up a hand. I'd given my word, and I wouldn't welch. The dragons had cautioned me to steer well clear, but they hadn't counted on Rowan's singlemindedness, nor on me asking her about her name earlier.

Naturally, she'd remembered the exchange.

I sat straighter. "Your name is Runa. Not so different in sound, but very different in meaning."

Something, perhaps recognition, flashed from her eyes. "Secret," she murmured. "It means secret, but who named me? And why did Mother call me something different?"

I had ideas about that, but they'd remain within me for now. I reeled in the truth spell I'd draped around her. No more need for it.

She blinked a few times and then shrugged. "I'm waiting, but nothing is happening."

"What are you waiting for?"

"Not sure. The skies to open up. Angels to sing. The secrets of the universe to show themselves to me."

The corners of my mouth twitched with annoyance. The dragons had led her to believe her name was the key to everything, when the reality was it was the merest of beginnings. Names took time to percolate, for the bearer to grow into them. Rowan meant tree with red berries, or little redhead. Innocuous as names went.

I wanted to reassure her things would change eventually. But we needed to unravel the secret of her birth before we did anything else. How the hell we'd beat the truth out of Ceridwen remained to be seen, but Nidhogg wasn't about to help. Probably in his dragon's mind, he'd already provided far more assistance than he thought we required.

Rowan pushed back from the table. "I should be going. I've infringed on your hospitality long enough.

I bolted to my feet. "We must locate Ceridwen."

She angled her head to one side. "Why? The only reason I had for laying eyes on the conniving bitch again was to dredge my name out of her."

I scrabbled for a reason that didn't include telling her about her dragon father. Nidhogg might forgive me for blurting her name, but he'd not take it well if I implicated one of his own in a forbidden alliance.

Never mind it was true. The evidence sat across from me at my old, beat-up table. "Don't you want to know who sired you?" I asked.

Runa rolled her eyes and stood. "I've asked. A whole lot of times. Mother refuses to answer. It will require time and energy to track her down. After our last exchange, she won't wish to be found, and she's powerful enough to hide behind wards that will tax my power."

"Aye. Yours. You'll have noticed our combined efforts are more than additive."

A predatory smile turned her beauty harsh and menacing. "I haven't forgotten. It would aid us in locating her, but have you found a reliable way to force words from someone who doesn't wish to utter them?"

She paused long enough to blow out a breath. "Besides, what earthly difference does it make who my father is?" The corners of her eyes pinched from old hurts. "If he knew about me, he didn't care enough to be part of my life. If he didn't realize he'd created a child, Mother must have had reasons for hiding her pregnancy."

I recognized a small chink in Runa's armor, and I drove a pick into it when I asked, "Aren't you curious what those reasons were?"

A scowl twisted her features. "Of course, I'm 'curious.' For years, I've been expecting to grow wings. Or a second head. Or be pulled into an alternative universe. Nothing unusual ever happened. Granted, the witches' magic is weak as dishwater, but none of them ever drew me aside to hiss a confidential message about me carrying werewolf blood. Or goddess forbid, vampire."

Her scowl deepened. "The more I've thought about it, the surer I was she'd lain with a vampire. The few I've seen have been gorgeous. Stunning bodies. Quick minds. Delightful conversationalists. I can see Ceridwen deluding herself she could control such a pairing, and then getting jerked off her moorings. Nothing trumps blood for power. And you can't punish something that's already dead."

"Why wouldn't she have destroyed the child?"

I chose neutral words, playing devil's advocate to get a point across without coming out and telling her dragon embryos were indestructible. Whether they hatched from eggs or wombs, once sperm and egg joined, a baby would result.

Runa turned her hands palms up. "I have no idea, and I've wondered about it. A lot. You weren't there, so you'll probably think I'm exaggerating, but Ceridwen never wanted me. I spent years telling myself I was mistaken, that she had an odd way of showing she cared, but finally I gave up."

"Why?" My heart hurt for her. The arousal from earlier had departed, replaced by fury at her goddess mother. Even if Rowan—Runa—refused to accompany me, I'd find Ceridwen and give her the rough side of my tongue.

"It wasn't just one thing," Runa murmured, "but a lot of little ones that were additive. She viewed me as more of a possession than anything else." A bitter laugh burst from her. "She loved that cauldron of hers. And she respected the other Celts—most of them. At least, she set whatever she was doing aside to pay attention when one of them stopped in to visit.

"I learned early that crying was useless. The occasional servant might pick me up, but it didn't happen often. I remember scrounging for food when I was so small I was barely walking. It's how I discovered I had magic. If I thought about something to eat hard enough, it would materialize in my hands."

"No one taught you?" Keeping my words even was a struggle.

She shook her head. "Nope. Self-taught. I always wondered how much stronger I might have been if anyone had taken the time to nurture my ability."

We stood staring at one another. Almost as an afterthought, she made a grab for her mug and drained it. Her voice was laced with reproach when she said, "You know things you haven't told me."

It wasn't a question, so I nodded. "I'm certain you know things you've not told me, either."

"Not the same. You know things about me, things you're not willing to share. Why? What the fuck is wrong with me that everyone pussyfoots around and talks in riddles?" She shook her head. "Never mind. I should have left once you gave me my name. Thank you for that. I only sound like an ungrateful bitch, but I very much appreciate whatever rules you had to bend to offer up my true name. I'll figure out the rest of this on my own."

Before I could come up with reasons to keep her in Vanaheim, she dragged magic around her and was gone. I didn't stop to debate the wisdom of following her. I just did. I assumed she'd return to Midgard, but I summoned power designed to track her energy. It would ensure we emerged in the same spot, and it saved me from guessing wrong.

I didn't know much more about her, but the element I'd chosen to keep to myself was important. It could mean everything as her future unfolded. Particularly if Nidhogg and Ysien were right about Midgard being in its death throes.

I emerged not far from the blood-soaked field where I'd spent so many hours. The reek of decay hit me like a wall. Sickly sweet and cloying. Damn it. The things I'd killed smelled worse dead than they had alive. As soon as the teleport spell spit me out in Midgard, I looked for Runa.

And didn't see her.

What the fuck? I'd followed her trail—unless she'd anticipated my moves and stymied me on purpose. Power arced from me. I employed seeking magic as I hunted for her unique blend of dragon and Celtic energy. Breath rattled from me. If I hadn't been determined, I'd have missed her entirely. She was here but swathed in wards.

Apparently, Ceridwen wasn't the only one who didn't wish to be found.

Too put out for subtlety, I barked a power word and the magic concealing her frittered to streamers swirling in a brisk, chilly breeze. She and I had talked far longer than I thought because dawn was breaking. A line of pink sat below the leading edge of a bank of ominous-looking clouds.

Runa didn't bother to close the distance between us. "Go away," she shouted. "My life. My problems. You must have your own to deal with."

I felt like shouting back she didn't know the half of it. Instead, I strode to her. "I'm not your enemy."

She angled a pain-laced look my way, brows furled and forehead creased into a web of fine lines. "At this point, buster, everybody but the witches are my enemy. The next time I see dragons, I'll leave."

"Oh really?" Sarcasm bled through my words. I made zero effort to temper it when I added in Norse, "And have ye tried running from dragons? How'd that go for you?"

"Like I told you. I'll figure things out. The same way I have forever. By myself. I don't need you. Or the dragons. Or anyone."

I wanted to slap sense into her. I wanted to drag her into my arms and crush my mouth over hers. She was beautiful. No Valkyrie could have outshone her. No, nor any of the goddesses in Asgard.

The same deep, rhythmic booming that had presaged the goblins and gnomes and trolls began under my feet. Then, my magic had been mostly present. Now, I was like a candle that had been burned from both ends. I twisted to face the worst of the noise, putting my body between it and Runa.

"What the fuck is that?" She wasn't having any of my attempt to shield her and stood by my side.

"Bad shit." I didn't have energy for better descriptors. "We can leave. Or we can fight. You choose."

One of the craters from the previous day heaved and rocked. The noise grew so strident, I shielded my ears with magic before the drums ruptured. I drew power and held it arcing between my hands as I waited for gnomes and goblins to burst through the expanding hole.

The gap in the ground developed a swirling appearance, and I felt the muted pull of a vortex. "Keep away from the edge," I said.

"What? Did you think I couldn't figure that out for myself? This isn't my first battle. Or my second. I—"

An impossibly large monster sprang through the hole.

Big as two elephants, it looked like a griffon on drugs, but the neck was wrong. Long, reptilian, and dragonlike, it supported a raptor's head. The rest of the beast was lionesque with patchy tawny fur. Instead of being smoothly covered, though, its body was riddled with brown pustules.

I could smell the poison from where I stood.

"What in god's name is it?" Runa didn't sound as rattled as I expected her to.

"Does it matter?" I shot back. "It's evil. We have to kill it." As I regarded its unblinking avian eyes, dirty amber and the size of dinner plates, I hoped to hell dispatching it would be possible.

"I get that part," she growled, "but are there more of them? I've never seen its like on Earth before."

The thing cawed a challenge. Its beak was black and shiny and probably sharp as fuck. So large it could have cleaved a man's head from his body, it snapped menacingly. Each time the edges clacked together I felt a jab in the pit of my stomach.

The list I'd constructed in my cottage courtyard came back to me. This was one of the many evils I hadn't recognized. I couldn't recall its name, but I did remember the mix of magics Nidhogg had said would work on it.

A wave of weariness washed through me. I shook it off. I was tired but not that tapped out. Dogged, determined, I started the process of weaving the net that should immobilize the hissing, cawing monster.

"Do you know, or are you guessing?" Runa asked in mind speech, which proved she'd been helping herself to my thoughts. I'd have to remember she could do that when I had

things I wished to keep private. Like her dragon blood. Luckily, it was a long way from the forefront of my mind.

"Little of both." I had no magic to spare on anything beyond my spell.

She didn't ask any more questions, but I felt power jolt into me as she joined her skills with my own. I welcomed her infusion of power. It could make all the difference between success—or the opposite.

Afraid I'd jinx our efforts, I couldn't bring myself to even think the word failure.

The griffon-thing wasn't into standing still while we plotted its destruction. Why would it? I've never had an enemy who's made things easy for me. It moved awkwardly because it was so huge. Until it spread wings I hadn't noticed. Black like the bird part of it, they were in far better shape than the rest of the beast.

It took a running leap and bolted into the sky.

I worked as fast as I could, but complex destructive magic takes time. Maybe more time than we had. The whoosh of its wings moved fist-sized rocks through the air.

"Duck!" Runa shrieked.

I feinted to one side as a rock that must have weighed two stone whistled past. I was just getting my feet back beneath me when I saw the monster, back feet extended, swooping toward Runa.

She saw it too and erected a ward with lightning speed. It glistened around her, ripe with the colors of her power. Blues and greens and violets.

My casting was almost ready. Almost. The beast pivoted until its front legs, tipped with sharp, nasty talons punched through Runa's ward. I heard an explosion as her magic gave way, and the monster grabbed her by the shoulders. She'd yanked a blade from somewhere and was chanting like a madwoman as she stabbed at the thing's clawed front feet.

The pulse of her magic that had been powering our joint spell dimmed. If I was going to make a move, it had to be now. I gave it everything I had and heaved netting studded with lethal darts over the thing's upper body. I did the same with a second net, but, this time, I captured its wings.

Chanting furiously, I upped the magical flow powering the snares. I have no idea where I got the strength. Maybe from Runa. Maybe from Midgard. Hell, maybe Nidhogg was hiding nearby and reluctantly helping.

Mostly, so he wouldn't have to train a new lackey.

He never had told me why I'd drawn the short straw. The Nine Worlds were full of likely candidates, most of whom would be better than me at keeping Midgard whole.

My spell was working, but not as quickly as I'd have liked. Runa was suspended a few meters in the air, still stabbing at the talons dug into her shoulders. At least she hadn't run into any of the poison-filled boils. I paid power out, funneling most of it at the netting around the thing's head. I hadn't counted on it nabbing Runa. Thanks to the netting around its wings, it wasn't flying very well anymore. If it fell out of the air, it would land right on top of her.

I couldn't let that happen. If it did, any number of boils would shower her with their contents.

Should I neutralize the snare around its wings? No. If I did that, it might fly off with Runa as its captive. I opted for another approach. Diversion. Focusing a thin beam of white-hot power, I took out one of its eyes.

Shrieking pain and outrage, it loosed its hold on Runa. She hadn't been expecting it, but she recovered admirably and fashioned a canopy to cushion the worst of her fall. Limping, she hustled to my side.

"Sorry. I never should have let it get me."

"Doesn't matter. Let's finish this." My words were rough, harsh. I didn't have much left, but the howling, bellowing monster couldn't know that. I dug deep, tapping reserves I didn't realize I had. Runa's magic laced with mine again, weaker than it had been, but still welcome.

Between us, we tightened both snares until the monster was trussed like a festival pig.

Finally, when I didn't see how the thing could still be airborne with its wings tangled together, it crashed to the ground a few meters away. The earth shook from the fucker's bulk landing. Its body started to come apart. Poison spurted and ran into the earth. Clouds of noxious gas scored my nose and lungs.

"Keep him busy," rustled through my mind.

I didn't bother to tell her I'd do the best I could. I was too busy pummeling the monster with magic.

Light on her feet as she avoided puddles of smoking venom, Runa went around behind the thrashing body. Grabbing onto protruding bones, she used them as a ladder. When she was high enough, she plunged her knife into the base of its feathered head, severing its spine.

I would have cheered if I'd had anything left. I'd tell her

how much her fearlessness impressed me, though. Once I caught my breath.

The abomination bellowed once, quivered, and then lay still. I gathered the tattered edges of my spell and my magic. Neither were required any longer. The thing was dead. I clapped a hand over my mouth to reduce my exposure to poison leaking from what remained of the thing's body.

Limping even worse than before, Runa joined me. Smudges streaked her face, and her clothing was torn where the monster's talons had dug deep. "We need to clean those up." I tapped her shoulder very gently.

She nodded. "Not much more for us to do here. I'll take us home."

She obviously had more juice left than I did because the field faded and the walls of the room I'd sat in a few hours ago formed around us. At least the air was clean. I took great, gasping gulps to clear the taint of poison from my lungs. And I took a good, hard look at Runa.

She was pale. Pain had etched lines into her forehead and around her eyes.

I touched her forehead. It was hot. Far warmer than it should be. "Sit," I told her, concerned some of the monster's poison had breached her skin.

"But I need to get water," she said weakly.

"My turn to take care of you."

A young, blonde woman raced into the room. "Ro. What happened?" She angled green eyes my way. "You're the man from the other night. The one who came with the dragon. I peeked out of the cave when there was all that ruckus and saw you."

"Tansy—" Runa began just before she crumpled to the floor.

"What's wrong with her?" Tansy wailed and knelt by Runa's side. "By the goddess. She's on fire."

"Get hot water," I told Tansy. "A big kettle of it, and linen to clean her wounds."

"But what's wrong with her?" Tansy persisted.

"She's been poisoned. Hurry." I clapped my hands for emphasis, and Tansy bolted from the room. As gently as I could, I pulled Runa's hair out of the way and levered off her tunic and vest. Red streaks were working their way down her chest and back. Her breasts were perfect, high and mounded, but I had a far different focus than the wonders of her body.

I dredged still more magic from Hel only knew where and barked power words. I told the poison to stop. To neutralize itself. To leave. I'd welcome any one of the three, and I wasn't taking any chances.

I traded from Runa's front to her back and repeated my words and my actions. Somewhere along the way, Tansy showed up and began cleaning the wounds. She sang in a high, clear voice, and her chant mixed with my power words. Finally, the red streaks began a slow retreat.

When I breathed deep, the stench of poison was gone.

"Will she be all right?" Tansy's voice was small and scared.

I dropped a hand onto her shoulder. "Yes. She will. Thanks to your help."

Tansy offered me a shy smile. "I have the healing gift,

but I've never had to use so much of it before. Let me get the dirty water and stained linen out of here."

I rocked back on my heels, so weary remaining upright was a challenge. My eyes might have shut of their own accord. What dragged them open was a large black cat who'd curled up on my lap and was purring as if he didn't have a care in the world.

CHAPTER SIXTEEN, ROWAN

I ran full tilt into the misshapen creature's wrongness when I was stabbing its clawed forelegs. That was when its blood first mixed with mine, creating an unpleasant jolt. Not something I expected. Griffons may be nasty pieces of work, but they don't spew venom. I knew right away I'd been poisoned, and I set markers in my body to protect myself. I believed they were working until I brought us back to the coven's lair.

Yeah. I also believed the worst of my injuries was a sprained ankle from when the bastard dropped me after Bjorn put out one of its eyes. Guessing wrong about shit can come back to bite you in the ass.

I've always been a champ at putting a good face on things. It's something I learned very young. Usually, I have time to set things right, but today when I recognized my inner warding had failed catastrophically, I was down for the count.

Except for an astral thread or two that detached from my body and watched Bjorn and Tansy fighting to bring me back. I'm immortal. The monster couldn't kill me, but there are worse things than being dead. Like being trapped in my body and unable to move.

I tried to help, but my magic was slow, sluggish. I'd burned through gobs of it, and it would take a while to recover. Maybe a long while at the rate things were going.

Bjorn was exhausted. I sensed what it cost him to keep on drawing power from somewhere, but he was intent on stopping the monster's poison—a gift that kept on giving even after its master was dead. Bjorn was a good man. He didn't care he'd moved well past when he should have quit. He'd keep right on going until he either brought me back from the dark, twisted corridors where most of me wandered or fell on his face.

I'd treated him abysmally when I bolted out of his cottage. Sunk in my own misery, I'd lost sight of what was going on with him. He'd been kind and flexible, given I'd dropped in unannounced when most of the world was sleeping. I had a million excuses, most of them circling back to my hideous childhood, but how long was I going to drag out those tired old vindications and parade them as an excuse for being an inconsiderate twit?

I felt the wrong places within me first grow smaller and then leave altogether. I was still unconscious, but I'd recover soon enough. Tansy gave me a kiss before she trundled off with the dirty water and blood-stained rags. I'd known she had some talent for healing, but she was more than capable.

Perhaps she could apprentice with Leif or Hilda, the two primary healers within the coven.

I made a note to talk with them about taking her on. After they were done with harvesting our crops.

Bjorn's eyes had closed. He still knelt over me, but exhaustion had claimed him. Or, more likely, he'd given up fighting it as soon as he was certain I was out of danger. It was as good an opportunity as I was likely to have to really look at him. Not that I hadn't grabbed the odd glance here and there, but I hadn't studied his face with its regal bone structure. After examining him from different angles, I realized he looked a lot like Odin. The real one, not the travesty who led the hunt.

Perhaps Bjorn was a bastard blowby? It would explain why power shimmered around him even in his depleted state. Blond bristles coated his cheeks and chin. He'd look wonderful with a beard, rough and steeped in masculinity. Not that he was lacking in that regard now, but his features were so striking he almost came across as too beautiful to be real.

I longed for my body. My astral self sensed things, more than experiencing them. I wanted to inhale his scent and murmur how sorry I was about leaving the way I had. We were born to fight together, he and I. If I'd doubted it before, the battle with the griffon-esque thing had wiped away any lingering reservations.

Mort stalked into the room. When he spied me crumpled on the floor, he abandoned all pretense of the feigned indifference common to all felines and raced to my side. He stuck his nose into my neck and licked me with his rough tongue. It took a while, but once he was satisfied I'd live, he jumped over me and curled up in Bjorn's lap.

Mort rarely let anyone else touch him, yet he'd sought out Bjorn. Surprise drove me back into my body. The collision of astral and physical selves was always brutal, which is interesting because the separation part is easy. Between my various hurts and the shock of being whole again, I groaned and dragged my eyes open.

The cat stared at me, purring.

Raw and needy from what Bjorn and I had lived through, I crawled close enough to curve my body around him and Mort. "You're awake." Bjorn's voice was raspy. He stroked hair back from where it had fallen into my face.

"You sound surprised." I threaded an arm around him. It felt right to touch him, and for once I didn't deny myself comfort.

"I am. Figured you'd sleep for hours." He coughed and turned his head to spit. "Let me get us water."

"Looks like I'm right on time," Tansy's voice rang from across the room. "I brewed tea for the both of you. And I brought Ro a fresh shirt."

Bjorn hugged me awkwardly given our positions with him kneeling and me plastered around his bent legs. And then he got up and walked toward Tansy. Where he'd been pressed against me felt empty, and I wanted him back. Displaced from Bjorn's lap, Mort rubbed his head against my upper arm as if to remind me I had responsibilities.

I scratched his head and got to my feet very creakily. I had hurt places that had never hurt before. When I weighted my one ankle, pain shot up my leg, and I yelped.

Bjorn and Tansy hustled to where I balanced on one leg, and Bjorn hooked an arm around me and helped me to the nearest table. "Sorry about your ankle," he said. "I didn't forget about it, but it wasn't nearly as important as everything else."

"It will mend." I focused a thin beam of magic at the place the ligament had torn. Not much because I didn't have much left, but anything was better than doing nothing.

Tansy helped me on with a fresh tunic, and then she spooned honey into the mugs, stirring it in. Fragrant with mint and rosemary, the tea slid down my abraded throat.

"Thank you," Bjorn told Tansy. "This is perfect."

"You're welcome. I'd do anything for Ro. She saved my life." When she looked at me, she added, "I ran your other clothes through the wash kettle. They're drying."

Before I could protest, tell her the debt—if there'd ever been one—was well and truly discharged, she walked quickly toward the kitchen. Mort ran after her, probably in hopes of a handout. Something besides mice.

"Tansy is a treasure." Bjorn sipped more tea. "Whatever's in this is perfect. My throat's a mess from when the venom turned into a gas. I tried not to breathe deeply, but it was a losing proposition."

I patted the spot next to me at the table, and he settled on the bench. "She's not the only treasure," I said. "I have no idea where all the power came from, but you just kept pouring it into me."

He smiled, and I felt my heart crack wide open. "I couldn't give up," he said. "We're partners."

I grinned back. "We are. I fought it, but how we click

when we work together can't be accidental. This will sound hokey as fuck, but the way our power meshes is special. I've never encountered its like."

He nodded. "Same conclusion I came to." His smile wilted, traded for a thoughtful expression. "Tansy still calls you Ro. Are you planning to tell the witches your other name?"

"No."

"Why not?"

"I haven't exactly thought things through, so this might sound disjointed, but names offer others power over you. The fewer who know my true name, the better. Earth is... different, for want of a pithier term. It's like the Breaking started something in motion, something that will end with Earth dying."

Bjorn opened his mouth, but I held up a hand. "I want to know what you think, but let me get through this first. Earlier, when I crawled up the monster to deliver a death blow, it seemed I had a foot in two worlds. This one and another that's far away but growing closer.

"Touching the griffon linked me to that other place, but briefly. As soon as someone—a guardian?—recognized energy that didn't belong there, they slammed the gate fast. By then, I'd killed the monster, so the link probably would have winked out anyway."

I drank more tea. My throat wasn't the best, either, and I hadn't been as close to the fumes as Bjorn. The air immediately around our adversary had been cleaner. "The third element," I went on, "is you and me. There are no coincidences. We met for a reason. We tested our magic together for a reason. This isn't a come on"—I exhaled nervously—"but it circles back to ground we covered earlier. We're meant to merge our magic."

He nodded and reached for the pot of hot water Tansy had left with the tea makings. Hefting it, he poured more into both our mugs. "I may pay for this, but the two pieces of knowledge I have that you're missing are these."

I set my cup down and laced my fingers together so tight the knuckles turned white. I'd criticized him roundly for holding out on me, but he'd had good reasons. "Hold up," I said. "If revealing secrets will cause problems for you, then perhaps you should let me find out on my own."

The same soft smile, the one that tugged at my heart, returned. "I'd decided much the same. Until today. I didn't sense the gateway to another world, but hearing you describe it worries me. A lot."

He spread his hands in front of him and looked at me in his direct way. "I'm not violating any confidences when I tell you I've been waiting for more fallout from the Breaking. It damaged Midgard's—Earth's—ability to protect itself. We've felt differences throughout the other Eight Worlds. For the first few decades, I assumed Midgard would heal its hurt places—or that Odin would conjure a fix. When neither happened, it concerned me, but I'm a tiny cog in a much larger wheel.

"No one wanted to hear from the chief sorcerer."

"I'm certain someone did," I broke in and unclasped my hands to grasp one of his. He didn't shake me off. I longed to ask about his possible familial connection with Odin, but it truly wasn't my affair.

"Aye, the common folk, but not the gods or goddesses. And they're who could have made a difference." He rolled his shoulders straighter. "And now, I'm moving into forbidden territory."

I tightened my grip on his hand and waited for the other shoe to fall out of the sky and clonk me over the head.

"Dragons, probably the same two who paid you a visit, have been after me too. Mostly the large golden one. His name is Nidhogg, and he's the Norse Dragon. For years, he mostly nibbled on Yggdrasil's roots, but he sought me out perhaps a fortnight ago and tasked me with watching over Midgard."

I blew out a tightly held breath. So far, this wasn't too bad.

Bjorn reached into a pocket and retrieved an egg-shaped piece of quartz that glowed with an inner light. His hands were just as filthy as mine, caked with blood and gore and grime. Once he'd laid the stone between us, it rocked gently.

"This is how Nidhogg keeps tabs on me, so if the skies crack open and I vanish—"

"I'll be on your heels," I said firmly. "No way am I letting anyone hurt you."

A soft laugh bubbled from him. "Thanks. I feel the same way about you."

His words wrapped me in warmth, tenderness. I leaned closer, letting our shoulders touch.

"The things you don't know," he went on, "are twofold. After years of doing very little, the gods are worried about Midgard. If it fails—and you're correct about it teetering on the edge of disaster—serious consequences affecting the other Eight Worlds will follow."

"As in?"

"The rot will spread, and it will be the beginning of the end of Yggdrasil and the worlds supported by the One Tree."

Breath whooshed from me. I'd known things were serious, but I'd assumed only Earth was implicated. The stone glowed brighter, and its gentle rocking became more pronounced. "Oh-oh." I reached for the stone, but Bjorn grabbed my hand.

"Not a good idea."

He was probably right. I was so tired, I wasn't thinking straight.

Bjorn shut his eyes for a moment and then stumbled to his feet and offered me a hand. "Come on. Time to pay the piper."

I was unnerved by how much energy it took to stand. My ankle wasn't much better, but I could weight it a little. "Pay what piper? Where are we going?" I asked.

"Outside."

The stone leapt up of its own accord and nosedived into his pocket. While I blinked stupidly at the place it had sat, the scent of Bjorn's power surrounded me. "We can't teleport," I protested. "Not enough magic."

"Normally, I'd agree with you, but we're not going very far."

The common room shimmered to nothing, replaced by the familiar beaten-down dirt in front of the hidden entrance to the cavern carved beneath Ben Nevis's bulk. As soon as Bjorn's spell cleared, I saw Nidhogg.

The golden dragon's huge hind legs were planted firmly, and he'd crossed his forelegs over his scaled chest. He regarded both of us before untangling his arms to shake a talon at Bjorn. "I told you to let her find her own way."

Bjorn stalked in front of the dragon and looked up at him. "I don't answer to you. Nor will I lie to my friends." He dug the stone out of his pocket and tried to drop it between him and Nidhogg. It made a U-turn midair and returned to Bjorn's pocket.

He rolled his eyes. "Cheap parlor tricks aside, why are you here?"

The dragon lumbered closer to me. "That one"—he hooked a talon at Bjorn—"is determined to deliver certain news. Since he canna keep what should remain hidden secret, I am stepping in."

"It's not as if ye told me aught." Bjorn had retreated to Norse. "I figured out the other on my own. Same as I unearthed her name."

"Pfft. Details." Nidhogg curved his neck. The motion moved his head closer to mine.

"Whatever this is," I growled, "would one of you spit it out so we can move on?"

"What I am about to tell you," Nidhogg said, "is no trivial thing. Combined with your true name, it will change everything."

I resisted the impulse to tap one foot and tell him I was waiting. I was tired and grumpy and annoyed my private moments with Bjorn had been upended.

The dragon leaned closer still. Heat from him was oddly

comforting in the chill of the night that had just fallen. "Long have ye wondered who sired you."

My eyes, which had been sitting at half-mast, snapped open wide. Shit. Was that what this was about? My long-missing father? "I suppose you're going to tell me he was a dragon," I muttered.

Fire shot from Nidhogg's jaws, missing me by millimeters. "Show respect, child."

"Sorry." I focused my hot, gritty eyes on him. "Go on." I'm no expert on reading dragon expressions, but he looked pissed.

"Your father was a dragon," he said in a firm voice that gave no quarter. Between the words and the tone, I knew what he said had to be true.

"Was it you?" I squeaked out.

"No. I know better," he thundered amid more fire, smoke, and ash. Good thing nothing flammable grew here.

"Son of a fucking bitch," I mumbled, meaning to keep my words in my head and failing. "Mother entertained a dragon. Ha. No wonder she couldn't get rid of me."

"Dragon younglings are precious," Nidhogg snarled. "We do not do away with them, no matter how thoughtlessly conceived."

Something about either his sentence or the meaning behind it didn't sit well. I tossed my head back and said, "I'm the innocent bystander here. None of this is my fault, but I suffered plenty because of Mother's roving eye and a dragon who couldn't keep it zipped."

Bjorn edged to my side and wrapped a hand around my upper arm. I got his message, even without him saying anything. I should both apologize and shut up before I dug myself in deeper. I couldn't quite get anything that sounded apologetic past my lips, but I could shut up.

Nidhogg straightened to his full height. "Well?"

I looked into his spinning eyes. "Well, what?"

"Ye should be delighted, thrilled. A million questions must be bursting through your mind."

"Really? I should be all those things because I host alien magic I know nothing about?" I clacked my teeth together, determined to ride herd on the rest of the sarcastic rejoinders crowded in the back of my throat.

"She doesn't mean it." Bjorn spoke for me. "We're fresh from a battle, and—"

"What battle?" Nidhogg roared the question.

"One of those abominations you described crawled through a gateway. In this case, it was a griffon with a long, snakelike neck."

"Where?" Nidhogg thundered.

"Same spot where you dropped me into the midst of the last batch of atrocities."

He spewed fire, and his eyes spun so fast I had to look away. "Worrisome," he pronounced. "I understand why ye came around to deciding to reveal her dragon side."

I expected Bjorn to roll his eyes. Instead he bowed briefly and said, "Thank you, sire."

Nidhogg turned his attention back to me. "Ye, Runa, are a Dragon Heir. It means many things, but your studies must begin immediately. I only hope we are not too late."

I've never been into bowing and scraping. And I quit being accommodating when I was about ten. I stood tall and yanked my arm out of Bjorn's grip. Once it was free, I crossed my arms beneath my breasts. "I welcome instruction in magic, but I have a life here. People who depend on me. I refuse to drop everything and turn my existence inside out just because you finally decided I was important enough to merit your attention."

I should have stopped there, but I was on a roll, and holding my tongue has never been one of my strong suits. "How long have you known about me?" I demanded. "From the sound of things, you've been aware of me since my birth. You could have come to me anytime. But you waited until now.

"Fine. I respect whatever internal reasoning led up to today, but you must respect me too. I'll do my damnedest to learn your magic, and do whatever else is required of my newly uncovered status as a *Dragon Heir*." It was hard, but I didn't imbue the words with exasperation, not too much, anyway. "I'll do all those things," I went on, "but in my own way and on my own timetable."

I waited and held eye contact. No way was I about to back down. I'd cut my teeth on Celtic arrogance. This was just one more sanctimonious bastard who was stuck on himself. I'd absorb what this whole dragon thing meant later —when Nidhogg wasn't breathing down my neck.

The dragon ripped his attention away from me; it felt like my top layer of skin came along with it. "Reason with her," he snarled at Bjorn just before the air around him turned into a mélange of color and he vanished.

Bjorn made a grunting noise. "'Tisn't wise to anger a dragon," he mumbled.

"Yeah well, wisdom isn't my middle name." I was still furious at being ordered about. "I'm going back inside. Are you coming?"

A corner of his mouth twitched. "I've had warmer invitations from alley cats guarding a kill, but yes, I'll be right behind you."

CHAPTER SEVENTEEN, BJORN

I'm not sure quite what I envisaged once I figured
out Nidhogg planned to tell Runa about her
dragon blood. But I expected her to react in some fashion.
He might have told her she was part unicorn or part Fae for
all the difference it made.

Maybe it would take time to sink in, but my overarching
impression was she didn't give a fuck. This was just one
more drain on her resources, and she would have been
equally happy never knowing. Probably happier. I beat back
a smile. I'd respected her before, but she'd vaulted to a whole
new level.

I caught up with her in the doorway to the common
room. "We need to talk. Will this chamber remain empty?"

"Probably not. Come this way." She did an about face
and marched along a curved corridor. The bite of Celtic
power was strong in these tunnels. It surprised me because
centuries had passed since they'd bided here. Except for

Runa. For some reason, I tended to discount the other half of her blood: the Celtic one.

The way her mother's kinsmen had treated her was abysmal, and I was angry with them. Odin could be a fucker, but then so was Thor. And Loki was so bad I kept well clear of him. The other deities in the Norse Pantheon had good hearts for the most part. But even Odin had a soft spot for children. If he'd wronged any, I'd not heard about it.

Runa ducked beneath hangings off to the left, and I followed her into a small, rounded room. Lights flickered into being without obvious magic from her, so they were probably keyed to her energy. A bed was tucked into one corner with covers rucked up toward the near end. Hooks lined the wall opposite the bed, and a variety of garments hung from them.

She turned to face me and folded her arms beneath her breasts. "First off, my name is Rowan. If you keep calling me Runa in your mind, someone will pick up on it, and the secret of my name will no longer be an advantage."

I nodded agreement. She was correct. Enemies not knowing her true name might not confer much of a benefit, but things were going downhill fast in Midgard. She was wise to hang onto every single edge she had.

"Next item," she went on, apparently satisfied I'd comply with her request. "Is Nidhogg my father?"

My eyes widened. I hadn't expected her to ask that. "No. He already told you as much, and dragons don't lie. They are masters at twisting the truth, but he answered you directly when you questioned him."

"Mmph. So who is?"

"I have no idea, which is why we still need to pay Ceridwen a visit."

Runa—Rowan—made a face that looked as if she'd chomped on something bitter. "I really don't want to, but I don't see where there's much choice. I know enough to make things uncomfortable for her, and—"

I shook my head. "What makes you think the rest of the pantheon didn't sense your dragon blood? It was obvious to me."

"Your point?" She set her mouth in a tight line.

"Twofold. Either they didn't care, or they had some investment in sparing your mother embarrassment." I blew out a breath. "Your mother is a seer—and a damned talented one. The Celts value her prophecies. They also might have felt sorry for her."

"Pfft. I doubt that." Rowan rolled her eyes.

"You do know the tale about her other children?"

"Of course. Everyone knows how she brewed up wisdom to make up for her son being ugly, but the casting went awry."

I shifted my weight from foot to foot to keep myself from giving in to exhaustion and sinking to the floor. The large black cat who'd sought refuge in my lap jetted into the room, meowing like a mad thing. Rowan held out her arms; the cat leapt into them and then used her body to crawl to her shoulders.

Watching them, I was certain they'd executed this maneuver hundreds of times. I chose my next words carefully. "You only see one side of Ceridwen—the one you hate." I hurried on before Rowan transferred her ire to me.

"She deserves every bad thing you feel about her, but there's another side to the story."

"Like what?" Rowan's words could have etched glass.

"She couldn't avoid giving birth to you, but she had many choices once you were born. She could have sent you away. She could have locked you onto a borderworld. Instead, she kept you by her side. Granted, she ignored you, but—"

"Spare me," Rowan broke in. "However I feel—or don't feel—about Mother, it's long past time to get over it. I was just thinking that when my astral self was watching you and Tansy combining your magic to help me."

I sank into a crouch because I couldn't help myself. My legs didn't want to hold me upright any longer. Rowan perched on the edge of the bed. "I can drag a chair in here," she offered.

"I'm fine." Something else had occurred to me, and it was a perfect time to toss it out there. "This will sound farfetched, but another potential reason Ceridwen kept you where she could see you is she holds knowledge about your future. You wield a potent combination of power. There have only been a handful of other Dragon Heirs scattered throughout time, and—"

"Tell me about them," she demanded and leaned forward.

"It might be easier if you asked specific questions," I countered. "I need my library to give you names, dates, lineage, and suchlike."

She nodded solemnly. "Will I be able to shapeshift?"

"I'm fairly certain the answer to that is no."

A wry grin curved her mouth. "Damn. It would be so advantageous. Have there been others with Celtic blood?"

I scrunched my forehead until my eyebrows probably touched. "I don't know for certain. The Dragon Heirs who come to mind are all Norse blends. It makes sense since dragons live in most of the Nine Worlds."

"Dewi doesn't," she pointed out.

"Another reason for us to pay your mother a visit. We'll want to include the Celtic dragon. She and Nidhogg must know one another."

Rowan was nodding slowly. "Some things are coming together. No wonder Mother cautioned me to steer clear of Dewi. The dragon goddess might have taken pity on me, moved me under her wings, and cared for me." Rowan fisted one hand and punched the air. "No matter what kind of spin you put on it, I was a possession. Ceridwen might not have wanted me, but she didn't want anyone else to have me, either."

"Aye. That would add to my suspicion she knows something about your future. The role you have yet to play."

"But why create the Breaking?"

I considered the question. "Perhaps she didn't mean for it to cut so deep. If her primary goal was to drive you back to her side, the Breaking was overkill."

Rowan snorted. "Major overkill." She patted the bed next to her. "Get up off the floor and sit here. I'm feeling like a shitty host."

I wanted to sit next to her, so I didn't argue the point or tell her how comfortable I was squatting on the floor. It took more effort than I would have guessed to unfold my body.

Once I was on my feet, the few steps to reach the bed were easy.

I'd no sooner settled next to her—keeping a small space between our thighs—when the cat jumped to my shoulders. "Oomph. He weighs more than I expected."

She turned a surprised look my way, eyebrows raised, mouth half open. "Mort is very particular. He rarely lets anyone else touch him. He found me when he was a scraggly kitten and hasn't been far from my side since."

"Animals tend to like me." I reached up toward the cat, and he nuzzled my filthy fingers. At some point, I needed to clean up.

"I like you too," she said and scooted so her body leaned against mine.

My reaction to her touch was instantaneous. Heat began in my midsection and rolled through me. Before I wrapped my arms around her and turned her so I could kiss her, I had at least one more thing to accomplish.

"You didn't say much outside," I prodded.

"What was there to say?" She shrugged. "Over the years, I've imagined my father was anything from a demon to an elf to a vampire. A dragon isn't that far removed from all my other theories."

Before I could say anything else, she went on. "I've always known my magic was strong enough to rival the full blooded Celts, so I assumed my father must have been a powerful magician. Besides, Mother was selective about who she took to her bed. I couldn't see her diddling the help."

"Did you have servants?" I quirked a brow.

"Not usually. Magic is far more efficient, and you don't

end up with bodies that need food and shelter when they're not cooking and cleaning for you." She laid a hand on my leg and tucked her head onto my shoulder, partially displacing the cat who clawed his way to our laps.

"I don't know," she said, sounding wistful. "This whole thing with my father was like an obsession. I wanted to know so badly, I would have offered up my firstborn." She chuckled. "But like all obsessions, now that it's no longer a secret, knowing isn't nearly as satisfying as I imagined it would be."

I understood perfectly. Meeting the Norse gods for the first time had been kind of like that. I'd placed them on such high pedestals, the experience couldn't come close to my expectations.

And it hadn't.

I laced my fingers in with hers. She squeezed lightly and murmured, "The magic part should worry me, but it doesn't. I figure maybe there's a slightly different mix to accomplish some of the things I do, but I can't believe I have a rich vein of alien magic that's been there all along. If I possessed such a thing, I'd have stumbled across it. I've been in some dicey situations where I was pulling out all the stops. If I didn't trip across it then, it's not there to be found."

She angled her body until she more-or-less faced me. The cat squalled indignantly and jumped to the floor. Having her so close to me was heady. My chest tightened; my heart beat faster. My nether regions came alive with heat and need.

Looking right at me, she said, "The one thing that makes an enormous difference in how I wield my power is you. We strengthen one another. I doubt there's an enemy who could stand before us."

I cupped the side of her face and said, "Enough of an army assembled against us would tax even our resources. It worries me because someone seems intent on drawing us out and challenging us."

"Which means we're not the only ones who know how synergistic our magic is."

Somewhere between our impromptu trip to Niflheim and battling the griffon, the same thought had occurred to me. Not much I could do about it, though. Because it was easier than addressing thorny puzzles, I focused on Rowan, her enticing scent and the press of her body against mine. Her skin felt smooth, silky beneath my fingertips. A quick glance at my hand brought me up short, and I moved it. "I'm really dirty. I shouldn't be touching you."

Rowan waved a hand in front of my face. Grime had caked beneath her fingernails, and her fingers were streaked with dried blood and greasy soot. "We're a match in that regard."

I craved her far worse than I wanted to clean up. A basin and ewer sat on a stand across the small room, but I couldn't use them. I'd pollute the water and the scrap of towel neatly folded next to it. What I needed was a creek. One flowed not far from the entrance to these caverns.

"Bjorn."

The way she said my name stoked the flames raging through me, and drove all thoughts of anything but her out of my mind. I angled my head and kissed her. Soft, tentative, I offered her a choice. In case I'd read her wrong. Her lips were lush beneath mine, and her wonderful mint-and-vanilla scent thickened around us.

She kissed me back hungrily and wove her arms around me. I gripped the back of her neck to hold her in place. The taste of her lips was enticing as we licked and bit and sucked. When she opened her mouth to my tongue, I teased the inside of her mouth, exploring its sweet folds, and imagined trading my cock for my tongue.

Rowan molded her upper body to mine. The curves of her breasts pressed into me, nipples forming hard points of desire. Our mouths were still glued together, and our breath came faster. She was just as aroused as I was, and the knowledge delighted me.

The hand she'd had on my thigh found its way to my painfully erect cock, and she rubbed it through my trousers. I snaked a hand between us to capture one of her breasts and twirled the nipple between two fingers. Her breast felt amazing. The image of her naked chest returned to me.

Her breasts were high and full and tipped with golden-brown nipples the size of old-fashioned coins. I plunged my tongue into her mouth again, and she sparred with it and pressed her breast deeper into my hand.

Savagery ran through me. A need to possess the woman in my arms. I'd had sex before, not lots but some. The heat and need and urgency had been nothing like what I felt now.

She tumbled backward onto her pallet, dragging me with her. Lying side by side was a definite improvement. She tossed a leg over one of my thighs, and the heat from her seared me. Rowan ripped her mouth from mine. "What are we doing? The world could be ending. We should be out there practicing fighting, and—"

"We belong together, you and me." I brushed my dirt-caked thumb over her lower lip that was swollen from our kiss. "I don't know how or why, but we're meant to be together."

Her eyes had turned to molten gold, liquid with lust. "I've never believed those fated-mate connections, but holding you, being with you, feels right."

"Right enough to make love?" Suddenly cautious, I didn't want to force myself onto her if she wasn't sure."

She grinned and thrust her pelvis against my leg. "More than right enough. Maybe we could clean up first and do this properly? I know a pool not far from here. It's small, and we could heat it with magic."

Visions of stripping off our clothes and making love in the pool blasted through me. I could almost feel the press of her breasts and the slick tightness of her vault closing around me. My cock jumped against her touch.

"I'll take that as a yes." Her smile had widened into an expression that Aphrodite would have approved of.

I kissed her again, lingering over the feel of her full mouth working beneath mine. Now that I knew we'd be lovers, we could take our time, tantalize one another, enjoy exploring each other's bodies. I wanted to make her come a hundred times, but first we had to let go of one another long enough to find this pool of hers. After a final lick, I began untangling my limbs from hers.

"Why stop at a hundred?" She laughed, and the silvery sound of pealing bells made my heart glad.

"No thoughts of my own, eh?"

"Maybe a few. I'll teleport us there. It will be faster." The feel of her magic rose around me, thickening the air with promise and the potential of what she and I could be together.

Lovers and warriors. I relished the combination, and it almost made me laugh. Up until a very short while ago, I hadn't cared much for anything that had to do with warfare. Having Rowan by my side changed everything.

The walls of her room were replaced by a circle of standing stones with a pool in the center of them. I couldn't wait to undress her, but first I sent power arcing around us to make certain we were alone. We were, but we also weren't exactly in Midgard any longer.

I wrapped my arms around her. Touching her was such a novelty and such a delight, I didn't even try to resist. "What is this place?"

"A world between worlds. Not exactly Earth, but not too far separated from it, either. It isn't a borderworld, but it is private."

"How'd you find it?"

"A long time ago, before the Breaking, the Celts were still in Inverlochy Castle. No one ever cared where I went or what I did, so I explored every tunnel, every cave, every possibility that led away from the castle. I got skilled at concealing my tracks, and I spent a lot of time here. One other place was almost as good, but without the pool."

She let go of me with one hand long enough to flick magic at the water's smooth surface. After she'd chanted a small spell to warm the pool, she turned to me and began unbuttoning my blood-saturated clothing. It would be a relief to put some distance between my shirt and jacket and nose. Rowan's delicious scent overpowered the stench of the monster but didn't obliterate it entirely.

She pushed my jacket aside, followed by my shirt, and ran her hands over my bare skin. "Such a beautiful man."

Her words pleased me. For the first time ever in my lengthy life, I wanted to be appealing to another. I've always valued being viewed as competent, capable. Those are different from being thrilled a woman found me desirable.

I reached for the bottom edge of her shirt and worked it carefully over her head, making certain not to disturb the wounds that were healing on both shoulders.

"You have the most amazing breasts." I filled my hands with them, luxuriating in their firm fullness and rapidly hardening nipples.

"You saw them before," she said playfully.

"Aye, but I had other priorities." Bending forward, I licked a nipple. She moaned softly, so I licked the other one. Meanwhile, her fingers were busy with my trousers. I kicked off my soft leather boots before the pants pooled around my feet.

My cock jutted from my body. She made a grab for it, but I said, "Nope. Bath first." If she touched me, we'd never make it into the pool. At least, not for a long while.

Before I could undo her trousers, she whipped through the fastenings and stepped out of them. Breath swooshed from me, and my chest got tight. Her breasts were only the beginning. Hips flared beneath a sculpted ribcage and narrow waist. Her ass was almost generous, and her legs long and shapely. If she'd had shoes, they were long gone.

She held out a hand. I kicked out of the tangle of my breeches and clasped it. We walked into the pool together. The bottom was mostly sand with a few rocks. Half a dozen steps brought us waist-deep, and I gathered handfuls of sand to scrub the dirt off my hands. Dipping my face into the water, I washed it too.

I felt Rowan working on my back. When she was done, I turned her around to return the favor. She had a long, graceful spine and strong, broad shoulders. "The claw marks are healing," I told her.

"They should be gone by now," she said. "And they would be if my magic had fully recovered."

After rinsing sand from my hands, I gathered her close, her back to my front, and reached around her to cup her breasts. They fit perfectly into my hands, and I angled my head to string kisses up the side of her neck. She nestled against me and murmured, "I can't believe how good you feel."

My erection pressing into the curves of her ass told her without words how amazing she felt in my arms. I luxuriated in the heat coursing through me and dipped a hand to the spiky mat of red curls between her legs. Her nub was distended and slick, and I teased it with a finger.

She went from leaning against me, mewling with delight, to ramrod straight in the space between two breaths. "What is it?" I turned her in my arms so I could see her face. "Did I do something wrong?"

"Not at all. You can't hear the same as me because this

spot is married to Celtic power. Something's gone horribly wrong at Inverlochy Castle." She chugged out of the water and started dragging clothes over her wet body.

I stood stock-still, blood pumping through every vessel, cock ramrod straight and begging for release, before I rose beyond the swamp of lust my body had turned into and ran out of the pool. A jolt of magic dried me and got most of my clothes on except my boots. Never have figured out how to finesse them with anything other than the old-fashioned method.

"Talk with me," I urged. "What's happening?" By now, I was sitting in the sand, dragging my boots on and getting the laces out of the way.

"Mother." Rowan spat the word like a curse. "Mother is at Inverlochy. The witches are defenseless against her. We have to hurry."

"I'll be directly behind you." On my feet, I ran lightly after her right through something I could have sworn was a solid cliff. It parted the moment I touched the illusion and spit us out in a place that stank of Celtic power.

Readying myself for damn near anything, I put out a call to Nidhogg. If we needed firepower, his was as potent as it came.

CHAPTER EIGHTEEN, ROWAN

I longed for Bjorn with an urgency that ran far deeper than wisdom or reason. My plate was unbelievably full. I did not need a love interest mucking things up. Except, he wasn't going anywhere. We were destined to fight together. Apparently, that destiny ran deeper than comrades in arms. It had taken a whole lot of self-discipline not to unbutton his trousers back in my bedroom. It would have been so easy to extract his incredible cock and ride him to ecstasy.

But we were filthy, and I had an inexplicable need for our first time to be special. Something other than rutting in the dirt like a couple of animals. I've never had much use for men beyond the occasional roll in the hay. Bjorn was different. He wasn't roll-in-the-hay material.

It should have scared the living daylights out of me. Quickies didn't mean anything. Hell, I didn't even have to like the guy. I wasn't signing on for anything beyond a cursory fuck. The moment Bjorn's mouth came down on mine, sweet and hot and irresistible, I was lost. I may as well have stenciled an "I'm yours" heart across my forehead like the cutesy little Valentine candies mortals used to be so fond of before the world broke.

Blinded by lust and heat and need, I brought him to my private pool. The one no one else knew about, and we bathed, washing each other. He stood behind me, the hard muscled planes of his body a delight against my back. The swell of his cock enticing. A sudden rush of Celtic power followed by outraged shrieks brought me thumping out of my fantasies of Bjorn filling me with his hot, hard dick. There was trouble at Inverlochy. Celtic trouble. And it had Mother's name stamped all over it.

Goddammit! If she harmed so much as a single one of the witches, there'd be hell to pay. Maybe I could leverage my linkage to dragonkind—a connection my Celtic kin probably all knew about—to mete out punishment.

I didn't expect Bjorn to come with me. This was my problem, but I was quietly pleased when he simply assumed he'd be by my side. He dressed fast and asked for as many details as I had about the problem. It was starting to feel like my days of being on my own were over, but that was dangerous ground. The best way to avoid disappointment would be to keep my expectations nonexistent.

He fed power into my travel spell, and we came out in the deserted castle courtyard. At least the beginnings of the garden were still intact. Now that we'd breached the veil separating Inverlochy from the stones and pool, I sensed

Arawn and Gwydion too. Mother hadn't come alone this time.

Had something tipped them off about the witches being here, or had they come across them by accident?

I dashed up the stone stairs with Bjorn right behind me. There'd been a stretch—a rather long one—when Mother intimidated me, but that time was long gone. Thank the gods —the other ones, not her—for small favors. After the witches initial volley of outraged shrieks, they'd been silent. I picked out their energy signatures, one by one.

No one had killed them. Not yet, anyway.

I felt Bjorn kindle defensive magic and weave it in with mine. Good to be ready. I'd been so intent on making sure my friends hadn't been harmed, it had been the only thing in my mind. We barreled into the sizeable chamber the witches had claimed in time to hear Ceridwen's chilly voice.

"Ye will leave this spot and never return."

"But you've just signed our death sentences." Patrick stood up to her. It made me proud of him.

"Why should I care?" Ceridwen countered.

"That's always been the problem," I shouted as I burst into the room. Bjorn flanked me, and we stopped just inside the door. "You've never valued anyone's existence beyond your own."

"Ye're being overly hard on your Mum," Arawn said. Tall and gaunt, he wore his customary black robes. Dark hair spilled around him to waist level, and his dark eyes missed very little. The god of the dead was a man of few words, so hearing him speak surprised me.

"You think so?" I turned my attention his way. "Do you know who my father is?"

He shot a pointed glance at Gwydion; magic crackled between them as they employed shielded telepathy. Striking like all the Celts, the warrior magician and master enchanter was as fair as Arawn was dark. He was garbed in sky-blue robes sashed in white, and his ever-present magical staff carved with cunning runes and symbols shone with its usual inner light. The collection of leather pouches he normally carried everywhere hung from hooks on his sash.

I chopped a hand downward. "I already know my parentage. All the effort you put into hiding Mother's dirty little secret was for naught. These things have a way of coming out."

"Whatever are ye talking about, child?" Gwydion looked at me as if I'd grown two heads.

I tossed a truth spell over him. Before he could break it, I said, "Do you mean to tell me you didn't know my father is a dragon?"

The shock stamped into his patrician features was genuine. I didn't need my spell any longer, so I reeled it in. Gwydion stared at Ceridwen. "A dragon, eh? Ye did a masterful job hiding that little tidbit from us."

"How about if we move this discussion upstairs? To the council chamber?" I added a megadose of compulsion to my words. "Then the witches can get back to their garden."

"They canna be here." Mother focused eyes twin to my own on me.

I hustled forward and planted myself between her and the witches, aware of Bjorn maintaining a position where he could defend me. His unconditional support warmed me. I'd never had anyone stick up for me—until I joined the coven.

I settled my hands on my hips. "And why not?" I asked Ceridwen. "They're not hurting anything here. You don't require this place. For us, it's a matter of survival. Too many evil creatures are roaming free to plant anything outside."

"*Us* should be employed to mean you and the Celtic pantheon," Mother retorted.

I blew out an exasperated breath. "You fucked a dragon, for chrissakes. You hid my parentage to salvage your sorry reputation. You treated me like shit. When I refused to return to your side like an obedient puppy, you fucking broke the world."

Anger boiled up hot from my guts. "You didn't give a good goddamn how many mortals you mowed through, or what a tough time the few survivors would have. Nope. It's just like always. All about you. The witches you hate so much took me in. We're running out of food, and I will do everything in my power to ensure we can grow what we need. Right here in Inverlochy castle. I'm a Celt. I have as much right to the use of it as you do."

"When you broke Midgard," Bjorn's deep voice growled from next to me, "you opened gateways that had been locked tight for good reason. It's taken a few years, but pathways have formed. Channels that allow wicked creatures access to a world they've always desired."

"Who are you?" Arawn asked.

"Aye, ye've a Norse feel about you," Gwydion added.

"I am Bjorn Nighthorse, master sorcerer for the Nine

Worlds," he replied coolly. "No need to offer your names in return, I know who you are well enough."

An uncharacteristic groan ripped from Ceridwen. After a string of curses in multiple languages, she muttered, "Goddess be damned. The cauldron never lies."

"What exactly does that mean?" I was close enough to thump her in the chest with my index finger. No more respect from me. She didn't deserve any.

"We'd like to know as well." Arawn turned his bottomless black eyes on Ceridwen.

"While ye're at it," Gwydion sniped, "how many other secrets have ye been sitting on?"

I narrowed my eyes to slits. "We will move this discussion upstairs." I thumped Mother once again for good measure. "I want your absolute word you will leave the witches alone. They'll only be here long enough to see their crops through to harvest."

"What about the next planting?" Ceridwen snapped.

"If Earth lasts that long, there will be another planting," I agreed. "You will leave them alone then too."

Arawn and Gwydion moved to either side of Mother. "Leaving?" I asked caustically. "It will only put off a long-overdue talk. And inconvenience the hell out of Bjorn and me because we'll have to track you down."

"We shall reconvene in the council chamber," Gwydion informed me. A jolt of power dropped over Mother, ostensibly to teleport her, but maybe the master enchanter knew her well enough to expect her to try to make a run for it. Mother never did like to lose the upper hand. Thorny discussions weren't her favorite, either.

When the air cleared, they were gone.

The witches looked rattled. "Do you think it's safe for us to remain?" Patrick asked.

"Aye," Bjorn said. "I was certain the other Celts knew about Rowan's parentage. Clearly, they didn't. They'll be annoyed enough with Ceridwen for withholding the truth that having you here growing a few vegetables won't even rise to the level of a minor inconvenience."

"A dragon, eh?" Patrick's drawn face relaxed into a warm smile.

Hilda rushed forward and hugged me. Leif and several others gathered close. "We'd still love you if your da was the Devil himself," she murmured.

I returned her embrace. "You're all special to me too. Bjorn and I are going upstairs, but you can get back to work."

"Check in with us before you leave," Patrick told me. His instructions were transparent as hell, but he needed to make certain I was all right. Blood might be thicker than water, but if I had kinfolk, it was my witch family all the way.

"Sure thing." I patted his shoulder before Bjorn and I walked out of the room.

"We could teleport," he pointed out.

"Yeah, but I want to give them time to grill Mother about opening her legs when she should have known better." I smiled, but it had a lot of teeth and no mirth at all.

"There is that. Also I had the distinct impression they weren't aware your mother was responsible for the Breaking. Or not totally responsible."

I hadn't picked up on that part, but I'd be damn certain to rip the scab off that wound too. We traipsed up many flights to the Celts' council chamber. It sat on the fourth floor at the tail end of a long, wide hallway. The farther up we moved in the castle, the more intact it was.

Wall hangings depicting Celtic glory were interspersed with bronze statues and ivory carvings. A fortune in art sat within these walls. A useless fortune. Money didn't buy anything anymore. I paused a couple of meters from the double doors that led to the council chamber. They were shut, but I'd expected them to be. A cursory jab of magic told me the Celts had shielded it from prying ears too.

I turned toward Bjorn. "That thing you said earlier."

"Which thing in particular?"

"The one about the Breaking kicking open paths for bad shit from other places to rampage through to Earth."

He nodded. "It's the only explanation that makes sense. Midgard would have been well on its way to healing after the Breaking, but the magic that split the world became self-perpetuating. As big a bitch as your mother is, I don't believe she cared enough to keep an infusion of destructive magic flowing."

"I might be deluding myself, but remember how I said I might be able to gradually repair the damage? I didn't realize Mother was behind the Breaking until quite recently. Once I understood it was her power that spawned the destruction, I started considering how to counteract it. Only problem is things keep popping up, so I haven't been able to focus any attention on how to address the problem."

Bjorn made a wry face. "Things *popping up* is an understatement. Even without them, though, your idea might have worked a decade ago. In the meantime, this thing

—whatever it is—has developed a mind of its own and terminal velocity. Magic that renews itself is the hardest to alter."

"But we're strong together," I argued.

"We are, but probably not strong enough. All we need are a few more griffons or trolls or other monsters to crawl out of the dirt." He blew out a tired sounding breath. "They'll figure out damned fast we want to cut them off from their playground, and they'll pull out all the stops to keep their portals wide open."

"Maybe the dragons would help—" I began.

The doors to the council chamber slammed open. "Ye dinna strike me as someone who'd be waiting for an invitation to enter," Gwydion said sourly.

"We were talking," I told him.

He turned on his heel and stalked into the room. Despite years of disuse, it was lovely. Light reflected through crystalline windows, casting colorful shadows on an enormous marble table. Ringed by benches and chairs, it could have seated forty.

Mother stood in her customary spot near its head, and I wasn't surprised to see her cauldron. The thing followed her everywhere. Steam rose from it, and the hissing sound of bubbling liquid was loud in the cavernous hall.

Bjorn and I walked into the room, pulling the great doors shut behind us. Better than three meters tall, they were carved with likenesses of animals, mythical and otherwise. When I was a child, sometimes the carvings came alive if I looked at them long enough. A great stag had started to detach once and scared the living hell out of me.

"Did you come to any decisions?" I asked as I covered the distance to the front of the table where all of them were milling about. No one was sitting, which spoke to how exasperated everyone was.

"About?" Arawn raised one dark brow.

"For starters," Bjorn took over, "since one of yours broke Midgard, what assistance are you willing to provide to at least attempt to stem the tide of wickedness?"

"If Odin requires our assistance, he can request it." Ceridwen glanced up from the boiling mess in front of her. It was hard for me to look at her for very long, probably because we're so much alike. Same height. Same build. Same hair. Same eyes. She favored hunting leathers, which have never been a favorite of mine. I find them hot and itchy.

Today, though, she was garbed in robes like the men. Hers was a deep violet shade sashed in teal. A copper ankh set with rubies hung from a golden chain around her neck, and her hair had been pulled into a simple bun low on her neck.

"Odin doesn't know you were behind the Breaking," Bjorn said. "An omission I will correct as soon as I return."

"Ye doona want to do that, son," Gwydion said.

"I don't?" Bjorn sent a "yeah right" look at the master enchanter.

"War between us and the Norse gods willna make things better." His words were smooth and laced with coercion.

"Ye doona have to live here." I mimicked his brogue. "If Midgard fails, the other eight worlds willna be far behind. The One Tree will sunder, and goddess only knows what impact that will have. Even on the distant borderworld ye call home."

Ceridwen had been chanting softly in the background. It was irritating as hell. I strode to where she bent over the cauldron and dropped my phony Scottish inflection. "Stop that," I hissed.

It took a moment for her to look up. When she did, fury shot from her eyes. "So we have come full circle, have we, child? Where ye tell me what to do? I think not."

"You lost the right to call me child long ago. You were a spoiled brat after you couldn't abort me—and don't bother to insult my intelligence by denying you tried. I've moved on. I don't care about the rest of it. What did the cauldron predict? Why did Bjorn's name send you off into a cursing fit?" I gripped the edges of the table, ready to stand there all day if need be.

"Before you answer," Bjorn cut in, "does Odin suspect there's a prophecy with me dead in its center?"

"If he does, the knowledge dinna spring from us," Gwydion muttered.

"Aye since we dinna know about it," Arawn added and shot a black look Mother's way.

I glanced from him to Gwydion and back. "Mother parleys with Odin. She hired him to hunt me down—a bounty as it were. Once I was found, she neglected to pay him."

"How do ye know of this?" Gwydion's words arrived the same moment a truth net dropped over my head.

I welcomed it and tossed my shoulders back, standing tall. "The Hunt showed up near my home. Worked out well for Odin since he'd been searching for me. We struck a bargain, so the Hunt would leave a young witch alone. In exchange for her freedom, Odin tasked me with locating Mother, said she'd taken something that was rightfully his. He gave me two days, but I didn't need that long. Once I found her, she dragged me back here to Inverlochy. Odin showed up and said something about the errant spawn having been located and for her to pay up. Do you need to hear more?" I asked sweetly.

The netting shattered around me, dropping onto the marble floor with little clicking sounds. Gwydion glided to Ceridwen's side. "What else have ye not told us, *Sister*?" He emphasized the last word until it sounded more like blasphemy than a familial endearment.

"Many things. I doona answer to you." She tilted her chin at a defiant angle.

"Aye, but ye do when your actions bring disgrace on your Celtic blood," Arawn's voice was low, smooth, dangerous. "What did ye see in yon kettle?"

"I see many things."

Arawn crossed to her so fast all I saw was a blur. He gripped her shoulder. "Specifically, Ceridwen, Celtic Seer, what did ye see that relates to Bjorn Nighthorse—and your half-dragon daughter?"

I kept my expression as neutral as I could. He'd just tendered a formal request, one Celtic god to another. Mother couldn't refuse him without penalty. Just what those consequences were comprised of had never been clear to me, but it didn't matter. What did was Mother would be motivated to talk.

Maybe Bjorn and I could use the information to save Midgard.

Ceridwen took a step back from her kettle. After a wave of her hand and a power word, the large, black, cast-iron pot vanished with a cracking noise as if it had been sucked into a vacuum.

"I may not have been a candidate for Mother of the Year," she aimed her words at me, "but neither was I as horrible as ye've depicted me. After ye left, I assumed ye'd return. I gave it plenty of time. When ye dinna show any signs of reclaiming your rightful spot with the rest of us, I cast a small spell to push you in the proper direction."

"Small spell?" I rolled my eyes. "Like fuck it was small."

"Were ye always so rude? I wasna finished."

I clacked my teeth together to keep from blurting out no matter what weak suck excuse she came up with, I would always hold her responsible for the Breaking.

"Please continue," Bjorn invited in a tone that could have meant anything.

"At least one of you has manners," Mother muttered. "The casting got away from me." Her nostrils flared. "Go ahead. Test my words with a truth spell. The harder I tried to regain control of it, the larger the schism grew. Finally, I gave it up for a lost cause and suggested we move the pantheon off world. No one seemed to mind."

"Aye, but we did," Gwydion said. "It might have helped if ye'd been forthright about exactly how the world broke. If we'd addressed the problem with our combined magics when it was fresh, we'd have made a difference."

Ceridwen shrugged. "Spilt milk, *Brother*."

"Just because you did a bad thing that was far worse than your original plans scarcely excuses you," I said.

"Say what ye will, 'tis still spilt milk," Mother retorted. The air around her developed a shimmery aspect.

"You're not going anywhere," I said.

"In this case, I agree with your spawn," Arawn growled. "What did ye see in that kettle of yours?"

"Many things I see never come to pass."

"I ken that part," the god of the dead's voice was as chilly as the souls he tended.

"If you saw anything that relates to me, I would know what it is," Bjorn spoke firmly.

"Ye have your own seers. Ask them."

"Christ, Mother. And you accused me of being rude," I sputtered. "What is it about people befriending me? Being kind to me? Somehow it offends you, and you do your level best to shit all over them. Like the witches. They never did anything to you. For me, they provided all the things you never did. Love. Succor. Fellowship. They took me in. Accepted me without questions. Supported me."

I paused long enough to take a breath. My throat was unpleasantly thick, and I hated that her indifference still grated. Bjorn dropped a steadying hand lightly on my shoulder.

"Ye are still under a geas to answer me," Arawn told my mother. "If ye demur, ye will face the punishment of my choice."

She didn't even look rattled as she arched her red brows. "Really? And what do ye have in mind?"

"A few centuries in a cage with the dead."

"Where ye can visit me at will?" she sneered.

"Ye flatter yourself. I'd not visit at all. Talk or be banished."

Bjorn's hand slid down my arm until he clasped my hand, offering silent support.

I waited, more curious than anything. What would Mother decide? She was immortal and might not mind a few hundred years underground.

Next to me, Bjorn stiffened and angled his head to one side, listening. I pricked my ears to greater sensitivity, but nothing reached me. "Hold up," he said in Norse. "We shall have company presently."

"I sense no one," Arawn growled.

Gwydion tapped his staff on the ground. It went from glowing white to a pale bluish tinge. "I do. Probably for the best. Odin will be here quite soon"—his eyes rounded in surprise—"with a dragon."

"Two dragons," Bjorn corrected him.

The magic shimmering around Mother swirled faster. "Don't let her leave," I shouted.

Quicker than I could follow, Arawn moved behind her. When he stepped away, a finely woven silvery cord bound her wrists. I tried to find it within me to feel sorry for Mother, to have some compassion, but I came up short.

CHAPTER NINETEEN, BJORN

I'd almost forgotten sending an emergency message to Nidhogg. Apparently, it had gotten through, and he'd rounded up Odin. I was almost certain the second dragon was Ysien, and I would have given a lot to know his connection to Nidhogg. All dragons are related at some level, but there had to be a specific reason they'd paired up.

I'd cast a few sidelong glances Ceridwen's way. Her resemblance to Rowan was unnerving. The two women could have been twins, but the similarity crashed and burned once I moved past physical appearance. Ceridwen was cold, haughty, contemptuous. Rowan had a heart. And a damned big one. She put others before herself without a second thought.

The smell of the sea rolled through the room, along with a thick mist. When it cleared, Odin was there looking larger than life. Unlike when he led the Hunt, his skin was intact.

Dark hair braided in two thick plaits hung down his chest. Tall and broad, he wore leather breeks, a linen shirt, and a vest made from what might have been reptile hide.

His huge battle axe, Jarnbjorn was strapped across his back, and twin drinking horns draped around his neck from leather thongs. The ravens, Huginn and Muninn, sat on his shoulders cawing like an unleashed tempest.

Nidhogg burst through a gateway of his own, wings extended, and flew a few laps around the council chamber before landing heavily at the end of the room and regarding everyone through eyes that spun slowly and shaded from silver to green and back again.

Odin narrowed his single fog-colored eye at Ceridwen. Sometimes, he employed a glamour to hide the fact he'd traded an eye for wisdom and magic, but he hadn't bothered with it today. "No matter where I travel," he growled, "I seem to fall over you." He strode across the room and stuck a thick finger beneath her chin, forcing her to look at him. "Ye owe me, Celtic slut."

The ravens cawed agreement.

"She owes a lot of us," Gwydion muttered.

"Aye, get in line." Arawn inclined his head, first at Odin and then at Nidhogg. "Welcome to our council chamber. I doona recall inviting you, but your appearance is timely."

"Ye dinna invite me," Odin said. "My dragon said we might be needed, and I did a bit of digging."

"I am no one's dragon," Nidhogg roared. Fire shot from his mouth, bouncing off the crystal walls.

Odin waved a hand. "Och. Stand down. Poor choice of

words." He refocused on Ceridwen. "Rumor has it ye are the force behind the Breaking. Is this true?"

I kept glancing about, wondering where the other dragon was. I still sensed him—her?—skulking about.

"It might be." Ceridwen met his single-eyed gaze directly. "What of it?"

He snaked out a ham-sized hand and slapped her so hard the crack reverberated off the walls. Her head snapped back on her neck, but she remained silent, apparently not willing to give him the satisfaction of hearing her cry out.

Odin bent his head so it was almost level with hers. "What of it, eh? I'll tell you since ye're too stupid to figure it out for yourself. I rule Nine Worlds. They are interconnected through magic and Yggdrasil. If one world sickens and fails, shockwaves travel to all the others. The One Tree's roots link each world to it and to each other, and—"

"I ken it well enough," she cut in and sneered at him. "Magic got away from me. I dinna mean for it to feed on itself."

"Did she tell any of you what she'd done?" Nidhogg demanded in his deep growl of a voice.

"Not us." Gwydion shook his head. "Nay, nor any of our kin, either. News such as that wouldna have remained secret."

"No matter how ye regard us," Arawn said, "had we known, we'd have gathered our forces and not rested until the damage was mitigated. We liked living on Earth. My realm remains here because the logistics of moving the dead are beyond even my magic."

"She's hiding a prophecy that involves me," I spoke up. "It was what Arawn and Gwydion were attempting to dredge out of her when you arrived."

Odin's face darkened, and he drew his thick black brows into a harsh line. "What prophecy?" he thundered.

"Most of what I see in my cauldron never comes to pass," she hedged.

"What prophecy?" he repeated. "If ye doona tell us—"

"I have first rights to condemn her," Arawn told Odin. "She will bide several centuries with the dead in my halls. Assuming she canna find her tongue."

"Pfft. I have a far better idea." Odin grinned nastily. "She can be fodder for my Hunt. She likes being fucked. My men would adore passing her around. The Valkyries too."

I swallowed a knowing snort. The winged warrior women were supposed to be virgins, Odin's handmaidens who escorted worthy dead to Valhalla. But I'd always suspected the maiden part was a sham. My sense of the second dragon was fading. Had it left? Or was it merely cloaking itself better?

Rowan stood unmoving by my side, fingers tightly laced with mine. I tried to read her expression, but her face was smooth, enigmatic. Was she pissing on her mother's grave or was her generous heart getting in the way?

"When Bjorn requested my assistance a short while ago," Nidhogg rumbled, "I believed our task here would be straightforward. It is past time to combine our talents into a push to salvage Midgard. If we wait, the breach will be so large no magic will be able to close it."

"Where does it go?" Rowan asked. "I know where it

begins. I've kept an eye on the Breaking site almost since the beginning. Bjorn and I corralled some of the worst of the residual evil, but it's a temporary fix at best. Where does the Breaking fissure lead, and why have my attempts to block it been unsuccessful?"

"I have some of those answers, but not all," the dragon replied. "First, though, I would hear of the prophecy that involves our master sorcerer."

I wasn't all that sure I wanted Ceridwen to reveal it, but that was sheer cowardice on my side. Knowledge was power. I should welcome both.

"The gist of the seeing is about the Norse wizard and my daughter." Ceridwen broke a lengthy silence. "The two of them must not remain together."

Rowan stiffened where she leaned against me. "That's sheer crap, Mother. You made that up. You hate it when I'm happy. You resent anyone who treats me like I'm worth something."

"Ye've all been facile with truth spells." Ceridwen had dropped all pretense of bothering to look pleasant. Her eyes had turned to slits, and she'd skinned her lips back from her teeth. "Cast one now and test my words."

"Lies come in many colors," Odin said. "Ye've conveniently neglected to say why ye came to that conclusion."

"When they put their power together, it's enough to defy any of us. Enough to break worlds—"

Rowan burst out laughing. "That's rich, Mother. You beat us to it."

"Power like yours shouldn't exist," she shot back. "I never

should have birthed you, yet I had no choice in the matter. I couldna kill you. Whenever I tried to banish you, the verra next day, there ye'd be, back beneath my nose."

Rowan jerked her hand out of mine, but I made a grab for her upper arm and held fast. "Not worth it," I told her.

"Ye tried to kill your own daughter?" Gwydion's question held incredulity and deep sorrow.

"She just admitted as much," I said. I wanted to rip Ceridwen from stem to stern with my bare hands. I wanted Nidhogg to fry her with fire. Most of all, I never wanted to lay eyes on her again, but even absent seer ability, I didn't think I'd be that fortunate.

"Nay, I never tried to kill her." Ceridwen struggled against the cord binding her wrists to no avail. "I knew better. I would have failed."

"We made certain she remained with you," Nidhogg said. "Ye dinna deserve such a treasure, but we kept her in a familiar place for her. Children never understand being spirited away from their home, from those who've raised them."

"Thanks for the thought," Rowan snarled. "I would have welcomed such a change."

"Ye only think ye would have." Nidhogg softened his voice until it was almost gentle.

"You've been watching over Rowan ever since she was born," I said. It was obvious from the dragon's words.

"Aye. We take care of our own. She may not have taken her dragon form yet, but she is still one of mine," Nidhogg said.

"Hold on." A startled look skittered across Rowan's face. "Bjorn said I won't be able to shapeshift."

"There's never been a Celt and dragon mating afore, child," Nidhogg told her. "We doona know what ye'll be capable of."

I listened with interest. No wonder I hadn't been able to come up with any Celt and dragon blends. There weren't any.

"Does Dewi know about me?" Rowan asked.

"None of us did," Gwydion said. "For all her bluster, Dewi has a generous nature. If she'd understood a young dragon bided among us, she'd have made a point of spending time with you."

"Doona say it," Ceridwen told Rowan. "Another ally I withheld from you. Another nail in my coffin." She scanned the group with her cool-eyed gaze. I had to hand it to her. She didn't buckle under pressure, and apologies weren't part of her lexicon.

"Prophecies have life to them. The one involving Rowan is far from complete. It jumped to the forefront when she and that one"—Ceridwen jerked her chin my way—"met one another. I had a feeling he had to be the central figure from the first part of the foretelling, but I wasna certain until I heard his name."

"We have our own seers," Odin said. "I am one thanks to my kinsman, Mimir, and his spring. Freya, too, has the gift of divination."

"Aye, but ye need me," Ceridwen insisted.

"They may, but I'm questioning if we do," Arawn growled.

"Leave us out of this," Nidhogg said. "Ceridwen is your problem. No one from our realm would be so thoughtless with their power, or so anxious to cover up their misdeeds."

Ceridwen tried to spread her hands in front of her, but the silver cord limited her movement. "If ye toss me aside, ye'll lose the use of my cauldron. It answers only to me."

"Since ye're, ahem, selective about which parts ye share, how is that a loss?" Gwydion looked down his nose at her and thumped his staff centimeters from her feet for good measure.

She shrugged. "Bind me with spells. Force me to—"

"We shouldna have to bind you with aught. What happened to decency?" Arawn's question was without inflection, but his face was screwed into a mask of anger.

"Ye're one to talk—" she began.

"'Tisn't about me. None of us has magic to spare to bind you. Not if we're engaged in a battle to salvage what's left of Earth."

Nidhogg puffed smoke and ash. "I propose a temporary compromise. As ye'll recall, the Morrigan bides half the year in Fire Mountain and half the year in Hell. Your domain." He sent a pointed look winging at Arawn. "We're already riding herd on one of your rejects. Adding a second—for a limited time—willna tax us unduly."

"I liked my idea about feeding her to the Hunt better," Odin muttered.

"Aye, I liked it well enough myself." Nidhogg's jaws opened in a parody of a smile. "Only problem is none of your Riders are powerful enough to hold her, and she'd be gone the second ye turned your back."

"I refuse to share the same air with the Morrigan." Ceridwen rolled her shoulders straighter.

"World breakers doona get choices," Arawn said. He turned to Nidhogg and bowed deeply. "Thank you, Dragon Lord, for your generous offer. However many months ye control her will be a burden lifted from us."

"Ye're most welcome," Nidhogg replied. "Her cauldron can travel to Fire Mountain with her. The Morrigan is deep within a cave system. I'm certain she'd relish the company of one of her sisters."

"That hag is no sister of mine," Ceridwen screeched.

"One problem down." Odin ignored her and dusted his hands together.

"Aye, the easy one." Nidhogg turned his spinning gaze on Rowan and went on. "In front of your kin, I name ye Dragon Heir. As such, ye have responsibilities to dragonkind. Your first task is to claim your true name."

She pulled out of my grip and walked closer to the golden dragon. "I accept my true name, but not parading it about offers me protection from those who would harm me. I apologize for my behavior when last we met, yet nothing in my life has changed. The witches need me. I can't just pull up stakes and travel to Fire Mountain—or wherever—to learn about my dragon side."

"I thought long about your words." Nidhogg puffed steam until Rowan was surrounded by clouds of it. I took it as a good sign. Dragons only produced steam when they were in a nurturing mood. "Try as I might," the dragon continued, "I canna fault you for caring about those weaker than yourself."

"That's my daughter," Ceridwen spouted. "The original bleeding heart. Goddess only knows where that trait came from."

"Not from you," I said firmly in hopes she'd shut up. Among her other despicable qualities, she craved attention and did what she could to ensure the limelight fell on her.

"Thank you for understanding," Rowan told the dragon.

"While I empathize with your predicament," Nidhogg went on, "it doesna excuse you from your tasks as a Dragon Heir, so we will come to you to ensure your lessons proceed apace."

"What does that mean, exactly?" she asked.

"A dragon—the one most conversant with your current requirements—will find you each day. Ye will absorb knowledge and practice new skills." Nidhogg's gaze fell on me. "Ye will be there as well."

The thought of never leaving Rowan's side thrilled me, but I still asked, "Why? Have I been relieved of my duties as chief sorcerer for the Nine Worlds?"

"Of course not." Odin looked at me as if I were brain damaged. "Ye'll have time for both pursuits."

I didn't correct him, but I didn't see how, unless I gave far worse service to my clients than I'd been in the habit of. I'd just have to be less available. Way less available.

"The reason"—Nidhogg continued to spear me with his unrelenting eyes—"is your conjoined power is additive. Synergistic. It has a role to play as we battle to save Midgard, but none of us fully understand how to maximize that benefit. Not yet, anyway."

"I do," Ceridwen trilled.

"Ye lost your chance for a seat at the table," Gwydion said firmly.

"If ye doona pay heed to my knowledge, the two of them—my daughter and that Norse sorcerer—will rise up and destroy the lot of you."

"And now you're making things up." I'd had a bellyful of Ceridwen and strode near enough to add, "Silence. If you say anything more, I'll spell your mouth closed."

"Why wait?" Arawn asked pointedly. "I tired of listening to her years ago."

"You have power." I eyed him. "No one is stopping you from using it as you wish."

"Power over the dead," Ceridwen sniped.

A jolt of black lightning shot from Arawn's hands and wrapped around her bound wrists. The cord snugged until it cut through her skin. Blood dripped onto the floor, but she didn't cry out.

I'd half forgotten about Ysien, or whoever the second dragon was, until his bright blue scales popped through a gash in the air. Wings spread, he flapped over Nidhogg's bulk and said, "At your service, sire."

"Take her." He waved a foreleg at Ceridwen.

"Same cell as the other Celtic whore?" Ysien raised both scaled brows.

"It'll do."

Ysien flew above Ceridwen. "Your air taxi has arrived, bitch." He brayed laughter, coating her with fiery ash, and landed.

"Wait a moment." Rowan ran lightly to where her

mother wobbled on her feet, face twisted with pain. "Mother."

"What? Ye were always more trouble than ye were worth."

Rowan shook her head, and her eyes sheened with tears. I started to go to her, but Nidhogg's voice in my mind held me back. *"Her task, not yours."*

Dragons were big on task assignments, but maybe he was right this time.

"No, Mother. I was never any trouble at all. You were blinded by hating me, so no matter how little I required, it was always more than you had to give. I may be a fool and weak as fuck, but I forgive you.

"For everything."

A tear glistened and rolled down Rowan's cheek. When it left her face, it turned to a large red jewel before it landed on the ground at her feet.

"Hating you was eating me up," Rowan went on. "I'm done with all of that. We could have been so much together, you and me. Instead, we're strangers. It makes me sad, and I feel sorry for you, but I'm not wasting any more of my precious time wishing you were someone warmer, more loving—or loving at all. I accept you. I love you. And I'm sorry things couldn't have been different."

Rowan was crying in earnest now. A pile of multihued gemstones formed around her feet. Nidhogg be damned, I went to her and cradled her in my arms.

"You don't deserve her," Ysien told Ceridwen just before he bound her with magic and leapt through a gateway that formed out of nothing. One moment the air was empty, the next a fire-ringed portal blasted into being. And was gone just as quickly.

"I'm all right," Rowan snuffled and wormed out of my arms. Turning to Nidhogg, she said, "I accept your offer and welcome the dragons who will come to teach me. I will work hard and make you proud of me."

"I'm already proud of you, Dragon Heir." He breathed more steam. It wafted across the room and wrapped around Rowan and me.

"Thank you again for taking Ceridwen off our hands," Gwydion said.

"'Tisn't forever," Odin cautioned him. "Only long enough for us to get a handle on how we address the enemy who would destroy Midgard—and the other worlds linked to it through Yggdrasil."

"We understand," Arawn said. "Both she and the Morrigan are our problems, not yours. We shall take both of them back once Earth's fortunes are looking brighter."

"Do the two of you speak for the other Celts?" Odin asked.

Gwydion shook his head. "If decisions are to be made about how to address Earth's problems, we must convene far more of us than Arawn and me."

"My word binds my people," Odin said, "as Nidhogg's binds dragonkind, but I would prefer including Thor, Loki, Frey, Freya, and others as we develop battle strategy."

"Be sure to include Hel," I blurted, followed by, "Never mind. It's not my place to say aught."

"More your place than ye imagine," Odin said.

Before I could ask what he meant by that, he nodded sharply at Nidhogg. "We have work to do."

"Agreed," the dragon said.

The ravens started cawing again, as if they'd suddenly come awake from being in some kind of trance.

"When will I see you again?" Rowan asked Nidhogg. "You, or the dragons who will teach me."

"We will find you, Dragon Heir. Meanwhile, Bjorn has lore books. Immerse yourself in them. Learn about the dragon side of your heritage."

"Will you be able to locate me if I'm in Vanaheim?" she asked.

Nidhogg laughed. It broke the tension that had thrummed through the room. "What do ye think?"

Rowan grinned. "Sorry. It was a stupid question. You'll take good care of Mother? I shouldn't give a fuck, but—"

"That one has always been a master of taking care of herself." Gwydion spat the words. "Apologies from me. I had no idea how miserable your youth was."

"Nor did I," Arawn said. "And Dewi will be devastated."

Gwydion turned to Odin. "I will gather my kinsmen. When and where would ye like to meet?"

Odin tipped one of his drinking horns to his mouth and swallowed deep. Once he capped it, he said, "Asgard. Three days hence. Will that give ye sufficient time?"

"It will," Arawn said and stuck out a hand. Odin shook it. Gwydion did the same.

"We are bound," Odin said. "Shall we formalize it with blood?" He pulled a small dirk from a sheath that hung from his belt.

"Fine by me." Gwydion chopped a short gash in the ball of his thumb with a knife of his own. Odin did the same, and they slapped the cuts together. Once they were done, Arawn stepped close and offered his own blood bond.

Nidhogg had lumbered near. "Hold up your hands," the dragon instructed and bent his long neck until he could snake out his tongue and lick blood from each of them.

The feel of the power dancing through the room changed as Celtic, dragon, and Norse magic slotted together. It grew stronger. Richer. And it gave me hope. Maybe the fight for Midgard wasn't as hopeless as I feared.

Rowan stood, hands clasped behind her. Together we watched as first the Celts and then Odin and Nidhogg shimmered into nothingness. Rowan bent and scooped two handfuls of gems into her pockets.

"I don't get it," she said. "I've never cried jewels before."

"Nor did you acknowledge you were a Dragon Heir," I reminded her. I didn't point out she'd not only cried gems, she was also gathering them for the beginning of her very own hoard.

"Maybe that's the difference," she said. "It would almost have to be. Let's go down and reassure the witches I'm still alive and no one will disturb their garden."

"Do you have plans for after that?" I smiled. My heart was full of unfamiliar emotions. Love. Tenderness. Fierceness. Pride. Nidhogg had said he was proud of her, but I was too.

"Many." She paused. "But they depend on you. Are you good with catching some rest and then digging into your lore books?"

"Do you suppose we could work in a meal, either before or after sleep?"

"Only a meal?" She batted her eyelashes my way.

"Didn't want to get too presumptuous," I teased back, but my body came alive with wanting her.

"Presume away," she said and threaded her fingers in with mine. I ached to kiss her, but we'd have time alone later. The witches were probably worried sick about her, and it wasn't fair to make them wait any longer than they already had. They loved her.

Just like I did. The realization hit me hard, but I didn't fight it. I was too tired, and she was too precious to me to play games denying my feelings.

I was such a sap. Such a softhearted fool, but if I hadn't opened my heart to Mother, it would have made me as big a bitch as she was. I felt sorry for her. Giving voice to my sorrow over our failed relationship made me a better woman, not a worse one. For all the clarity I had around Ceridwen, though, my feelings about Bjorn were cloudy, tangled up in my obsessive need for independence.

I yearned for him, and we could make love from now until forever. I'd never tire of him, but the simple sharing of our bodies wouldn't be enough. Neither of us would be able to leave it at that. We'd want more, and that more would get in the way—of everything. We'd been within moments of joining our bodies. Once we did, we'd belong to each other.

Part of me welcomed it—the part that had fallen hard for his muscled body, Greek-god gorgeous face, and brilliant mind—but another bigger part worried it was the worst idea ever. We'd need all our resources as we slogged through one enemy after another doing our damnedest to salvage Earth. If he was more worried about me than himself, he might make a fatal error. One that would rip him from me forever.

There it was.

I'm immortal. He isn't.

At least, I don't believe he is. His magic feels different to me. I figured it was a byproduct of me not running into very many from the Norse worlds, but Odin and Hel have a common thread flowing through their power. Not that I met her, but her magic was woven into her blankets. Bjorn has it too—that particular magical feel—but it's mixed with a bunch of other elements.

As we walked down the stairs to find the witches, I decided he and I needed to talk—about a lot of things. And the conversation needed to happen when we weren't so tired the simple act of keeping our eyes open taxed us.

I found the witches hard at work in the garden. Small, green shoots stood a few centimeters tall already. The witches must have felt me approaching because by the time I got there, they'd all straightened and were dusting dirt from their hands.

"You're still in one piece, lass." A slow smile lit Patrick's face. "'Tis glad I am to lay eyes on you."

"We were never in any danger." I smiled back. I started to step around what had happened to Mother, but the witches had a right to know. "Ceridwen is on her way to Fire Mountain. The dragons promised to hold her there."

Hilda whistled, long and low. "The dragons' home world. She'll not be bothering us again."

"No. She won't," Bjorn agreed.

"So we can let this batch of seeds grow naturally?" Patrick waved an arm to the side. When I nodded, he said, "Excellent. The plants will be larger and hold more nourishment that way."

"Ceridwen was only one danger," Bjorn cautioned.

"She won't bother you, nor will the other Celts," I said, "but it still isn't safe traveling between here and Ben Nevis."

"You didn't make the other creepy-crawlies go away, eh?" Leif came as close to smiling as he ever did, which involved a slight uplift to one side of his mouth.

"Much as we'd love to have accomplished that, sadly, we haven't," Bjorn told him. "Not yet, anyway."

"We can transport some of those bins of food you located," I said to the witches. "There're limits to how many we can take in a single teleport trip, so if we take some each time we're here..."

"Eventually, we'll have them all," Bjorn finished the thought for me, and then added, "Naturally, we'll leave the provisions you require to complete your planting project."

I looked from one witch to the next. They were all special to me. "Do you need anything that's not already here?" I asked.

"Nay," Patrick said. "We have tools and seeds and food aplenty. Far more than we've had in many a long year. Eating our fill will strengthen us and make it simpler to tend the growing crops."

"Where will you go from here?" Hilda asked me.

"Home. Neither of us have had much rest since we battled the griffon. From there, we'll be in Vanaheim for a while."

"Battling a griffon sounds like quite a tale." Patrick nodded knowingly. "Some evening, around a fire, I'd love to hear about it."

"We'd be happy to accommodate you." Bjorn smiled.

"Why Vanaheim?" Hilda raised her gray brows into question marks.

My life was so intertwined with the coven, they had a right to know. I wasn't certain if my new role as Dragon Heir was supposed to remain hidden, but I wasn't about to keep a secret like that from my family.

"It's all right," Bjorn urged. "Go ahead and tell them."

"Tell us what?" Patrick's question held a protective edge. Bjorn wasn't the only one who'd go down fighting to protect me, but the witches were fragile by magical standards. I wouldn't let them take on any more danger than they already faced.

"You already know I carry dragon blood." I took a measured breath. "Apparently, a title comes along with that. I'm what's called a Dragon Heir. Precisely what that means has yet to emerge, but Nidhogg—"

"The Norse dragon, Nidhogg?" Patrick asked in a tone tinged with wonder. "Was he the one who killed all those goblins and trolls the other night?"

"Yes to both," Bjorn said and gestured for me to go on.

I nodded. "Anyway, Nidhogg told me he'll be sending dragons to teach me that side of my magic. The lessons will begin immediately."

"Good for you," Leif said. "You've always had more magic than you've known what to do with."

"Will you be able to shapeshift?" Hilda asked breathlessly.

I laughed. "First thing I asked too. Bjorn said no; the dragon said maybe. I'm hopeful in that regard because flying would come in so handy."

"Where does Vanaheim slot into things?" Patrick asked.

"I have a cottage there," Bjorn said. "'Tis filled with lore books and ancient scrolls. Nidhogg tasked Rowan with learning all she can about dragonkind, their history, and their magic."

"Do what you need to." Patrick's tone was solemn. "We'll be fine now since that mother of yours isn't breathing down our necks."

"Oh I won't be gone long." I glanced at Bjorn. "I haven't exactly run this by you, but I was thinking maybe we could gather up a few source materials and bring them back to Earth. Once we're done with them, we can trade them out for the next batch."

"We can experiment," he said. "Some of the scrolls might not take kindly to leaving my cottage, let alone Vanaheim."

Hilda walked to me and gave me a long, hard hug. "I've always known you were destined for greatness, child. I've seen it when I cast my runestones and in my tea leaves."

I hugged her back, holding her close as her cinnamon and fennel scent soothed me. "You never told me."

"No reason to. I might have been wrong and gotten your hopes up for nothing."

Laughing, I let go of her. "Ha! My fears more like. Destined for greatness sounds like enough responsibility to crush anyone."

"Aye, but you'll do just fine." She patted my arm. "Now get moving. You've better things to do than to stand around chewing the fat with us."

"See you soon," I said. "Where are those bins of food? May as well begin transferring them."

Two witches scurried around the side of the castle. When they returned, they carried hard-sided containers. I took three. Bjorn tucked two beneath one arm.

His power, with its scent of the sea and sunbaked clay, settled around us. He built a travel spell amid a chorus of goodbyes. Inverlochy's courtyard faded, replaced by the walls of my small chamber beneath Ben Nevis.

"Wow! Precise," I told him. "I'm lucky if I get within a meter of the cave entrance." I set my three bins off to one side.

Bjorn piled his next to mine and shrugged. "Once I've been somewhere, I can always find it again. Oh my. Someone was expecting us back."

My eyes followed his gaze, and I saw a small loaf of bread, chokecherry preserves, a tureen that probably held soup or gruel, and the ever present pot of tea. Crossing to the food, I knelt and lifted the lid of the teapot, inhaling the fragrant herbal mixture.

"This is Tansy's work," I said. "Come eat."

I settled on the floor in front of the low table. Bjorn sat across from me. For long moments, we ate without talking. Finally, he said, "Toward the end there, when Odin and the Celts were blood bonding, did you notice a change in the feel of their magic?"

I set down the cup I'd been drinking vegetable soup from

and thought about it. When thinking didn't get me very far, I reconstructed the scene with a touch of magic, and smiled.

"Yes. A definite change, although at the time I chalked it up to being tired and emotionally wrung out." Picking up a piece of bread made with potato flour, I sopped it into the soup and ate it. "Why did you ask?"

"Mostly to reassure myself I hadn't imagined it," he said around a mouthful of food. Once he'd swallowed, he added, "It was really kind of Tansy to leave this for us."

"It's her way of doing what she could to ensure our safe return. I'm certain the food was imbued with witch charms meant to draw us back."

He scooted around the table until he sat next to me, and then he draped an arm around my shoulder drawing me against him. I should have pulled away, but he felt so good. Warm. Solid. Caring oozed out of every pore. The combination was impossible to resist.

He tucked my head into the hollow between his neck and shoulder. Desire for him kindled. It had never really gone away. He stroked the side of my face and my tangled hair. If I'd been a cat, I'd have been purring.

As if on cue, Mort ambled into the room, tail high, ears pricked forward. With a heartfelt meow, he vaulted into my lap and made himself at home. For once, he didn't chide me for being gone, just made it obvious he was happy to see me.

Bjorn ran a calloused thumb across my lips. Despite my thoughts from earlier, the ones where I'd predicted being lost forever if we made love, I angled my head so my lips hovered near his.

Our breath mingled, hot and sweet, before he kissed me.

Nothing gentle about this kiss. His mouth crushed down on mine; his tongue thrust into my mouth. Somehow, I ended up crosswise in his lap, arms around his neck, as we kept right on kissing each other.

Mort did a bit of clawing for purchase, but he clung tenaciously to his spot on my lap even though he was smushed between our bodies.

We traded deep kisses for little light butterfly ones. Sometimes, I strung kisses over to his ear. Sometimes he ran his mouth down my neck. He cupped one of my breasts and rubbed the nipple. The flutters in my belly turned to a torrent of lust. Reaching between us, I pulled my tunic up and out of the way to give him contact with my bare skin.

His cock swelled and hardened against my thigh.

Breath burned my lungs as my heart rate accelerated. If we were going to stop, we had to do it now, before my entire brain turned to a lust-saturated quagmire.

Bjorn stopped what he'd been doing, moving a hand from one breast to the other and flicking my nipples with his fingers. He raised his mouth from mine. "You're uncertain about this." His words were gentle, not accusatory at all.

I nodded, not sure how to articulate what I needed to say.

He dipped the hand that had been caressing my breasts to the vee between my legs. "We don't need to make love until you're ready. You've been through so much, I'm amazed you haven't made a break for a borderworld. Let me pleasure you, darling. And then we'll sleep."

I should have said no, but heat thrummed between my thighs. I was so close to release, I'd come embarrassingly quickly. The sensation of his hand on my vulva, his fingers drumming a tattoo on my sensitive nub were impossible to resist. My legs separated, and I undid the fastenings on my pants to give him better access.

Mort had twisted out from between us and lay on the floor still purring.

Bjorn pushed my pants down enough to touch me. He inscribed small circles around my engorged nub, murmuring endearments. I wanted him to rub harder, faster, but he teased me, tantalized me. Brought me almost to the edge, and backed me off until I thought I'd die if I didn't come.

In a single movement that I didn't follow at all because I was focused on the heat pouring through me, he rose to his feet with me still in his arms, and laid me on the bed. Next, he knelt between my legs and covered my clit with his mouth. Fire surrounded me as he licked and sucked. I threaded my fingers into the silk of his hair and rocked my pelvis against his face.

The climax that had spooled in my belly, eluding me, crashed over and through me. I came so hard I may have blacked out as I turned into a panting, screaming, writhing mess with Bjorn's mouth still attached to my clit.

A second climax seeded itself from the first. Now that I was on a roll, it blasted through me with all the subtlety of a runaway train. He didn't show any signs of stopping, so I wriggled from beneath him with an agenda of my own.

"Ye're not done," he said in Norse. "I promised ye a hundred of those."

"Not all in the same day," I panted and crawled to where I could unlace his breeches. It was awkward, so I pushed until he lay on the bed and turned him over. His cock was hard, hot, and heavy as it sprang into my hand.

I swirled my tongue around the velvety head of him, licking fluid that had pooled from the opening. He tasted of musk and salt and desire. Still so aroused all I could think about was sex, I took as much of him as I could into my mouth, making up the difference with my hands.

He groaned and made deliciously male noises as I worked him between my hands and mouth, paying special attention to the sensitive head. He wove his fingers beneath my hair, holding my head as he fucked my mouth. I may have cheated and added magic to heighten his pleasure, but I wanted to give as good as I'd gotten.

I knew when his control shattered. I felt it go as he abandoned all pretense of going slow. I sucked hard, tightened my grip on his shaft as I willed him to climax. His cock quivered in my hands just before shudders ran through it. It swelled even bigger than it was, and semen pumped into my mouth. I swallowed and swallowed, until there was no more.

With his cock still buried in my mouth, he reached for me, moving me around until he could tongue my sex one more time. My pants had slid down a few more centimeters, and he jammed a hand between my legs, slid two fingers inside me, and licked my swollen nub.

Third time's always a charm. I came fast because bringing him off had been such a high I was almost there anyway. Waves of sensation swept through me as I sucked hard on his still-erect shaft.

We collapsed against each other, breathing hard. I don't

remember how we ended up lying side by side so we could kiss again, but we did. "You taste like me," I murmured.

"Aye, and ye taste of my jism," he said, still in Norse as he smoothed hair off my sweaty face. He kissed my forehead. "However we love one another, 'tis a gift."

I tried out combinations of words, and opted for the simplest ones. "Part of me wants us to be together. Another part is scared as shit."

"We have all the time in the world, darling. Ye'll let me know when you're ready."

I nestled into his arms. I didn't believe his assessment about having lots of time. Every magical sense I had was screaming time was running out, but I didn't want to ruin the moment by saying so. What we'd shared was mystical, magical. It may not have bound us in the same way as actually making love, but it wasn't far off, either.

He cradled the back of my head in one hand. "Sleep. When we wake, we'll go to Vanaheim."

I didn't need encouragement. My eyelids were heavy, and I couldn't have stayed awake if I'd tried. Being surrounded by his arms and legs and the scents of the sea and sunbaked clay made me feel safe. Alarm bells tolled, but weakly and from a great distance. Nothing and nowhere was safe, and I'd be an idiot to forget it.

It's so tough to decide how to break these long tales into three books, but this feels like as good a spot as any to end this one. A lot will happen in book two as Rowan learns about her magic, the threats to Midgard escalate, and Bjorn and Rowan's relationship hits a few rough spots. She's not the only one carrying secrets around her birth, and his may well tear them apart.

Dragon Heir continues in *Dragon's Blood*. Read on for a sample.

BOOK DESCRIPTION, DRAGON'S BLOOD

After discovering she's half dragon, Rowan figures it can't be any worse than being related to the Celts. That's the thing about assumptions, though. They come round and bite you in the ass.

The second book in a magic-laced, fast-paced, fantasy trilogy. With dragons.

I'd rather fight than study, but I'm stuck poring over dusty scrolls. I promised I'd learn about the dragon part of my magic, but I'm having a hell of a hard time believing there's some concealed strain of power just waiting for me to kindle it. Meanwhile, my friends the witches are playing fast and loose with remaining hidden.

My Celtic kin won't bother them anymore—at least I

don't think they will. But far worse things rove Earth than the Celtic gods. The Breaking has developed an energy all its own. The longer it runs wild, the harder it will be to contain.

Soon, very soon, no magic in the Nine Worlds will be enough to counteract it. Once that happens, the few remaining mortals will go first, but the rest of us won't be far behind them.

DRAGON'S BLOOD, CHAPTER ONE, ROWAN

Fire painted the sky and the ground, so much fire I saw red even through my closed lids. Keeping my eyes shut was a very bad idea, though. Dragons surrounded me. Maybe not more than a dozen, but they were so freaking big, it felt like more. They were ostensibly teaching me how to fight, except I already possessed that particular talent. In between salvos, they chittered merrily among themselves like a pack of oversized crows. Occasionally, I picked up bits and pieces of their mind speech.

Coming out victorious in a good scrap has always been high on my list. I haven't had a hell of a lot of choice in the matter. Mostly, it was fight or be vanquished. It's not possible to kill me, but there are many, many punishments that would make me long for my own death.

Anyway, it surprised and annoyed the crap out of me when a red dragon who hadn't introduced himself—herself?

—announced that today we'd shore up my battle talents. If he'd asked, I'd have replied, "No thank you."

I'm at the bottom of their pecking order, though. Probably less than the bottom. No one ever asks me jack crap.

A cloud of ash and smoke billowed around me, followed by trumpeting. Clearly, one of my tormentors—er, teachers— had discovered my attention was wandering. Wracked by coughing from all the smoke, I resorted to telepathy.

"Stop!"

Ysien, one of the blue dragons, hooted laughter. "Aye. And the enemy will surely cease if ye but tell them ye've had enough."

No one made fun of me. No one.

Trapped between embarrassment and fury, I made a grab for Bjorn's power. He had to be out there somewhere beyond the impenetrable blanket of smoke. We were amazing fighting together, but today for whatever reason, the dragons had apparently told him to sit this one out. He's not the type to take orders, so they must have forced him to remain off the field.

Blech. Dragons.

When Nidhogg, the chief Norse dragon who was conveniently absent today, told me I had to learn about the dragon half of my blood, I'd reluctantly agreed. I'd had zero idea about the non-Celtic sector of my parentage until a scant handful of days ago. Anyway, at the time Nidhogg floated the idea about tutors for me, he'd intimated a single dragon would show up each day.

I had no fucking idea why I merited the attentions of so

many. Were they bored? Had they come to examine the one and only Dragon Heir ever who was a mix of Celtic and dragon bloodlines?

Was one of them my father?

So far, everyone had been closemouthed about that little tidbit. So secretive, I wasn't expecting a dragon to burst out of the ether and scoop me up in his scaled forelegs, greeting me as fathers did in my imagination. The dragons had known about me since my birth, and no one bothered to show up with flowers and a pile of excuses about why they'd left me in Ceridwen's care. Or non-care, which was closer to the way things played out.

My thoughts may have taken off at Mach 10, but I can think and fight. My current mission was lobbing jolts of defensive magic to clear a circle around me. My bid to locate Bjorn had failed, so the dragons' barrier between us must cut both ways. If he could have reached me, he would have.

Bjorn Nighthorse is another mystery, but I didn't have time to pick it apart right now. With his ice-blond hair and eyes like a restless ocean, he's so striking it's sometimes tough for me to look at him. Feels like I've fallen off a cliff into a dangerous no-man's land. One where the only way out is to wrap my body around his and never, never let him go.

My defensive perimeter had expanded to a ring a meter wide. Within its boundaries, the smoke had almost cleared. Being able to get a full breath into my lungs helped.

I resorted to the same strategy I've always used. Nothing fancy about it. When I'm surrounded, I pick 'em off one at a time. I live in a body that looks human, but most of the bastards I fight are bigger than me, or they have thick hides or horns or scales or other impediments—like poison—that make it tough to do anything straightforward. Like reaching inside them to stop their hearts. Hell, some of them, like trolls, don't even have hearts. Goddess only knows what keeps them upright.

From somewhere far away, I heard Bjorn shouting. He sounded furious and worried. From the tone of his curses, he'd been trying to break through to me from his end of things exactly as I'd suspected.

I focused my attention on a single dragon. And I sort of cheated because I picked the smallest one, small being relative. This one was green and stood a bit over two meters tall. I'd never vanquish it in straight-on combat, so I teleported onto its back where it couldn't reach me with fire. Breathing shallowly, I tried to bring some of my protective bubble along with me.

Didn't work very well. Teleport spells are picky like that. I didn't want to take the time to resurrect my shielding. Besides, the smoke had only been bad next to me—before I'd gone into full attack mode. The dragon I'd selected was bellowing and wrapping power bands around itself to either shake me off or press me into its thorny hide so hard its scales would cut into my flesh.

Couldn't let that happen. My blood would give it power over me. Enough power to immobilize my efforts. I unleased my instincts, pulled the dirk I always carry from its sheath banded to my thigh, and used scales for purchase to crawl up its neck.

Sticking the point of my dagger in the one place beneath its jaws not coated by scales, I shrieked, "Surrender."

Everything around me went quiet. No more bellows, trumpets, or bugles. For the moment, no more fire.

Ysien lumbered close. "Well done, Dragon Heir."

"No lack of guts." The dragon beneath me shook itself again, but I had a good hold on it. Its praise pleased me, but words were cheap.

I wasn't in a hurry to cede my advantage, so I left the knife in place. Dragons are immortal too. I couldn't do much damage, but I wanted to hang onto the illusion of having the upper hand.

"Runa!" Ysien's tone had developed an edge. "Stand down."

"Don't call me that." I couldn't risk taking my attention from the hand that held my blade.

"'Tis your name, and high time ye claimed it."

"We are done for today," I announced.

"I told you to sheathe your weapon. Dragons do not raise their talons against their own."

"So, it's only acceptable if you're attacking me?" I clung to my almost nonexistent advantage and repeated, "We are done for today. Once you agree, I will jump down."

A sheet of fire roared past me. Roared was an understatement. It sounded like a giant blowtorch and felt like someone had opened a gateway into Hell. Sweat sheened my body; I curled my damp fingers tighter around the hilt of my knife.

"Agreed," Ysien snarled.

Blade still in hand, I climbed down Greenie's neck, jumped lightly to the ground, and tucked my weapon away. Ysien furled his wings, but I shot in front of him and said,

"Hold up a moment." I tacked, "please," on as an afterthought.

He didn't fold his wings, but he didn't flap them, either. The dragon stared at me with his whirling gaze. Maybe because of my dragon blood, I can look directly at them without becoming snared in whatever spell they choose to weave.

I settled my hands on my hips. "I have claimed my name. I'm not using it because true names offer power over the bearer."

Smoke puffed from his nostrils. "But we all know your name. We've known it since your birth."

Awk. There it was again. Proof of one more set of relatives who could give a fuck less about me. At least the Celts hadn't made a secret over not giving a crap. Discovering a second batch who'd considered me irrelevant should be like water slipping off a dolphin's back. Except it wasn't. Their indifference stung.

I cursed myself for a chump.

"The length of time you've known my name is irrelevant. If it's rolling around in your minds, anyone with magic could discover it. I've been Rowan since my birth, and Rowan I shall remain until I tell you different."

Before he could protest or tell me it wasn't my choice—which it goddamn well was—I went on. "When Nidhogg told me I'd have assistance learning the dragon portion of my magic, he said one dragon would show up each day. One." I flapped my hands for emphasis before resetting them on my hips.

"What the fuck?" I went on. I was on a roll, and not in

the mood to shut up. "Why are all of you here? Don't you have anything more interesting to occupy your time?"

No one answered, but twelve sets of whirling eyes bored into me. Unpleasant doesn't come close to describing how creepy that felt. I forged ahead, anyhow. What choice did I have? When you clue bullies in that they're getting to you, you're screwed. I shoved my shoulders straighter and said, "I thought part of my training was to push the boundaries of how my magic slots with Bjorn's, but you blocked us from each other. Why?"

Ysien did answer that question. "To see how ye did on your own. Why else?"

"Pfft. I've been 'on my own' practically since I was born." I would have stamped my foot, except it felt juvenile. "I'm starting to feel like some kind of circus attraction. Does Nidhogg know all of you are milling about practically salivating over the anomaly you've known about but ignored for centuries?"

A red dragon took a step toward me. "We had our reasons."

"And they were?"

"Ye shall know at the proper time," Ysien told me. He's always had a patronizing way about him that grates on my nerves.

Breath swooshed from my lungs. I wanted to punch him, but he wouldn't have even noticed, no matter how much force I put behind the blow. "You're as bad as Ceridwen," I growled. "At least she was honest about how much she hated me."

"Apologize," Ysien hooded his eyes and bent his neck so

his head was more on a level with mine. "I am nothing like your Celtic whore of a mother."

My temper has always been a stumbling block, and I reined mine in. Still, I wasn't about to grovel. I settled for saying, "Insofar as I know, no dragon has lied to me directly." I stopped before launching into how lies of omission weren't any better.

"Dragons do not lie." He snapped his jaws with their double rows of teeth shut. The *clack* sounded like a small canon exploding.

Yeah, but you're masters at twisting the truth.

I cleared my thoughts fast. Among their other talents, dragons are exceptional mind readers. I'd been excited to discover I had a brand new extended family, but the novelty had faded fast. My commitment to learn about how to maximize my dragon-linked magic was waffling too.

I wanted to return to Midgard—Earth—and the witches who'd offered me home and hearth and family after I'd walked out on the Celtic pantheon. The witches were worth my time and my magic.

Instead, I was in Vanaheim standing in a substantial clearing not far from Bjorn's cottage. Made of cunningly interlocking stones with very little mortar between them, it looked as if it had been here for hundreds of years. Who knows? Perhaps it had. Unlike Earth, where most didn't wield magic, everyone I've met in Vanaheim had at least some.

Bjorn possessed far more than "some." He's the master sorcerer in all the Nine Worlds, and his power defied description.

"We shall leave you to your *student*," the red dragon told Ysien. From the beast's voice tones, I was fairly certain it was female. Her emphasis on student made it sound like what she meant was, "good luck corralling that headstrong monster you were stupid enough to invite into our midst." But perhaps I was overreacting.

"Ye will leave when I dismiss you," Ysien stopped staring at me long enough to glare at her.

I fully expected the Red to tell him to piss up a rope. Instead she bowed her head ever so briefly. The only indication she wanted to strangle him was the smoke wafting from her nostrils and around her jammed-shut jaws.

"We have one final task today while many of us are here," Ysien announced.

Crappity crap. There was that tone again. The one that screamed he ran the universe. Why the others put up with it for a second was beyond me. He scanned the dragons and crooked a talon at a copper-colored one. Dragon talons are blood-red, maybe ten centimeters long, and razor sharp. They're beautiful if you can get past how deadly they are.

The coppery dragon ambled forward. Not built as heavily as some, it was tall with a graceful set to its long neck. Ysien said, "Zelli, meet Runa."

I nodded at the dragon and managed, "Pleased to meet you." It wasn't as if I could shake hands. The name, Zelli, argued the beast was female, and unlike Ysien, she hadn't done anything to alienate me.

Not yet.

She puffed steam my way, a good sign from a dragon.

"Pleased to meet you as well, *Rowan*." She stressed my proper—as opposed to my true—name, and I loved her for it. Maybe she and I were destined to get along.

Ysien glared at her. She glared right back and said, "'Tis a small enough thing. I say we accommodate where we can."

Before Ysien could correct her or order her to call me Runa, I smiled brightly and said, "What is this one last thing we have to do? Whatever it is, could we hurry it along? Bjorn and I were heading back to Earth in a little bit."

"Why?" Ysien bit off the word.

"Now you look here." I craned my neck back to attempt to look him in the eyes. "I don't answer to you. My life and my *home*"—I stressed the word home—"are there. I do not require your leave to return home. Besides, I want to experiment to see if I can move some of the lore materials from world to world."

"Mmph. Does Nidhogg know?"

"I don't answer to him, either," I replied tartly.

Zelli pushed between us. "How would ye feel about riding me? 'Tisn't something dragons normally offer, and it was the death knell of our relationship with the Celtic gods. They would have used us for steeds." She turned her head, and the steam turned to a rain of ashy smoke.

My eyes widened. I'm sure my mouth fell open, but I shut it fast. Of all the things she might have said, her invitation to jump on her back was the last one I'd have anticipated. I'd ridden on the occasional airplane back before the Breaking, but this was different.

"Rowan?" Zelli prodded.

"Uh, sure. I guess it would be interesting," I stammered. I'm not usually at a loss for words. "Why would I be doing this?"

"None of us are certain what ye'll be capable of. Ye may find your own dragon form. In the meantime, ye must needs practice aerial warcraft. For that, ye require a companion who can fly." After a hesitation, she added, "I volunteered."

I had a feeling she hadn't had any competition. More than once, I'd thought how convenient wings would be. For one thing, they offered a superior view of the battlefield. For another, flight would move me out of harm's way for some predators.

Her jaws lolled in an approximation of a smile.

Magic jumped to my summons and I vaulted onto her back. "What about Bjorn?" I asked. "We're a team. We fight together."

"I haven't forgotten," Ysien said sourly and jerked his head to one side.

The smoke had finally cleared enough for me to make out Bjorn astride a black dragon, who'd just leapt skyward. I reached for him in mind speech, not expecting much, but I broke through. *"Hey there."*

"We'll talk later," he said. I knew him well enough to hear the controlled fury beneath his words. He hadn't liked it at all when the dragons had erected a barrier between us.

"Ready?" Zelli spread her great wings. When I glanced over a shoulder, I was awestruck by how big they were closeup.

"I think so. Anything I need to know?"

She bugled laughter. "Doona fall off."

I settled myself farther forward until I could wrap my arms around her neck. A pair of horns sprouted from the juncture where her neck attached to her back. They looked like a better bet balance-wise, so I gripped them.

She edged away from the group and sprang into the air. The transition felt effortless. One moment her hind legs were planted on the ground, the next, we were flying. *"Just a little bit here to get you used to things,"* she spoke into my mind.

I must have been more nervous than I thought because I had those horns in a death grip, and my eyes were shut. I pried them open as we banked left and right and flew in a figure-eight. Next, she climbed steeply enough, I pressed my legs into her hide. She was warm. Might come in handy on a cold day. We hit some kind of zenith because she dove toward the ground, pulling up at the last moment. A heady exhilaration ran through me, and I whooped for the sheer joy of moving through the skies.

"How are you doing?" she asked.

"I love this!" It wasn't an exaggeration. Riding Zelli was a lot like when Bjorn and I had first joined our magic. Destiny had speared me that day, making it abundantly clear our power was created to work together. Riding the dragon had a familiar feel to it, as if I'd done it in another lifetime.

"Ready to fight?"

"Yes!" I gathered defensive magic, while warding myself. Should I ward her too?

She must have been in my mind because she said, *"Worry about yourself, Dragon Heir. I will be fine."*

I scanned the ground. While we'd been experimenting,

Ysien—or someone—had been busy. Targets lined the far side of the clearing. Bjorn and the black dragon were heading right for them. Power burst from Bjorn, and the two targets on the end disintegrated.

We waited for them to clear the area before we did our own strafing run. This was easy. Too easy. While I recognized that no enemy would just stand there and wait for me to mow them down, my aerial perch added a whole new dimension to my offensive strategies.

Fighting aside, riding the dragon sang to something deep inside me. It held a rightness that filled me with giddy joy. I'd have whooped again, but it wasn't dignified. Beneath us, dragons replaced the spent targets, infusing smaller ones with magic to make them harder to hit.

"Once more," I shouted, too excited to hide my enthusiasm. I felt like a kid who'd just been handed the best toy ever. A glance at Bjorn told me he was as caught up in the whole dragon-riding gig as me. His usually stern face had relaxed into a smile. Power crackled around him, adding to his unearthly beauty.

And then it was our turn again. Zelli added her power to mine, and we annihilated the entire rest of the row. I did whoop then, and she bugled. Maybe my crude shrieks were buried by her victory cries. I hoped so.

I wanted to fly and fly and fly, but we thumped onto the ground, and she folded her wings. Turning her head, she puffed steam around me. "Thank you," I said. "That was unbelievable."

"Doona tell anyone," she whispered into my mind, *"but I enjoyed our flight."*

"It will be our secret." I hesitated before adding, *"Until next time?"* I held my breath. There had to be a next time. This had been too brilliant not to have a repeat.

I tossed a leg over her side and jumped down, disappointed she hadn't confirmed there would be a next time. I was almost across the clearing to where Bjorn stood when she said, *"Until next time, Dragon Heir."*

I spun to face her and raised a hand in farewell. My throat was thick with emotion, and I didn't want her to leave. She puffed smoke my way, spread her wings and circled to gain altitude. One by one, the other dragons left as well. I was grateful to avoid another confrontation with Ysien. I was a disappointment to him. I read those signs well enough. Mother had been a master at teaching them to me.

Bjorn covered the remaining distance between us and draped an arm around my shoulders. "Flying was unexpected. And delightful."

I leaned my head against him for a moment. It had been all those things, and a whole lot more. I didn't want to muck about describing what had felt surreal. Words might ruin it, so I asked, "What's next?" It was past midday from the angle of the sun.

"Ysien reminded me I need to commission several magical blades. He and Nidhogg worked on a list with me before we battled the griffon. Since then—"

"We haven't had any time," I cut in. "Yeah, I'm well aware of that." I looked away from his direct gaze. It wasn't as if we were mated or anything. We could—no, should—do things separately. "How about this?"

I wriggled out from beneath his arm. Leaving his side harder than getting off Zelli had been, and both those things worried me. I'd gotten by being strong, needing no one.

"How about what?" Warmth and caring streamed from him. I could lose myself in his blue eyes, fall into their beauty and never surface.

Alarm bells tolled deep in my mind. "I'll go inside and finish the section I was working on in that one scroll. If you're not back by the time I finish, I'll teleport to Earth and look in on the witches."

His smile faded a notch. "Sure, Rowan. Will you meet me back here, or—"

"Either way," I said. "I'll be at one of the two coven strongholds. When I'm done there, I'll head back this way. Might be a couple of days, though. Is it still all right for me to try to take one of the lore books with me?"

He nodded. "It will let you know quick enough if it doesn't want to leave." Before he was even done speaking, power flickered around him as he built a teleport spell.

I wanted to grab his arm, tell him I'd go with him, that we'd do everything together, but I kept my mouth clamped shut and hopefully concealed my stupid, ridiculous neediness. We had a job to do. A world to save. Once we'd pulled Earth out of the gutter, we could focus on each other.

I nodded a farewell and sprinted for the house not trusting myself to stick around. I'd bought us a little space from one another. May as well make good use of it. I was certain I'd done the right thing, but desolation scoured me.

I didn't get it. Before, I'd always been enough for me. I shook myself from stem to stern. I had to locate that solo headspace again, and pronto. Bjorn's cottage was not the place to accomplish it. The second I got near the place, his scent reached for me. The sea mingled with sunbaked clay tugged at my heart. My soul.

Resolute, I trotted to the place I'd been working and picked up the scroll. I'd promised, given my word I'd work through this one scroll. When I finished it, though, I'd be gone.

ABOUT THE AUTHOR

Ann Gimpel is a USA Today bestselling author. A lifelong aficionado of the unusual, she began writing speculative fiction a few years ago. Since then her short fiction has appeared in many webzines and anthologies. Her longer books run the gamut from urban fantasy to paranormal romance. Once upon a time, she nurtured clients. Now she nurtures dark, gritty fantasy stories that push hard against reality. When she's not writing, she's in the backcountry getting down and dirty with her camera. She's published over 75 books to date, with several more planned for 2019 and beyond. A husband, grown children, grandchildren, and wolf hybrids round out her family.

Keep up with her at www.anngimpel.com or http://anngimpel.blogspot.com

If you enjoyed what you read, get in line for special offers and pre-release special reads. Newsletter Signup!

Witches Rule

Dragon Heir (Summer and fall, 2019)

Dragon's Call

Dragon's Blood

Dragon's Requiem

Dragon Lore

Highland Secrets

To Love a Highland Dragon

Dragon Maid

Dragon's Dare

Dragon Fury

Earth Reclaimed

Earth's Requiem

Earth's Blood

Earth's Hope

Elemental Witch

Timespell

Time's Curse

Time's Hostage

GenTech Rebellion

Winning Glory

Honor Bound

Claiming Charity

Loving Hope

Keeping Faith

Ice Dragon

Feral Ice

Cursed Ice

Primal Ice

Rubicon International

Garen

Lars

Soul Dance

Tarnished Beginnings

Tarnished Legacy

Tarnished Prophecy

Tarnished Journey

Soul Storm

Dark Prophecy

Dark Pursuit

Dark Promise

Underground Heat

Roman's Gold

Wolf Born

Blood Bond

Wolf Clan Shifters

Alice's Alphas

Megan's Mates

Sophie's Shifters

Wylde Magick

Gemstone

Lion's Lair

Unbalanced

STANDALONE BOOKS

Branded, That Old Black Magic Romance (paranormal romance)

Edge of Night (short story collection, paranormal and horror)

Grit is a 4-Letter Word (nonfiction)

Heart's Flame (post-apocalyptic romance)

Icy Passage (science fiction romance)

Marked by Fortune (post-apocalyptic coming of age story)

Melis's Gambit (historical paranormal romance)

Midnight Magic (paranormal romance)

Red Dawn (post-apocalyptic paranormal romance)

Shadow Play (historical paranormal romance)

Shadows in Time (Highland time travel romance)

Since We Fell (contemporary romance)

Warin's War (paranormal romance)

www.ingramcontent.com/pod-product-compliance
Lightning Source LLC
Chambersburg PA
CBHW071118180726
48291CB00007B/2078